The Illuminated Man

Books by Eleanor Fitzgerald:

The Ministry of Supernatural Affairs

Night People

The Black Carnation

Children of the Rat

The Midnight Aviary

Our Forbidden Future

Shaken to the Bone

The Illuminated Man

Other Works

Oxford Junction

The Forest

Hymns for the Gallows, Volume One: The Trial

Hymns for the Gallows, Volume Two: The Last Meal

Hymns for the Gallows, Volume Three: The Hanging

Anima, Volume One: The Signal

This is a work of fiction. Names, characters, places, and incidents either are the product of the author's imagination or are used fictitiously. Any resemblance to actual persons, living or dead, events, or locales is entirely coincidental.

Copyright © Eleanor Fitzgerald, 2024

The moral right of Eleanor Fitzgerald to be identified as the author of this work has been asserted in accordance with the Copyright, Designs, and Patents Act of 1988.

All rights reserved. No part of this book may be reproduced in any form on by an electronic or mechanical means, including information storage and retrieval systems, without permission in writing from the publisher, except by a reviewer who may quote brief passages in a review.

Cover Art Copyright © Eleanor Fitzgerald, 2024

First paperback edition November 2024

ISBN: 9798327600140

Published Independently

Contents

Author's Note: Content Warnings.............................ix

Part One: Sweet Summer Sadness...............................1

Chapter One – Strange Questions, Desperate Requests
....3
Chapter Two – Lady of Fortune................................11
Chapter Three – A Very Bad Omen...........................19
Chapter Four – The Midnight Train..........................27
Chapter Five – Rooftop Musings...............................37
Chapter Six – Baby Steps, Again...............................45
Chapter Seven – Feasting and Fawning.....................55
Chapter Eight – Old Habits Die Hard........................63
Chapter Nine – Unsettled Skies.................................73
Chapter Ten – Designer Shirts, Knee Length Skirts..83
Chapter Eleven – Westbound and Down...................95
Chapter Twelve – A Three-Pointed Circle...............105
Chapter Thirteen – A Bite in the Morning...............115
Chapter Fourteen – From the Air and the Land.......123
Chapter Fifteen – If I Can Shoot Rabbits................133

Interlude One – Awaken, My Love..........................141

Part Two: Something Wicked in the Bay.................145

Chapter Sixteen – Trick Shot...................................147
Chapter Seventeen – An Attempted Release............155
Chapter Eighteen – Seeing the Wood for the Trees.163
Chapter Nineteen – Wrong Place, Wrong Time.......171
Chapter Twenty – The Stopped Clock.....................179
Chapter Twenty One – Hungry for Truth.................187
Chapter Twenty Two – Armchair Politics................195

Chapter Twenty Three – Playing Make-Believe......205
Chapter Twenty Four – The Dot Connector............215
Chapter Twenty Five – On the Trail........................223
Chapter Twenty Six – Destined for the Scene.........233
Chapter Twenty Six – You Missed the Starting Gun 245
Chapter Twenty Seven – We Rise with the Dawn...253

Interlude Two – Behind the Mask............................263

Part Three: Night Terrors...269

Chapter Twenty Eight – A Bad Day to Die..............271
Chapter Twenty Nine – Cargo Cults........................279
Chapter Thirty – Better the Devil You Know..........289
Chapter Thirty One – All Hell Breaks Loose..........297
Chapter Thirty Two – Ante Up.................................307
Chapter Thirty Three – Chained to the Rocks.........315
Chapter Thirty Four – You See Her When You Fall Asleep...323

Epilogue – Someone or Something to Show You the Way..333

Acknowledgments..347

About the Author..351

Author's Note: Content Warnings

I have drawn from my own experiences and knowledge to create this novel as well as some fairly extensive research. This is a horror novel, above all else, and it is a tense, frightening narrative. As such, there are some content warnings that I would like to point out in advance, although I will not be too specific; I do not wish to spoil the plot, after all! This will be the last mention of these warnings so that the story may unfold uninterrupted. This list is not exhaustive, however.

- **Body Horror**
- **Drug Abuse**
- **Torture**
- **Graphic Violence/Bloodshed**
- **Institutional Violence**
- **Mind Control**
- **Kidnapping**
- **Suicide/Self Harm**
- **Child Abuse**
- **Erotic Horror/Horror-themed Non-consent**

I know that this last one might be especially triggering, but it is important due to the nature of the characters and their gifts, and I tried to telegraph it pretty hard so that you should be able to see what's coming. If you would still like a more detailed breakdown of trigger warnings on a chapter by chapter basis, feel free to email me. My details are in the About the Author section at the end of this book.

Thank you for choosing this novel, dear Reader. I hope you enjoy reading it as much as I enjoyed writing it.

THE MINISTRY OF SUPERNATURAL AFFAIRS

Pugnamus In Obumbratio

This book is for James Bullock, one of my closest childhood friends.

We used to go on writing holidays to Torquay, and the first germ of this book certainly took root on one of those little trips.

Part One: Sweet Summer Sadness

Chapter One – Strange Questions, Desperate Requests

Gavin

Gavin Strangeways perched on his desk, tie loosened and top button undone as he faced his class of Year Twelve Chemists. There were only about fifteen minutes left of the lesson; the last one before the summer holidays, and the listlessness in the room was palpable. The chain of the silver locket he wore gleamed brightly against the tanned skin of his neck.

"So," he said after a moment, "end of the year, with just a quarter of an hour left to us. Technically I'm supposed to be teaching you right up until the minute the bell rings, but I don't really want to do that; you're a good class and you've worked your bloody socks off this year.

"I'm not going to give you a quick-fire quiz or a worksheet to do, but we are going to do some science." He hopped down from the desk and looked at his ten students, hands on his hips. "From now until the end of class, it's open season on science; ask me anything you want to know, and I'll do my best to explain it.

"No restrictions, and remember that there are no stupid questions; only people lacking curiosity."

He looked at his class eagerly, despite the oppressive July heat, but they did not respond. In fact, their silence was deafening. He sighed, his shoulders slumping, and leant forwards, resting his bare elbows on the empty table in front of him.

"Nothing?" he asked, raising an eyebrow. "Not a damn thing?"

Silence, and a few awkward stares at the desk.

"You've got all the answers you need, is that it?" Gavin said, trying to keep the annoyance out of his voice. "That's the problem with this place; we teach to the exam specification, but we never encourage you to look past the narrow syllabus."

Fuck it, he thought, *let's ask them individually. Someone will have something to say, surely.*

"Alice," he said, gesturing at a tired looking girl with dark hair and untidy clothes, "is there anything you want to know? You've always been a bright spark; ask me a question."

She paused for a moment, almost fearfully, and then she spoke.

"Why do whales strand themselves on the beach?" Her voice was barely a whisper, and she glanced nervously at her classmates, clearly expecting mockery for her question.

"That's a good question, Alice," Gavin replied. "Honestly, we're not a hundred percent sure; it could be confusion from the noise of boat propellers, or it could be illness, or a dozen other factors. The thing we do know for certain, however, is that it's a warning sign that things are not right in the local ecosystem.

"Strange behaviour in animals is often a symptom of a deeper, more dangerous problem."

One of the boys, sat nearby, snickered and stared at the girl, who looked down at her desk like her life depended on it.

"You'd know all about strange behaviour, wouldn't you, Alice?" he said nastily.

"Hey, Darren," Gav said sharply, "cut that shit out.

There's no need for it anywhere, and especially not in my classroom."

"Yes, Mr Strangeways," Darren said, a smug grin on his face. Gavin had been having problems with the lad all year, and he was dreading the class's return in September. Unfortunately, Darren Green was one of the brightest pupils at the school, and he knew it. "Although anyone could've told her that we don't know about that. It was obvious."

"Darren," Gavin warned, adding an edge to his tone.

"Sorry; it was obvious, *sir*." He laughed more loudly this time, and Gavin was about to chastise him when Alice spoke up angrily.

"Where does colour come from?" she asked, staring at Darren.

"Objects either reflect or absorb light; the stuff they reflect is the colour we see. Fucking hell, Alice, that's a GCSE question!" Darren sat back smugly in his chair, radiating arrogance.

"What happens to the light that's absorbed?" Alice asked immediately, and Gavin couldn't help but smile. *Nice one-two punch, kid.* "Come on, Darren, isn't it *obvious*?"

"It, uh, it gets, uh," Darren floundered. As much as Gavin wanted to see the self-satisfied grin wiped off the little bastard's face, he did not want to encourage public humiliation in his classroom.

"It causes energetic excitation in the electron structure," Gavin said. "We'll be touching on it next year, but in order to explain it fully, we'd need to get into some quantum mechanics, along with a bit about crystal structures."

He smiled at the red-faced boy kindly.

"If you remind me next year, I'll tell you how the

touchscreen in your smart phone works." He grinned broadly as the bell rang out. "Trust me, Year Twelve, it will blow your minds. Have a great summer and don't do anything that I wouldn't do!"

His students gathered up their books and bags, shuffling out into the corridor for six weeks of freedom. As Alice went to leave, Gavin called her over.

"Can I have a quick word, Alice?" he asked, and she nodded.

"I'm sorry I snapped at Darren, sir, but he's... he's such a cunt sometimes."

Try as he might, Gavin could not stifle his giggle.

"I couldn't possibly comment," he said after a second of silence to regain his composure. "Don't worry, though, you're not in trouble. You do seem a bit, well, *off* today, Alice; are you alright?"

"Just tired, sir," she said with a forced smile. "I haven't been sleeping well, although it might just be the heat."

"Alright then," he said, not really believing her. "Remember, I'm here if you want to talk at all. One last question, if I may; why did you ask about whale strandings?"

"I had a dream about it last night," she said sheepishly.

I thought so, but Gavin decided against voicing this. Instead he wished her a pleasant summer and sent her on her way. *Poor girl,* he thought. *She has no idea what kind of world she's waking up into.*

He sighed and paced around his classroom, tidying papers away and neatening up his desk; it was certain to gather all kinds of dust and detritus over the next six weeks. He drummed his fingers on the wood, looking at all the chemical burns and scars from the past few years.

"I wonder if my soul looks anywhere half as bad?" he muttered, gently touching the locket. He was about to reach underneath his desk to pull out his various hex-bags and charms when there was a knock on his classroom door.

"Mr Strangeways, sir?" asked a familiar student. Gavin's heart ached a little when he saw her; the girl's mother had been on the same cancer ward as Lucy, and they'd died within a few days of each other.

"Hi, Jacinth," Gavin said, slumping into his chair. "What can I do for you?"

"Well, I, um, I need your help, sir," she said awkwardly. "I've told the other teachers, but they say they can't do anything."

"What's happened?"

"It's Libby Styles," Jacinth said, her voice wavering as she spoke. "She's disappeared."

Gavin frowned as he listened to Jacinth explain the situation, occasionally handing her a tissue as needed. The broad picture was a strange one, but not inexplicable; Libby's family had been on the school's radar for a while, especially where truancy was concerned. The fact that she hadn't been seen for a couple of days at the beginning of the summer wasn't odd, especially for a fourteen year old.

"Maybe her parents just decided to head out on holiday early, Jacinth," Gavin said patiently. "It wouldn't be the first time Libby has taken off for a while; I know her home life is a bit turbulent, and the heat has everyone's tempers a little frayed."

"That's what Ms Robbins said," Jacinth sighed,

clearly frustrated. "I know you're supposed to do things properly, but no one is even trying to help me!"

The girl stared at Gavin tearfully.

"This isn't like the other times," she whispered. "Libby would always tell me when she was gonna run off, but now she's just gone. I tried to ask her mum about it, but it was like she didn't even know who I was talking about.

"It's as if Libby never even existed in the first place."

Gavin sat up a little straighter in his seat; he could tell from the girl's tone that something was seriously wrong. *There's been something amiss in the air for a couple of weeks,* he thought. *Maybe this is related.*

"My mum said that if anything weird or unexplained ever happened, or if I was in any danger, that I should come and talk to you. She said that you'd help me." Jacinth's lip trembled at the mention of her late mother, and Gavin nodded solemnly. "She said that... well, that you could do magic. Like, *real* magic."

Gavin reached underneath his desk and pulled out one of the more recently constructed hex bags, showing it to Jacinth.

"I try, but it doesn't always work. Still, better safe than sorry. Here you go," he said as he tossed the bag to her. "Put that above the doorway of your house and it should keep you and your family protected from whatever is happening.

"It is worth mentioning, though, that the ordinary things are often much more dangerous than the weird and wonderful, so take care."

"You'll help me?" she asked, and he nodded. She smiled and took a moment to examine the little leather bag. "What are these funny patterns all over it?"

"It's Ogham; a very old kind of writing. I've got some on me, too," he said, gesturing to the tattoos on his exposed arms. "The Headteacher prefers me to keep them covered up, but in this heat, she's more lenient than usual."

"This is a hex bag, isn't it?" Jacinth said, and he gave her a thumbs up. *Never underestimate a teen's interest in the occult.* "Everyone says that you're a wizard, Mr Strangeways."

"Is that so?" he asked with a smile.

"Mhmm." Jacinth looked at him with a suspicious gaze. "Are you?"

"Not quite," he chuckled. "I'm just a student of the Old Ways."

"Thank you, for the hex bag," Jacinth said gratefully. "It's nice to know that someone cares. Oh, I'm not sure if this is important, but my brother said there's been a strange person hanging around the promenade at night. He mentioned that Libby's dad was talking to him about a week ago, opposite the chicken shop where my brother works."

"I'll look into it," Gavin said. "Is that Fatboy's Chicken Shack?"

"Yeah; do you know it?"

"A mate of mine is one of their regulars," Gavin said with a smile. "It's a good place to start. Go on, Jacinth; you better head on home. Remember, the hex bag goes above the front door."

"Will do." She turned to look at him from the doorway. "Thank you, sir, for giving a shit. I hope you find her."

"Me too," Gavin said as the teen girl trotted off down the corridor, protection charm still in her hand. "Take care, Jacinth."

Gavin looked out the window of his classroom as the palm trees swayed gently in the light breeze that had swept in from the sea overnight, providing a little relief from the heat. The gulls cried outside as they swooped through the cloudless afternoon sky.

"So much for an uneventful summer," Gavin said as he gathered up the rest of his charms and spell bags. "One of these days I'll have a normal day, but it won't be any time soon."

Chapter Two – Lady of Fortune

Flora

Flora traced her fingers through the warm water in the bathtub as it slowly filled. It was pleasantly scented, with rose and lavender oil, and several yellow candles burned in the wrought iron candelabra that dangled above the bath; it could easily be raised or lowered with a nearby crank handle.

The tub itself was massive. It was a roll top, free standing with ornate brass taps and clawed feet supporting it above the intricately tiled floor. On the wall behind the bathtub was a rich red velvet curtain, patterned with gold thread.

The entire scene exuded luxury, which was exactly what Flora Cain wanted.

Once the bath was deep enough to suit her needs, she closed the taps and walked to the other side of the bathroom. She hummed happily as she went, stepping lightly on her freakish, yet oddly appealing, feet.

Flora Cain's legs ended in three-toed deerlike feet, which gave her access to uncanny nimbleness and agility. She had inherited these strange limbs from her father, who was a full-blooded Faun. Unlike his, however, Flora's feet were completely hairless. She did share his mane of curly hair, though, along with a small pair of curled horns atop her head and a little fluffy tail at the base of her spine.

"My Money-Makers," Flora said gleefully as she glanced down to admire her feet; whilst most people would balk at the sight, a certain subset of people were completely obsessed with them. Flora had also found out, much to her delight, that the latter group were willing to pay obscene amounts of money to watch her paint her toenails, dance around a room, or step on all manner of foodstuffs.

Whilst she had received some requests to crush small mammals, crustaceans, and other living creatures beneath her Faun toes, she had refused. Thankfully, the crush fetishists were in a minority and her usual audience were perfectly happy with her regular content, showering her with enough money and gifts to live a most lavish lifestyle.

Still, she thought as she checked the cameras that stood across from the bathtub, *it is nice to push the boat out now and again.*

Although her regular videos and livestreams were doing well, Flora had grown artistically frustrated before too long, and had worked hard to find a more niche, experimental outlet. What she had settled on had turned out to be her most lucrative venture of all, although sometimes she wondered if making such extreme videos, as she would be that day, spoke to a deeper flaw in her personality.

The Mark's first gentle overtures, perhaps? Still, she shook her head to clear the notion from her mind. *No, it's not going to happen; I won't let it.*

"A darkness exists in your soul, Flora," she said, repeating a close friend's words with faux sincerity as she examined the framing of the shot; the bathtub was perfectly centred, with just enough at the edges to allow her co-star to lurk in the doorway at the beginning of the scene. "Well, at least I'm not as fucked up as some of my audience are."

Flora's particular line of work was not without serious risks; even with all the anonymity the internet was able to provide, one of her more *obsessive* fans had shown up at her door with a chainsaw, desperate to take her feet as some kind of perverse trophy.

Even with the usual undercurrents of misogyny and transphobia that existed in the murky waters of fetish content, the problematic element of Flora's audience were often motivated by her appearance. As the daughter of both a Faun and a Rusałka, she was not only supernaturally beautiful, but downright disturbing in just how attractive she was.

Hell, I've had people physically be sick when they see me for the first time, she thought sadly as she checked the slow motion setup. *I wonder what it's like to look at someone like me, and to be affected by the Glamour?*

I guess I'll never know.

"How are things coming, Flo?" asked Jazz, her co-star, from the bathroom doorway. She was a muscle-bound woman that towered above the waiflike Flora, and she wore a sleeveless leather jumpsuit and a domino mask.

The differences between them did not stop at height and build; Jazz wore her hair short, was a regular full-blooded human, and was cisgender. Flora had been working with the striking woman for almost eighteen months and the two had become firm friends.

"Everything is ready to go," Flora said with a sigh, "but..."

"Are you having doubts again?" Jazz asked, and she nodded. "We don't have to do this today, Flo. Hell, I've made enough money with you to see me through the next couple of years quite comfortably."

"I know, I know," Flora said, running her perfect hands through her even more perfect hair, "but I know this one is gonna look *fantastic*; it'll be our best flick yet. Besides, I've already teased it all over socials and I don't want to burn my cred just because I got cold feet."

"Then what's the problem?" Jazz asked, putting a reassuring arm around the smaller woman. "After all, it's not really a snuff film if you don't actually die."

"I'm just not sure if making a sexualised video of you drowning me means that I've got some kind of awful internalised misogyny or some other fuck-up in my brain or..." Flora trailed off, shrugging her shoulders. "Fuck it, I don't know."

"Listen, Flo," Jazz said kindly, "I've said before that if you're going to make this kind of content, you should probably see a therapist, just to talk this kind of thing out; I do, and it means that I get to go into this and have fun with it.

"The world is full of books and films that are brimming with this kind of stuff; Hostel, Saw, Final Destination, anything by James Herbert. The important thing is that this isn't real; you even make sure that you get a chance to show the audience that you're alright at the end of each video.

"Making these things doesn't make you a bad person, and it's okay to enjoy making them, because we both know that it's just a game; we're just pretending. Let's be honest, all we're actually doing is having me shake you around a bit under the water to make a good video; there's not even a risk of me actually drowning you."

"That's true," Flora said with a small smile. "Being half Rusałka does have its benefits."

"Also, you're not making this shit blindly, either. You're thinking about this and approaching it in a proactive way. You have all the power in this situation, Flo; it's your set, your flick, and you can call it off whenever you want to." Jazz grinned at her. "That alone makes it subversive."

"I guess I never thought of it like that," she said, feeling a little of her former mojo return to her.

"Not to mention that you're an untucked non-op trans woman in very small pants getting 'attacked' by a cis woman in a bathroom." Jazz grinned at her. "Babe, Hitchcock could never even come close."

"I guess no-one is really getting exploited here, are they?" Flora asked.

"Fuck no! Like I said, Flo, I make more money in one day with you than I have on every other shoot combined." Jazz looked at her with mock sincerity. "This is a pretty sweet gig for me, Flo, so let's not mess with a good thing."

"And I do enjoy it," Flora said, nodding now. "It fulfils an artistic desire that I need to vent somewhere."

"Still got writer's block?" Jazz asked, and Flora shrugged.

"Is it really writer's block if you've never even started in the first place?" She chuckled and slipped off her thin silk robe. "If you get into position we can get this video rolling."

Jazz nodded.

"As always, Jazz," Flora said as she set the cameras recording, "it will be a pleasure to be drowned by you."

"The pleasure is all mine, Flo," Jazz said as she positioned herself menacingly in the bathroom doorway. "Let's get to it!"

Later that afternoon Flora was sitting in her editing suite, reviewing the footage from the recording session. She had been right; it was certainly the most artfully shot of her drowning videos, and the slow motion video of her freakish feet thrashing amongst suspended droplets of water were downright mesmerising.

So lost was she in the footage that she didn't hear the phone in her bedroom ringing for the first few seconds. She leapt to her feet and trotted down the creaky wooden corridor and into her room, picking up the receiver of the vintage phone as she collapsed on to her massive four poster bed.

"Hi, hi! This is the Hotel Montresor; Flora Cain speaking!" Her voice was warm, welcoming, and musical, with an almost warbling resonance to it. "I'm afraid that we are not taking reservations at this time; we are unfortunately closed for refurbishment."

Flora looked around at the peeling wallpaper, mould darkened boards, and general ramshackle appearance of her room. *I doubt we'll be taking reservations ever again.*

"Oh," said the man on the other end of the line. "I... uh, this Hotel was recommended to me."

"I see," Flora said, sitting up in her bed, suddenly serious. She tried to ignore the quiet scampering of little clawed feet as something strange slipped out of sight around her doorway. "Is there a representative of the Hotel you were instructed to contact?"

"The Stationmaster," the man said nervously.

"This is she," Flora said, her mind now sharp as a tack. "I hope you don't mind me saying so, but you sound tired, sir."

"Yes," the man said quickly. "I struggle to sleep in

the summertime."

"Likewise," Flora replied, giving the next part of the pass phrase. "Is it the stillness of the air?"

"No," the man answered, his voice now confident. "I wake with the dawn."

"Understood, sir," Flora said, her mind racing. "You're in luck; we've just had a room open up. When can we expect you?"

"A little after eleven o'clock tonight."

"We will meet you at the door." Flora listened for the telltale echo of a tapped line, but it seemed clean to her. "We offer complimentary meals to our guests; will you want something light, or something *hot*?"

"Hot, please."

Fuck. Flora sighed heavily. *Why is nothing ever easy?*

"Your request is noted, and we are pleased to accommodate you. Will you be travelling alone?"

"Ideally," the man said, "but I will inform you of any unexpected accompaniment."

"Much appreciated, sir," Flora replied, her teeth now on edge. *Whoever this person is, they're running from the Ministry, and they're a trained operative.*

It's going to be a hell of a day.

"Is that all?" The man sounded anxious to end the call.

"One final thing," Flora said, doing her best to maintain her professional demeanour, "we will need a name for the booking."

"Of course," the man said, hesitating for a second before continuing. "My name is Reginald Kellogg."

Oh shit. Flora paused for a second, but tempted as she was to turn him away, she didn't. *It wouldn't be what Lucy wanted.*

"We'll see you tonight, Mr Kellogg," Flora said. "Travel safe."

There was a click as the line disconnected, and Flora waited for at least a minute, but there were no echoes or other anomalies, confirming that it had been a clean line. Flora hung up the receiver and stared into space for a moment.

"Oowoo," peeped the little creature as it peeked around the edge of her doorway. It moved out of sight as soon as she turned to look at it, scampering away down the corridor.

"Not now, you wretch," Flora said. "I suppose I better tell everyone what the score is."

The pipes in the wall groaned and rattled, making the peeling wallpaper tremble in place.

"Yeah, me too, Monty." Flora picked up her phone and dropped a message into the house group chat, calling a meeting for that evening. "I hope Lucy's legacy doesn't end up with us all getting killed."

Well, at least my life is never boring.

Chapter Three – A Very Bad Omen

Gavin

Gavin strolled along the beach towards Paignton Pier, grateful for the slight breeze that had started to blow in from the sea as the scorching afternoon mellowed into a warm summer evening. He'd dropped his various books, hex bags, and teaching accoutrements at home before heading out.

After having a quick shower to wash away the sweat of the day, he'd decided to switch from his usual summer school garb of white shirt and linen suit to his more typical day-to-day outfit. He had a pair of comfortable sandals on his feet, matched nicely with his olive green cargo shorts and tie-die hemp tunic. His entire look was topped off with a wealth of wooden jewellery, a straw outback hat, and a pair of polarised sunglasses.

He still kept his hair in a long ponytail, but he'd taken the time to tie some juniper berries and sage leaves into his hair bobble; it made sense, given the strange turn the day had taken.

The waterfront was full of early holidaymakers taking advantage of the south-facing coastline; they were sprawled out across the entire span of Paignton Beach, with discarded trash littering the sand like landmines.

"Pick up your fucking rubbish," Gavin muttered as he picked his way through the crowd. Normally he would've stopped to deal with it himself, but today he was on a time limit, and he needed to talk to Leroy urgently.

"Hippie freak!" yelled one of the beach-goers, a man in his early twenties, clearly trying to impress his friends with his raucous bravado. "Go back to Woodstock!"

Gavin grinned, reaching up to touch the lenses of his sunglasses with his index and little fingers before twisting his wrist sharply to gesture at the man who'd insulted him. The man looked startled at Gavin's response, and shook his head dismissively.

Have a good evening, dickhead, Gav thought, and he let out a little chuckle as a small commotion arose when the man managed to somehow knock his drink on to his phone, frying the expensive device.

"Fucking hell, Jason, you're so fucking clumsy!" yelled one of the women the man had been trying to impress. "Such a fucking liability."

"Yeah, Jason," Gavin muttered as he kept on walking. He began to nod his head slightly as he neared the Pier and the music from the busy arcade drifted out across the beach. He was about to move from the sand to the promenade when a cloud passed over the sun, sending a cold shiver down his spine.

"Hmm," Gavin said, peering over his shades. He reached down and picked up a handful of dry sand, feeling its weight before letting it pour through his fingers. He watched it fall through the air, frowning as he saw the vortices and patterns in the drifting grains. "Yeah, that's not right."

"What the fuck is he doing?" asked a woman as she strolled past with her friends, and Gavin sighed heavily.

The hardest part about seeing the world for what it really is, he thought, *is dealing with all the normal people who don't even care to look.*

Still, I have a duty of care to them, although sometimes I wish I didn't give as much of a shit as I do.

He stood up brushing his hand clean on his shorts. The shrill cry of a gull wheeling overhead caught his attention, and he watched it for a moment, looking for further omens or portents. After a minute or so, he decided that it was just a hungry bird and went on his way.

Whilst Jacinth hadn't been entirely wrong when she said that Gavin could do magic, the full truth was a much more complicated matter. He was a member of the Dartmoor Druidic Circle; one of the Circle's three Arch-Druids, to be exact.

He was the youngest of the three by far, and had risen to prominence in the Circle in a somewhat controversial fashion. Whereas some of the other Druids of his generation were prone to wild and often dangerous experimentation, Gavin took a more practical, measured approach; watch, listen, and learn.

Whilst this in and of itself would be a rather traditional pathway to leadership, Gavin's meteoric rise came from his ruthless practicality. *Follow the rules as written,* he maintained, *and leverage any angle or loophole that you can.* Some attributed Gavin's proclivity for bending the rules in his favour to his Jewish upbringing, but in truth his late wife, Lucy, had taught him the virtue of an unconventional approach to things.

The other two Arch-Druids, Elmyra Vane and Peter Borage, did not always have the same sense of flexibility regarding the Druidic teachings which often caused them to butt heads with Gavin. Still, even after several years of working tensely side-by-side with him, they had not been able to find a transgression that would allow them to expel him from the Circle.

Closed minded old fools, he thought with a smile as he ambled along the pier. *If any weapon made of clay is an acceptable focus for a banishing rite, then half a brick is a perfectly valid choice.*

He stepped deftly to one side as a trio of gleeful teens sped past him, laughing and chattering excitedly; such was the promise of the impending summer holidays. Gavin couldn't help but feel a bittersweet sadness as he saw them go tearing along the pier.

I always wanted a big family, he thought, *but then again, I do have everyone at home.*

After all, blood isn't everything.

"I won't do it, Gavin," Lucy said as they looked out over the gentle moonlit waves. "I won't inflict my sickness on anyone else; this... this dies with me."

"Is it really such a burden, Luce?" Gavin asked, mesmerised by how her pale face shone so brightly in the darkness; it was as if she was cut from the moon herself.

"It is," she said, drawing her knees up to her chest and wrapping her arms tightly about them. "If you knew about all the things I've done, all the things I *could do*, you wouldn't come within a hundred miles of me."

Lucy sighed heavily and got to her feet, waving the night sky away with an idle hand. There was a flare of brightness as the moon was replaced by an evening sun in a cloudless blue sky. Lucy walked towards the empty beach, gesturing for Gavin to follow.

"I could keep us in here for years, Gavin," she said softly. "Centuries, perhaps millennia, if I really wanted to. In this world, darling, I am as close to godhood as I will ever get, and it took me half my life to choose to wake up and be the mortal that I was supposed to be.

"I'm older than you can comprehend, my love."

"We could have so much time together, Luce," Gavin said, joining her on the beach and slipping his fingers into her hand. "We could have as long as we wanted."

"It wouldn't be real, Gavin," Lucy said sadly. "All this is just a fiction; an illusion of my own making, and I know it. It might feel like life to you, Gav, but it's just a paper-thin lie to me."

She sighed heavily, and the evening began to darken as storm clouds rolled in from the horizon. Gavin tried to give her an uplifting smile, but she just burst into tears.

"I would tire of this, Gavin, but I would stay here for an eternity just to make you happy." She shook her head and turned away from him. "I'm only human, though, and I would soon grow to hate you for it. This place would become a living hell for both of us, and you wouldn't even remember that the waking world ever existed in the first place."

"But we would wake up eventually-" Gavin began, but Lucy wheeled around to look at him with a wild gaze that teetered on the edge of madness.

"How would you know that you really were awake, Gavin?" she asked, trembling with fear and incandescent with rage. "How could you ever trust the world around you ever again!?"

Is that what they did to you, my beloved? Gavin wondered, but he did not ask; he had promised to leave the horrors of Lucy's past where they belonged.

"I understand," he said, gently placing a hand on her tear-streaked cheek, "or, at least, I understand enough to not ask again."

"You..." Lucy closed her eyes and clenched her fists, "you have no idea what this power is in the hands of a child; all that limitless imagination combined with the endless terror of an unknowable world... There's nothing like it, Gavin, and the potential for evil is unfathomably high.

"Promise me, Gavin Strangeways, that you will never ask me to have children ever again."

"I promise, Lucy," he said, before kissing her softly. "You will always be enough for me; I need no other."

"Hey, man," Leroy Kapule said, reaching out for Gavin's outstretched hand. "Good to see you, brother. I wasn't expecting you to head on down this way, or else I'd have picked you up a little something."

Leroy gestured at the fast food bag beside him; several empty fry cartons and burger wrappers were on his little desk, and there was sure to be more food inside the bag. Leroy worked as an attendant at the Pier Arcade, which gave him ample opportunity to both eat and read at his leisure.

"What's today's light browsing, Lee?" Gav asked, and Leroy held up a textbook on colour theory in film. "Ah, I see you're back on the cinematography train."

"There are some good directors and visionaries out there, Gav," he said, reaching into his paper bag for another cheeseburger. He took a huge bite that almost halved the sandwich, with his razor sharp teeth glinting in the multicoloured arcade lights as he did so. Leroy continued to speak around his mouthful of food. "I mean it, brother; we're entering a golden age of film."

"I don't doubt it, Lee," Gav said as he looked shiftily around the arcade, but none of his students seemed to be present; he tried to keep his work and home lives as separate as possible, for the sake of both groups. "I wanted to have a bit of a conflab before Flora's special guest arrives tonight."

"For sure, for sure," Leroy said, finishing the burger in another satisfied bite. "You know, I can probably spare one of these, bro; you want one?"

"I wouldn't want to leave you short," Gav said sincerely. Even though Leroy was already a man of astounding size, his hunger was impossible to sate; such was the affliction of Ghouls worldwide, no matter how they were created. "I'm worried about this guy bringing Ministry heat down on the Torbay area, Lee. There's something strange brewing, and I've got a feeling that it's gonna get a bit hairy really soon."

"This about your student?" Leroy asked, and Gav nodded. "You any closer to finding out what's up with her?"

"I have my theories," Gavin said darkly, but before he could go on, there was a chorus of piercing screams from outside on the pier. Leroy was already halfway to the door by the time Gavin had gathered himself enough to start moving.

Damn, he's fast when he wants to be.

Both men were soon outside on the eastern side of the pier, looking down at the commotion on Paignton Beach as the previously relaxed sunbathers and swimmers fled the sandy shore in droves.

"Oh shit, bro," Leroy said, staring out at the chaos with his surprisingly warm undead eyes, "this is fucked. You were right; some shit is *definitely* about to go down."

Gavin nodded as he looked at the half a dozen Minke whales that had thrust themselves up on to the beach, wailing in pain and terror the whole time. They thrashed on the sand, groaning as the tremendous weight of their bodies crushed the very life out of them.

"I have fucked with a lot of shit in my time, Gav," Lee said anxiously, "and no matter where you are in the world, if the whales are acting strangely, there's sure to be even worse hot on their heels. This is gonna be bad, brother."

"Yeah," Gavin said, unable to look away from the horror unfolding before him. "The thing is, Lee, I thought this might happen; it's why I came down here."

"For real?" Gavin nodded. "How?"

"My student," Gavin said sadly. "I think she might be a Seer."

Chapter Four – The Midnight Train

Flora

"Where are the boys?" Coral asked Flora, who shrugged her shoulders. The Faun had been pacing nervously around the Silver Schooner; the Hotel Montresor's bar and the unofficial meeting place of its residents. After a solid forty minutes of movement, however, she had decided to take a seat.

"Oowoo," trilled a voice from behind the bar.

"Oh, fuck off," Flora said angrily, hurling an old newspaper at the shabby wooden bar. She was rewarded with the sound of pattering footsteps as the Peeper found a new place to lurk. "Fucking vermin."

"They aren't annoying anyone," Coral said, her knitting needles clicking and clacking as she worked on her latest creation.

"Of course they are," Flora said, looking at the twenty eight year old woman as if she was completely insane. "Coral, their whole purpose is to annoy us! That's literally all they do."

"They probably fill an important ecological niche," she replied smartly, "and I'm sure Monty doesn't mind having them, do you, Monty?"

The pipes in the ceiling rattled and the plaster on the mouldering walls groaned in response.

"They're definitely late," Flora said anxiously, looking through the bar's picture windows and out at the setting sun. The rich orange disk was just beginning to dip below the seaward horizon, its reflection glimmering on the surface of the choppy water.

"I saw Gavin when he popped in earlier," Coral said, finishing another row. "He said he had to go and speak to Leroy about something, so I'm sure they'll be along soon. They probably stopped off so that Lee could get enough food to see him through our little meeting."

"I'm sure you're right," Flora said, nervously scratching at the worn leather of her armchair with her perfectly manicured fingernails. "The impending arrival of our newest runaway has just got me worked up a bit, that's all."

"Is he going to be a problem?" Coral asked, raising a curious eyebrow.

"Probably," Flora said with a sigh, "but we take anyone who needs our help, regardless of the risk; that was Lucy's vision, ever since the beginning."

Coral remained pointedly silent as soon as Lucy was mentioned, and for good reason; a few months after the funeral, she had declared that she had discovered a wraith haunting the property. Gavin, Leroy, and Flora had humoured her for a while, but that all came to a crashing halt when she mentioned to Gavin that it might be the spirit of Lucy Strangeways.

We've never thrown anyone out of here, Flora thought as she looked at the younger woman, *but you came bloody close.* The memory of Gavin's absolute fury and the inconsolable despair that followed still shook the Faun to that day. Still, Coral had proven herself to be a useful member of the Exception Railroad; snooping Ministry Agents rarely suspected ordinary humans, so she was well suited to run interference where necessary.

"He's gonna be here in a few hours," Flora said, bouncing her feet nervously as she tried to sit still. "I'm gonna fucking brain Gavin and Leroy if they take much longer."

Coral sighed heavily, placed her knitting on the table, and then got to her feet.

"Where are you off to?" Flora asked, her voice more shrill than she intended.

"I'm gonna make a drink." Coral strolled over to the bar and began collecting bottles. She ducked behind the counter, fishing out the Boston shaker with a loud clatter. Her grey-haired head popped over the bar and she grinned at Flora. "You want one?"

"Go on then. What are you having?" Flora asked.

"I think I'll have a Vieux Carré, with an extra dash of grapefruit bitters and a fairy wash."

"A *what* wash?" Flora asked.

"Rinse the glass with Crème de Violette and ice before putting the cocktail into it. You want one?"

"That actually sounds amazing, so yes, please." Flora smiled at Coral. "It's pretty sweet having an in-house bartender, you know."

"I earn my keep," Coral said with a grin. She busied herself with making the drinks, but she winced in pain as she raised up the shaker. "Flo, would you be kind enough to dash to my room to get my stick, please?"

"Of course," Flora said, and she pranced across the bar and out into the main lobby of the Monty before making a hard left into Coral's section of the derelict hotel. The young woman lived on the ground floor, along with the main facilities of the old hotel, ranging from the bar to the pool. Leroy and Gavin lived on the second floor, and Flora occupied the entire third floor as she needed space for her video and photo shoots.

The first floor was kept exclusively for their more temporary residents, with three self-contained suites cobbled together out of the old rooms. The Monty had been in Lucy's family since the Victorian era, and she had left it to Gavin, along with a sizeable family fortune, when she died.

Her only stipulation was to continue running the Exception Railroad that she'd started.

Flora almost dashed past Coral's sleek black cane, but Monty shook the floorboards enough to cause the mobility aid to fall into her path.

"Thanks, Monty," Flora said, turning on the spot and trotting back towards the Silver Schooner. Although the hotel looked like it was barely standing, it was actually in a near-perfect structural state; the various aspects of disrepair were entirely cosmetic and were just signs of Monty's presence.

Still, Flora mused, *the mood of this place has definitely changed in these past few months.*

For at least a century the Hotel Montresor had been infested with a curious form of psychic mould. It permeated the entire building, seemed to be somewhat sentient, and was, at least for now, entirely benevolent, although the recent change in colour had Flora a little worried. Gavin, as a Druid, was absolutely fascinated by the mould, and had dubbed it Monty, for the hotel that it occupied.

So far his research had shown no other instances of the mould anywhere in the world, making it entirely unique. It wasn't long before the quartet had started referring to Monty as the fifth occupant of the hotel.

The Peepers did not count, especially when Flora Cain had anything to say about it.

"I've got it!" Flora said, swapping the stick for a perfectly shaken drink. She took a sip, savouring the gorgeous floral and herbaceous notes, all carried along by the warmth and sweetness of the bourbon. "Oh, this is fucking fantastic! Nicely done, Coral."

"I'm an artist," Coral said, oozing confidence. She was about to say something else when a little device at her hip began to light up and crackle with static. "Hoo boy, I think we've got something!"

She walked swiftly over to the table and began to make all manner of notes in her leather-bound journal. Flora sighed heavily and rubbed her eyes in frustration.

The two women had met in a community mental health support group for local residents suffering from depression; specifically those healing after acting on suicidal impulses. Whilst Flora's reasons were rather complex, Coral's were relatively straightforward.

The young woman had been sectioned more than once for believing that the town was brimming with supernatural entities and gifted humans. As most people simply ignored such things on an instinctive level, she was quickly diagnosed with all manner of conditions, which sent her into a suicidal spiral.

What helped her climb out of that pit of despair was meeting Flora at the support group and the realisation that she had been right all along. The two had quickly become friends and only a year had passed before she'd moved into the Monty permanently.

Still, whenever Coral spoke excitedly about aliens or one of her home-made psychic detectors sent her into a flurry of active research, Flora wondered if maybe *some* of the diagnoses attached to the grey-haired young woman weren't inaccurate.

It's been an interesting six years since, to say the very least.

"And then what happened?" Coral asked eagerly, nodding at the empty air as if listening to some floating spectre. "Fascinating!"

Poor woman, Flora thought. *It must be such a mind fuck not to be born into this world.*

Both Flora and Coral's attention was drawn to the door of the Silver Schooner as Gavin and Leroy ambled in, well over an hour after they should have.

"Where the fuck have you been?" Flora said. "We have some serious business to discuss!"

"Yeah," Gavin said, holding out his phone for Flora to look at. "Things are really amiss here."

"Are those whales?" she asked, and he nodded.

"Yes, they are," Gavin said darkly, "and something has potentially taken one of my students."

"This looks bad, Flo," Leroy said, settling into his favourite chair. "You better bring us up to speed on this new guy quickly, because we need to talk about how we're gonna shelter him when the Ministry is crawling all over this place."

"Right," Flora said, draining the rest of her drink to give her a little bit of courage. "This is gonna be a hard one, chat; his name is Reginald Kellogg, and he's the last survivor of the Familiar Project."

Leroy let out a low whistle as Gavin turned a deathly shade of grey. Coral, on the other hand, looked deeply confused.

"Is, uh, is that bad?" Coral asked, looking around at her friends for clarification.

"Oh, yeah," Leroy said after a while. "This is gonna be a fucking nightmare."

"Why?" Coral said, almost defensively. "It's nothing we can't handle, right?"

Jesus Christ, Flora thought as she pinched the bridge of her shapely nose, *where do I even start?*

The grandfather clock in the reception hall chimed midnight, and their new guest still had not arrived. The Montresor Gang were ready for trouble; Flora had changed out of her usual lingerie and robe combination into acceptable street clothes, and held a hockey stick wrapped in enchanted brambles in one hand. Coral had a taser and a butterfly knife tucked away in her jacket, and Gavin was arguing with Leroy over the Druidic origins of his own weapon.

"This is the brick all over again, bro," Leroy said, shaking his head in disbelief. Whilst the others were all armed, Leroy's natural gifts as a Ghoul made him more than a match for most threats. Gavin, however, was idly swinging a hiking sock filled with two pounds' worth of pennies from the arcade.

"The sock is made from hemp, which is a natural fibre and is permitted by the Circle," Gavin said defensively, "and the Circles of the Southwest allow the use of copper, tin, and lead in spells as they are readily available in the local environment."

Gavin twirled his makeshift flail gleefully in his hand.

"I think this fits the definition of a Druidic Weapon nicely."

"Gav," Flora said, almost trembling with stress, "I say this with all the love in the world, but I've never met anyone who has as much *just released from prison* energy as you."

"Letter of the law, Flora," Gavin said smugly. "Letter of the law."

"Man, this is why the other Druids don't like you." Leroy continued to stare at the gently clinking sock. "I'm serious, bro; if you hit someone with that, you're gonna fucking kill them."

"Not if I don't hit them somewhere vital," Gavin replied defensively, "and the other Druids *do* like me; they're just intimidated by an enlightened man, that's all."

Flora was about to interject when the front door opened. She immediately got to her feet and let her power flow into the brambles, causing the thorns to grow to over an inch in length and become stiff as iron.

A nervous looking man stared at the four of them as he slowly crossed over the threshold. He had messy dark hair that barely covered his horns, a long pointed tail that whipped back and forth, and an unkept beard that was clearly more of a disguise than a fashion statement. The man's skin was a ruddy bronze in colour, hinting at the Djinn that was mixed into his absurdly hybridised body.

The fingers of his left hand were gnarled and curled; they'd been savagely broken some time ago and never set properly afterwards. His other hand clutched a shining coin; a silver florin, one of the few ever made.

"Are... are you the Stationmaster?" he said shakily, looking at Flora. She nodded, and extended her mind already feeling for the first hints of his power beginning to latch on to her.

Much to her surprise, she found nothing.

"You're Reggie Brek, right?" Gavin asked, idly bouncing the sock in his hand.

"I, uh, I guess," Reggie said nervously. "I'm sorry I'm late; it took me longer than I thought to cross town. I had, uh, something I needed to do first."

"You've been in Torquay a while?" Flora asked, and he nodded wordlessly. She frowned as she stared at him. "Why didn't you say anything?"

"I was afraid that you wouldn't help me," he said nervously looking tearfully at his feet. After a considerable pause, he looked back at Flora. "Are you still going to help me?"

As much as every instinct screamed at her to say no, she instead looked at Gavin, who gave her a gentle nod. *For Lucy,* she thought.

"Of course we will, Reggie."

"Oh, thank you so much!" Kellogg smiled at them all as he clutched his ruined hand to his chest, as if trying to slow his clearly racing heart. "You don't realise how much this means to me!"

"I think you'll be surprised at just how much we understand you, brother," Leroy said, stepping forward and putting a hand on Reggie's back. "Welcome to the Hotel Montresor."

<u>Chapter Five</u> – Rooftop Musings

Gavin

Gavin watched as the crew from the Environment Agency removed the last of the whale carcasses from the beach; despite frantic efforts from onlookers and the authorities, not a single one of the creatures had survived.

"This is just the start, isn't it?" Coral said as she snapped several photographs of the scene before them.

"I think so," Gav replied quietly. "Say, you've not heard anything about people going missing in the past couple of weeks, have you?"

"No," Coral said after a moment's consideration, "but there's talk of a strange man walking the streets at night; a man who only appears to the truly lost and desperate. Maybe that's a good place to start."

"Jacinth did mention an odd man meeting Libby's father," Gavin said, glancing further down the beach at a sobbing woman. She was clinging to the railing with white knuckled terror and it was clear that she hadn't slept in days. "Tell me, Coral, was that lady here yesterday?"

"Yeah, she was," Coral said quietly, covertly taking the woman's picture. "Day before that, too; do you think she's involved?"

"Could be," Gavin said, "but she also might just be an environmentalist, upset at all the death on show."

"Maybe she's a Sensitive," Coral suggested, and Gavin nodded along; he didn't have the heart to tell her that 'Sensitive' wasn't really a thing. "Should we go and talk to her?"

"No," he said softly. "She won't give us anything useful if we confront her directly, but we will walk past slowly; do you have your tape recorder with you?"

"Always do," Coral said, producing the compact device from a concealed pocket. "You want me to see if she's saying anything?"

"Yes, along with a rudimentary EVP; something tells me that she's been touched by a creature from the beyond." Gavin put his hands in his pockets, suddenly chilly in the afternoon sun. "I can't say what my reasoning is, but my hunches aren't often wrong."

Except where Lucy's cancer was concerned, whispered a little voice in his head, but he pushed the words down deep. He sighed heavily and looked at Coral, frowning slightly.

"Say, you don't think Reggie has anything to do with this, do you?" he asked. "The timeline adds up, after all."

"I can see how a Familiar would have the ability to offer out dreams and wishes like candy," Coral said, "but it just doesn't feel right; Reggie's in too much of a fucking state to be a threat to anyone."

"Wishes?" Gavin asked, raising his voice slightly. The sobbing woman turned to look at them, as if he'd spoken her name. *Well, that clarifies that, then.* He lowered his voice for his next words. "You didn't mention wishes before, Coral."

"Sorry, Gav; I thought it was implied."

"I didn't mean it!" the sobbing woman yelled, marching towards them. "I didn't mean for any of this to happen!"

Coral reflexively clicked on the recorder as the woman neared them, and Gavin made sure to place himself bodily between the two; he couldn't help much if the woman got violent, but it was better than leaving Coral unprotected entirely.

"What happened?" Gavin asked. "What did you see?"

"I... I just wanted to see a whale," the woman said tearfully. "Just one more beautiful thing before I died; is that too much to ask for?"

"Not at all," Gavin said, keeping his voice as warm and approachable as he could. "Can you tell me who offered to show you a whale?"

"He offered me whatever I wanted," the woman said, her eyes fixed on the middle distance. "He said that I could have anything!"

"What did he look like?" Gavin asked, and she glanced at the cloudless blue horizon.

"He was made of the night sky, just blackness and glinting stars. That's all I can say."

"What did you promise him?" Coral asked, leaning around Gavin.

"Anything he wanted," the woman said quietly. "Absolutely anything."

"One last question," Gavin asked, looking at the woman's absolutely exhausted face. "Have you slept since you saw him?"

"Not a wink," she whispered. "Whenever I try I feel like something is going to come for me, to steal me away; I'm worried that if I go to sleep I won't exist any more."

That doesn't sound like something Reggie is powerful enough to do, Gavin thought as the woman continued to stare at the removal of the whale carcasses as it unfolded before them. *That doesn't sound like him at all.*

Gavin lay in bed that night, wide awake as his eyes studied the moonlit ceiling of his bedroom. The atmosphere at the Hotel Montresor that evening had been less tense than the previous few, but something had clearly upset Flora. If Gavin closed his eyes and strained his ears, he could hear the sad songs filtering through from the floor above him.

He'd known Flora since they were small, and he knew what that particular style of music meant, so he remained awake, waiting for the inevitable.

It was around one in the morning when the music stopped, and he heard a chair being dragged clumsily to the middle of the floor. He sat up with a sigh and reached into the little herbalist's cabinet beside his bed. His fingers danced over the bottles, unsure of which one to take upstairs when the moment finally arrived.

Poor Flora, he thought as he heard the chair clatter to the floor, followed a few seconds later as a second impact shook plaster dust from the ceiling. Flora's howl of anguish and frustration echoed through the Monty, and Gavin took that as his cue. He plucked a bottle of blackberry wine from the cabinet, slipped his bathrobe over his thin pyjamas, and headed upstairs.

He saw a flash of movement at the end of the corridor as he reached the landing; Flora's silk robe billowed in the moonlight as she slipped through the window and on to the roof. Gavin glanced into her bedroom as he passed, and the fallen chair, along with a length of rope, confirmed that it was one of *those* nights.

Gavin grunted and groaned as he climbed clumsily through the window out on to the flat roof. He scrabbled up the ageing wrought iron ladder on to the highest point of the Hotel Montresor, where Flora sat, silhouetted in the moonlight. She looked at him, tears streaming from her almost luminous azure eyes, and smiled sadly.

"Hi, Gavin."

"Hello, Flora," he replied softly. He offered her the bottle. "A little flavour for the sadness?"

"Thanks." She took the bottle from his hands, unsealed it, and took a long swig as he settled comfortably next to her. She handed the bottle back to him and they passed it to and fro, sipping it in silence for the next few minutes.

"One of those days, huh?" he asked after a while, and she nodded. "Monty still won't let you die?"

"Unfortunately not," Flora said despondently. "I wrote all my letters, made sure the knot was tight, and I even measured the drop to make sure it would be quick, but the fucking rope came undone, just like it always does!"

She let out a shuddering sob.

"It's not fair, Gavin," she said through her tears. "My life wasn't supposed to be like this!"

"I know, Flora," he said, putting an arm around her and holding her close.

"I was supposed to be a writer," she whispered. "An artist; a fucking visionary! I was supposed to be the Plath of our generation, Gavin."

"I know that's what you wanted," he replied quietly. "You were going to write the greatest English novel of our time, and then kill yourself whilst you were still young and beautiful."

"So very beautiful," Flora sobbed. "I wanted to be eloquent, and pretty, and selfish, and immortalised in tragedy, but..."

Her sobbing increased, and he could only understand her words because he'd heard them so often before.

"But I just can't stop helping people! I feel physically sick when I know someone is in need, and it's tearing my life apart. I just want to be a vapid bimbo, but I can't stop thinking about society and its problems.

"I know I should be grateful, Gavin, for everything I have, but I just feel so fucking guilty all the time. I know that no matter what I do, it'll never make enough of a difference, so why should I bother?"

"You bother because you care, Flora," he said as she wept in his arms. "I'm sorry, lovely, but you're just doomed to be a good person. You don't have a selfish bone in your body, and I know that hurts, especially when there's so much suffering in the world, but you can't solve it all, Flora."

"I know," she whispered, "but I have tried so fucking hard to be an unlikeable misanthrope, Gavin. I have worked ceaselessly to cultivate as bleak a life as possible, from living in a ramshackle hotel in a hopeless seaside town, creating art that fixates on my death, and even listening exclusively to sombre music, but instead of the all-consuming sorrow that I have strived so hard for, all I have is anger.

"Anger at injustice, anger at the Ministry, and rage at the way the world leaves the most vulnerable behind!" Flora took another swig of the wine. "I can't write when I'm angry, Gavin, and I know that Monty won't let me die until I've finished my book."

I don't think that's the reason it's keeping you around, Gavin thought, but he chose to remain silent. The whole situation would be comically dark if it hadn't been for the countless suicide attempts Flora had made throughout the decades they'd known each other.

"Finish my book," Flora said bitterly after another long chug of wine. "What a fucking joke! I haven't even started it."

She sighed heavily and looked at Gavin, her eyes glittering in the darkness.

"If I tell you that I love you, will you love me back this time?" She continued before he could respond. "No, that wasn't fair of me; I'm sorry, Gavin."

"It's okay, Flora," he said quietly. "I know what it's like to love someone that's forever out of reach."

"At least you had Lucy for a while," she whispered. Gavin sat in silence for a short time longer, but the mood seemed to have shifted; deep down he knew that the danger had passed. His feeling was confirmed when Flora let out a tearful chuckle. "Fuck me, Gav, this is good wine. You should give up teaching and go into brewing; you and Coral could make a killing."

"Nah, that's not for me," he said with a smile. "Besides, that's the special vintage; the rooftop reserve."

"Held under the counter for those rare nights that you have to talk your bestie down from the edge?" she asked, before clarifying. "Well, not that rare, nowadays, are they?"

"I'll be here, even if it means I spend my entire life on the roof with you, Flora." He smiled at her. "Besides, I know you won't really jump; not until the lads finally do you proud."

"That," she said with a giggle, "is a low fucking blow, Gav!"

"It's coming home," he said in a sarcastic, high

pitched voice. "At least you chose a spectacular night for it."

Flora nodded as the two of them stared at the full moon, its glow lighting up the sea in a plain of glimmering silver. The Faun sighed heavily as she turned to look at the Druid.

"My brother wants to meet me for lunch next week," she said nervously. "I have an awful feeling that he's going to ask to move in for a while."

"It'll be nice to have Paris here," Gavin said, but Flora groaned. "What? He's a sweetheart!"

"I know, but he's *so* fucking stupid. Like, even calling him a himbo is giving him too much credit. Besides, how am I supposed to keep up my air of melancholia with that upbeat grinning moron swanning around?

"He gets up early to make muffins, Gavin! It's just not compatible with my lifestyle!"

Gavin chuckled but just as he was about to respond, he was struck silent by what he saw in the sky.

A second silvery moon appeared alongside the first, and then another, and another. Soon the night sky was brimming with false moons, bathing the town in an eerie glow that turned Gavin's blood to ice water in his veins. Flora grabbed his arm in fear as the two stared into the luminous night.

"Gavin," she whispered, "what the fuck is happening out there?"

"I don't know," he replied softly, "but whatever it is, it's getting worse."

Chapter Six – Baby Steps, Again

Lola

Lola groaned as she gradually woke up, groggy and nauseous as the room slowly span around her. *Oh fuck,* she thought hazily, *they've changed something again.*

I hope they didn't take Thad away.

The past six months or so with Thaddeus Thane for company on Betony Island had made the monotony of imprisonment bearable; if they forced her back into the automated white room to suffer alone once again, she was certain to lose her mind.

Courage, Lola.
Remember, all roads lead to home.

She opened her eyes, and was astounded to find herself in a small bedroom with picture windows that looked out over the waters of the Thames Estuary. Her bedclothes were made of Egyptian cotton, and she wore her very own silver silk pyjamas; she'd never expected to see any of her extensive wardrobe ever again.

As much as she was thrilled to have at least some of her belongings back, she frowned at the expensive sleepwear.

"This doesn't feel like me any more," she murmured. Her voice had changed during her imprisonment as well as her taste in fashion, but like the former it was a reversion to her base state rather than an evolution.

Instead of the shrill, nasal voice that she'd affected for the decades after Lamplight, she now spoke in her native accent. She'd been born on Canvey Island and had buried the Estuary accent her entire life, but when it was only her and Thaddeus, it seemed wrong to hide who she really was.

Thaddeus had also told Lola her real name after a few weeks of imprisonment, but she wasn't quite ready to let her chosen moniker go yet. *I do sound more like a Michelle nowadays, though,* she thought as she looked out over the gentle waves.

She was intimately familiar with this part of the country, and she knew that she was still on Betony Island, but she was now in the large building that had housed the Project's research staff, instead of the underground prison she had been consigned to so very recently.

There was a gentle knock on her bedroom door, and she turned sharply at the sound.

"It's been a long time since anyone did that for me," she said softly, before raising her voice. "Come in."

The door swung gently inwards, revealing the tall powerful man behind it. She smiled at Thaddeus, pleased that her cellmate and friend of convenience had been allowed to join her on the surface. He walked slowly towards her, almost too stunned to speak.

"It's good to see you," she said, taking several quick steps backward, away from the door. "We don't have to do this all at once, Thad."

Whilst confinement had not been kind to him, he had worked hard to maintain his strength and agility in the small space that had been available. He still carried a considerable paunch, but it only served to make him all the more intimidating.

The skeletal bones of his fleshless hand twitched as he approached, and Lola took another stride away from the approaching Famine. This was the first time they'd been together without a barrier between them, and although she was confident in their friendship, something in his eyes made her full of fear.

Thaddeus was upon her quicker than she thought possible, roughly pushing her up against the wall and staring at her with a mad hunger that made her skin prickle into goose flesh. She could fell the yawning abyss of his gift; much larger than she expected, even with the regular diet of Ceps the Ministry had been feeding him.

"Are you going to hurt me?" she whispered.

At least if he kills me, it'll be quick, she thought, *unlike the decades I had to endure with Gideon.*

"Something about you feels different," Thad said, bringing his face close to her neck. "You feel strange, and you smell more enticing than the first time we met."

"A lot has changed since then, Thaddeus," Lola said softly. *I wonder if I could ensnare him now?* She immediately put the thought out of her mind; to do so would certainly mean that they would never, ever leave the Island. "Are you going to feed on me, or just do what everyone else does?"

There was a heartbeat of stillness between them, and then Thad let her go.

"I'm not going to harm you," he said after a moment. "You don't need to be afraid of me."

"Thank you," Lola replied, her heart hammering with relief. "There's a darker side to obsession that most never even think about. Whilst Gideon had his uses, the time we spent alone was monstrous.

"Truth be told, a part of me was glad to find out that Charity had killed him."

"And which part of you is that?" Thad asked, perching on the edge of her bed.

"The part of me that's in full control now." Lola joined him and they watched the summer sun shimmer on the waters of the Estuary. "Although I feel the presence of someone else pulling at our strings."

"What is this place?" Thad asked.

"This is where we live now," Lola said. "We'll be sent into the field soon, so we better start getting our skills sharpened up."

"Do they really trust us?" he said, genuinely surprised.

"Of course they don't," Lola said with a dark chuckle. "They've just found something more terrifying than we are. Do you remember what they used to say to me, Thaddeus?"

"I do," he replied before repeating the mantra she'd learned during Lamplight. "The Ministry always has a bigger stick."

"We better get practising," Lola said. "What are you going to drill first?"

"I've not done any shooting in ages, and some melee work wouldn't do me any harm," he said, stretching. "What about you?"

"I need to shake the dust off my major and minor support skills," she said as she opened the draw beside the bed. A broad smile broke out on her face when she saw that her special blue tinted glasses had been safely transported to the Island. "I'll give you three guesses as to what they are, but you'll never get them both."

"Spirit photography?"

"Nope."

"Field surgery?"

"Just one left, Thad." She grinned and he looked

inside her wardrobe, where several sets of work overalls were neatly hanging on the rail.

"Engineering?" he asked, blinking in surprise.

"Yep, both mechanical and electronic," Lola replied gleefully, "but engineering's just my backup. I did say that you wouldn't get them both, didn't I?"

"Then what is it?" he asked with a laugh.

"Coding."

His silence said it all.

"You don't believe me?" Lola asked, bristling slightly.

"You, uh, don't really seem like the type," he said awkwardly.

"Misdirection is another skill that is worth learning," she replied sharply. "For your information, Thaddeus, I've been coding since I was a child. When it comes to computers, I'm a fucking prodigy."

Lola's fingers danced over the keyboard as she peered through her protective glasses at the rapidly shifting screen. In the background, silhouetted against the window, Thaddeus was practising strokes with a large curved blade, most likely a kukri.

"Move your feet more," Lola called out. "Step into the strike; you're a big man, so make your body mass work for you."

"I know how to fight," Thad replied angrily. "Charity Walpole-"

"Charity is a sweetheart," Lola interrupted, "but she fights like an assassin, which you most certainly are not. You're strong and powerful, Thad, but you just aren't fast enough to fight like that. Why are you using an edged weapon, anyway?"

"It belonged to my Aunt Bella," he said, abandoning

the window and walking over to join her at the computer. "Silas Cherry used it to cut my fucking arm off."

"Did he..." Lola grinned at him, and he shook his head, which of course did not stop her, "... *disarm* you?"

"Fucking hell, Lola," Thad groaned, "that's bad, even for you."

"I'm serious about the blade, though," she said firmly. "If your opponent is a Cep, just grab them and eat them."

"And if they aren't?" Thad asked.

"Just break their neck or shoot them. You don't need to be fucking about with a weapon like that, especially when you don't have the training to use it properly. I bet Silas had that off you in fucking seconds."

"He did," Thad admitted with a sigh. "He moves like nothing I've ever seen."

"You would've had a better time without it," Lola said, stern as a schoolmarm. "A weapon you can't use well is just another tool for your opponent. That's part of the Ravenblade training; knowing your limitations."

"Everyone said that you were only a Ravenblade because of Gideon," Thad said softly, "but now I'm beginning to doubt that."

"Second highest score ever," she said with a satisfied smile. "Runner up to Helen Mickelson, who decided to be a doctor instead, so the highest of all serving Ravenblades, in fact."

"You were better than Gideon?" Thad asked, and she nodded.

"I carried him through the assessment, not the other way round. I thought it would be useful to set up a rumour that downplayed my talents, however, so I set it in motion and adopted the ditzy Rah-Rah persona that everyone knows so well."

"Oh."

"I'm a lot smarter than I look, Thad," she said, turning back to the computer. "I learned a lot in this place, but how to hide in plain sight was the most valuable lesson. People see what they expect to see, Thaddeus, which gives those of us who truly look beyond the surface a massive advantage.

"You aren't fast enough to fight like a Ghost, for instance, but you are much, much more agile than someone of your size normally would be. If you come out swinging at your top pace, with strength and accuracy, you'll have the edge over someone who expects you to be slower."

"Huh." He cocked his head to one side. "Can I ask you something about what happened on Hallowe'en, Lola?"

"You're going to ask why you all managed to get one over on me, even though I'm apparently so intelligent?"

"Pretty much," Thad said, and she chuckled.

"Sometimes people just get lucky, Thaddeus," she said with a casual wave of her hand. He looked at her for a moment, but then seemed to take her words at face value; after all, she and the Coven had put up a hell of a fight.

It would've been helpful if we'd won, but in the end I still would've been imprisoned here all the same, she thought slyly. Everyone had been so quick to throw her into solitary confinement in the bowels of Betony Island that nobody had even stopped to consider if that had been her plan all along.

That conversation, however, was one she would

need to have with Thaddeus in the future; for now, a plausible lie would have to suffice.

"You better put on your formal tie, Thaddeus," Lola said, turning to look at the sweating man. "We've got company."

"What do you mean, Lo-" His last word was cut short as something stole the breath from his throat, sending him crashing to the ground as the air was drained from his lungs. Lola settled back in her chair as she felt her own chest being emptied. She remained calm, however; this was merely a demonstration of power, rather than an attempt on their lives.

As quickly as it had left, their breath returned, leaving them both gasping, but alive.

A pale woman, seemingly spun from a light evening breeze, materialised in the room with the two breathless Exceptions. Everything about her was translucent and ever-shifting, like a twisting zephyr that stirs the morning fog in tight eddies, leaving only collapsing vortices as evidence that it ever existed at all.

A Sylph, she thought. *Now that's going to be a pain in the fucking arse.*

"Good day, Agents," the Sylph said gently. "My name is Miette, and I will be your handler from this point onwards. You have two more days of preparation before we set out on our first assignment.

"I will see you tomorrow evening, when I will explain the specifics of our case. Until then, I will be watching; any misbehaviour, and you will find that it is the last thing you will ever do."

The Sylph vanished as quickly as she had appeared, leaving the two Ceps reeling from her words.

Miette!? Lola thought as the name finally registered

in her mind. *She's one of Desai's best and deadliest! This is going to be a lot harder than I originally planned.*

She took a deep breath, and looked at the terrified Thaddeus.

"Take heart, Thad," she said in a comforting tone, "and remember that no matter what happens, all roads lead to home."

He nodded at her words, even though his eyes revealed that he had no idea what she meant.

Don't worry, darling, she thought sadly, *one day I'll tell you why we're both here.*

We just need to survive until then.

Chapter Seven – Feasting and Fawning

Flora

The wind had grown chilly in the intervening days since Reginald Kellogg had come to live at the Montresor. Flora had been kind and courteous to their guest, but had made sure to keep her distance where possible; it made perfect sense for him to imprint on her and that was something she could not allow to happen.

This is going to be hard enough without one-sided attachments getting in the way, she thought, *but I still can't feel him reaching out to me at all.*

How strange.

Thankfully, the heat that Reggie was certain followed him had yet to materialise, but Flora had called in every favour and contact to keep her finger on the pulse of the entire Torbay and Dartmoor area, just in case.

Something had the backs of the local Warlocks up too; their most recent meeting was supposed to be the Midsummer Dinner and Dance, but it had been cancelled last minute. Several of Flora's close friends were heading out of town for a while and although they gave no concrete reasons, she suspected that the mass stranding and the false moons had put the wind up them.

Them and me, both, she thought as she strode along the waterfront, through the Princess Gardens. The silver details of her fashionable black boots gleamed in the midday sunlight and the gossamer thin material of her sheer dress clung to her body in a way that no artist could possibly capture fully; her appearance was striking enough to stop people in their tracks, leaving them open-mouthed and gawping.

At least when I'm with Paris they'll stare at him instead.

Where Flora's supernatural beauty was enough to physically stun people to silence, Paris was on a whole other level. Their parents had ended up homeschooling him during his teens as his burgeoning glamour had literally driven several of his classmates out of their minds. One of Paris's best friends during school, an ostensibly straight teenage boy, had awkwardly asked him on a date only for the completely asexual Paris to gently rebuff him.

The boy had hanged himself in their front garden then next morning.

Flora sighed sadly. The crushing weight of the Cain siblings' gifts put a terrible responsibility on both of them, but it seemed to most that Paris was too simple and shallow for the tragic consequences of their beauty to affect him.

Flora knew better, however, and she knew that her brother's life was mostly lived online, as was hers, to protect those around him.

I wonder if a serious disfigurement would make our lives easier? Flora mused, and not for the first time. *Then again, I know that would bring me even more trouble than it would solve; what a cursed existence I get to enjoy.* Both of her parents had been counselled against their union by their respective families and the Ministry; if they were to have any children, they would have absolutely no chance of a normal life.

Still, love won out and the Cain siblings were born.

I think we did alright for ourselves, Flora thought as

the first eerie strains of music reached her ears, *and we've better learned to wield our supernatural appeal to our own ends.*

It was fairly common for Flora to hear Paris before she saw him; both were musically gifted, but his talents were geared towards instruments, instead of his voice. In his last email he'd expressed an interest in taking up the fiddle, and it was clear that he had taken to it like a Rusałka to water.

A sharp pain stung her heart as she grew closer to the source of the music; a part of her was deeply, profoundly jealous of her older brother and she sometimes, albeit only for a fleeting moment, hated him for it.

It was common for Rusałki and Fauns to be aromantic and asexual, at least where urges were concerned, but Flora had been unlucky enough to inherit her parents' capacity for both love and lust. *At least he'll never know the bitter hurt of unrequited love,* she thought angrily. Of course, she'd always have the temptation to turn her glamour on Gavin in order to make him obsessed with her, but she loathed herself for even considering it.

No, she thought as she neared the Marina and filtered through the small crowd that had gathered there, *if I am ever to be in a relationship with someone, they'll have to be immune to my charms.*

Gavin and I are destined to be friends alone, she accepted tearfully, *for better or worse.*

The music stopped suddenly and the people stood at the water's edge all stirred at the same time, as if waking from a collective dream. Paris waved eagerly at her from atop the sea wall, silhouetted against the bright sunlight.

"Good heavens, Rizz," she muttered as he leapt down and pushed through the crowd to see her, "what are you wearing!?"

Paris's raven locks were artfully tousled, mostly hiding his curled horns; not that anyone would even care if they did see them, though. What shocked Flora, however, was the flamingo pink hot pants and the matching crop top, along with a pair of Air Force Ones that were clearly customised to suit his particular brand.

"Hey, Flo!" Paris said, sweeping her up in a crushing hug. He towered above her, standing at just over six feet and seven inches; over a foot taller than her, and rippling with powerful muscles. *They should've called you Adonis,* she thought with a grin, *but Paris still works just fine.*

"Jesus, Rizz," Flora said once he finally released her, "are you trying to crush me to death?"

"Ah, sorry, sis." He took a moment to look at her outfit. "What's with all the black?"

"Oh, you know, pangs of despised love and all that," she said sheepishly. "Don't you think that your choice of brand deals are a little on the nose, Rizz?"

"Yeah, I guess the Jock might be a bit much," he replied blushing a little. "I don't get why Nike would be a problem, though."

God, give me fucking strength, Flora thought, even as a smile twitched the corners of her mouth.

"What?" Paris asked, clearly confused. "Come on Flo, what's so funny?"

"Never mind, Rizz," she said with a chuckle, leading him towards town. "Let's go get lunch."

"Oh, I have something for you," he said after his

fifth plate of food. He reached down and fished around in the small backpack that he'd brought with him, before finally producing a slightly crushed box. He handed it to her nervously and she opened it up, gasping with delight as she saw what was inside.

"Rizz," she said softly, "this is absolutely beautiful, thank you!"

Inside the plain white cardboard was a little nest of black tissue paper, at the centre of which nestled a simple golden brooch, shaped like an apple. It was elegant, expertly crafted, and as she picked it up there was a faded message engraved on the back of it.

To the fairest, she thought with a smile. She glanced at her brother, who had been giving her golden apple themed gifts ever since she'd first come out as trans almost twenty five years ago. *Sometimes I wonder if there's more going on in that head of yours than you let on.*

"I'm glad you like it," he said, beaming at her.

"Nothing makes me feel more seen as a woman than the gifts I get from you," she said kindly as she affixed her new brooch to her dress. "You're a good man, Paris."

"I try my best," he said, pausing for a moment before continuing. "So, Flora, I've got something I need to ask you-"

"Yes," she said, cutting him off with a chuckle, "I spoke to Gavin and he said that you can stay as long as you like."

"How did you know what I was going to ask?" he asked, wide eyed with surprise.

Your luggage arrived at the Montresor this morning, she thought. *I don't think I'll ever be able to tell if you're the best liar or the stupidest person I've ever met, but I guess it doesn't matter either way.*

"Women's intuition," she said after a moment of contemplation. "It comes in handy from time to time. Oh, marvellous!"

The waiter brought out their next round of dishes and another bottle of wine. Flora absolutely adored Lebanese food, both for its outstanding flavours and the generous portions that were provided. Fauns were natural feasters, eating only a couple of times a week but indulging to excess when they eventually did.

Of course, this put them into a state of euphoric torpor for several hours afterwards, which was an opportunity for those who wished them ill.

Whilst the Cain siblings retained their father's desire to feast, their mother's nature as an ambush predator meant that they could overcome their food-induced haze in a fraction of an instant if necessary, which made both Flora and Paris a true threat to any would-be attackers.

Always keep them guessing, Flora thought happily as she sunk her teeth into another slice of highly spiced sausage.

"I have to warn you, Rizz," Flora said after a few more ravenous mouthfuls, "that the Monty is rather busy at the moment. We've got one of our more, uh, *transient* guests staying with us."

"It's a hotel," Paris replied matter-of-factly. "Of course there are guests."

"I guess that's true," she said with a smile. *Sometimes the simplicity of his mind does make things easier.* "I just wanted you to know, in case anything untoward happens and all hell breaks loose."

"I'll be practically invisible, Flo; I know you've got your whole Sylvia Plath thing going on, and I won't get in the way of that." He paused for a moment. "Is Leroy still there?"

"Yes, he is," she said, her smile growing into a grin. Leroy and Paris were firm friends, and neither of the Cain siblings' glamour had any effect on him whatsoever, so it gave Paris a chance to be genuinely close to someone. When Flora had asked him about his immunity to their charms, he'd chuckled and muttered something about colonial beauty standards and being old fashioned, which did make sense.

"Oh, I meant to tell you this earlier," Paris said, pulling his phone out of his pocket, "but I saw something super weird when I got here this morning. I managed to get a video of it, though, and I thought you should see; it seems like something your crew would want to know about."

He set the video playing and passed the phone to Flora, whose eyes widened when she saw what was on the screen.

Oh no, she thought as the short clip looped around again, showing two colossal whirlpools spinning out in the deeper waters of the bay. Several seabirds and an unlucky kayaker seemed caught up in the tremendous currents as they swirled downwards to the sea floor.

"Is this, like, normal for this area?" Paris asked, trying to hide his nervousness behind a faltering smile.

"No, Rizz," she replied softly, unable to tear her eyes away from the mesmerising display before her. "This is completely unnatural. Look at the way they're rotating in different directions; that should be impossible given the geography of the bay.

"In fact, these don't even look like true whirlpools."

"Then what are they?" he asked, leaning forwards.

Flora looked past him, through the glass of the restaurant window at the clear, cloudless sky beyond. Still, the wind was gently picking up and the fronds of the palm trees were whipping back and forth in the strengthening breeze.

This all feels so fucking wrong, she thought as she glanced from window to video and back again. *Something tremendously powerful is out there, and it's clearly only just starting to realise how strong it is.*

This is gonna get bad real fucking quick.

"Flo?" Paris asked anxiously.

"Sorry, Rizz," she replied, handing back the phone. "I lost my train of thought there."

"You were saying that the whirlpools looked like something else; what is it?"

"Storm systems, Rizz," she said darkly, staring out at the summer sky once again. "Terrible, destructive storms."

Chapter Eight – Old Habits Die Hard

Lola

"Dead whales?" Thad said over breakfast on the morning they were due to leave. He'd been reading the report over and over since the previous night, when Miette had given them their briefing. "Optical illusions in the night sky-"

"-and now two whirlpools in water far too shallow for such a phenomenon," Lola continued, putting her fork down angrily. "You can keep saying it aloud as much as you want, Thad, but it isn't going to make any more sense than it already does."

He glared at her from across the table.

"Now clean your plate," she instructed firmly, "and we can get our shit together and get on the road. The sooner we get there, the sooner we can start investigating, and that will help all the pieces fall into place."

"Are you driving, or am I?" Thad asked, and Lola shot him a sharp look. His face flushed slightly and he stared at the table in embarrassment. "Sorry, Lo; I completely forgot. I'm still getting used to being the designated driver."

Part of Thaddeus's instruction during his imprisonment had been an intensive driving course, provided remotely, along with feeding him Ceps that were skilled drivers of all manner of vehicles. He had yet to physically get behind the wheel, however, and the nerves were clearly getting to him.

"Will you be alright once we're on the road?" he asked softly.

"I have my glasses and I've taken my pills," she replied. "If we can keep the driving to daylight hours, that would definitely be safer for me."

Whilst her talents as a Ministry Agent had not suffered during her confinement, the constant exposure to the fluorescent lighting of their subterranean prison had exacerbated an underlying condition that had plagued her since birth; one that was tied to the strange violet eyes of all Juliets.

Lola Oriole had epilepsy, specifically the photosensitive variety. Any kind of flickering or strobe light could very quickly put her out of action, which Thad had seen one morning a few months earlier.

The lights in her cell had malfunctioned, flickering rapidly instead of turning on fully, and they had triggered a full tonic-clonic seizure in her. Both Ceps had been sedated with an anaesthetic gas pumped into the cells before the Ministry doctors had attended her.

Thankfully, the incident hadn't been repeated, but her underlying illness had meant that she had never been able to drive, nor was she particularly keen to learn. Still, she was unused to anyone but the Ministry Superiors knowing about her epilepsy and it stung to be so openly vulnerable, even with someone as disarming as Thad.

She picked up her fork once again and gestured at Thad's mostly full plate

"Eat up, Thane," she said, more kindly this time. "They won't let us leave until we're deemed to be ready, which includes a full breakfast."

"How can you bear to live in such a regimented way?" Thaddeus asked after a moment of silence. "You do exactly what they ask of you, exactly when they ask; hell, if they told you to jump, you'd already know how high.

"Don't you ever get sick of it?"

"It's all I've ever known," she said flatly. "Even when I was a Ravenblade with minimal oversight, I still followed the rules they taught me as a girl."

"Why?" Thad asked, horrified.

"Because this is my home," she replied. "It's home for all of us, Thad; nobody really got off this island, and if they think they did, they're fucking delusional. Project Lamplight never stopped, Thaddeus; it just moved out into the wider world.

"They'll come home when they're ready," she said, popping a piece of sausage in her mouth, chewing it mechanically, and then swallowing without so much as tasting it. "When the time is right, it'll make sense to everyone.

"The important thing is to realise that there's always someone pulling the strings, Thane; no matter how free you feel, someone has planned out every second of your life already, so just go with it. Choice is an illusion; no matter which path you take, all roads lead to home."

"You could kill yourself," Thad said softly. "They aren't planning on that."

"Maybe they are," she said, almost without emotion as she speared another piece of sausage with the tines of her fork. "If they let me die, then it's part of the plan, but if it isn't, they'd stop me."

He stared at her, unblinking, as his cutlery trembled in his hands.

"Eat," she repeated. "Don't make me come over there and feed you."

"They really fucked you up, didn't they?" Thad said, barely loud enough to be heard. Lola simply smiled in response as she finished the last of her breakfast and placed her cutlery tidily on her plate.

"There's a freedom in knowing where you belong, Thaddeus," Lola said, placing her hands in her lap as she stared at him. "You'll see it, soon enough. Now clean your plate, and we can finally start looking for those answers that you want so much."

Thaddeus continued to stare at her in shock for a moment longer, but then he finally relented and began to eat.

Good, Lola thought as he dutifully ate every bite on his plate. *There's hope for him yet.*

"I thought you lived in Oxford," Thaddeus said as the little ferry carried them with the tide along the coast of the Estuary. Lola had given the pilot directions and Miette had assured him that there were no tricks afoot, so along the coast they went.

"I had a house in Oxford," Lola replied with a smile, "which was good for keeping up appearances and socialising, but I kept a safehouse in Allhallows just in case things ever went south and I needed somewhere closer to home."

"Home..." Thad echoed softly.

"You'll see Oxford again," Miette said to him, standing close behind the tall man, "if you continue to toe the line and fulfil your role within the Ministry."

"He's already frightened enough, Miette," Lola said as they approached the Allhallows Marina. "You don't need to threaten him any more."

She shivered slightly in the breeze that blew in from the channel; she'd only thrown on a light dress before leaving, as her old wardrobe had continued to feel alien to her. Thankfully, she had a stock of more suitable clothes in her safehouse, along with a vehicle for the unlikely trio to use to get to Torquay.

"Do we have any further leads?" Thad asked as their ferry chugged into the marina and headed slowly for their mooring point. "Aside from the whales, moons, and whirlpools, that is."

"We have one potential cause for the disturbances in the area," Miette said.

"Why wasn't it in the report?" Lola asked, rounding on the Sylph. Miette glared at her but Lola did not back down. "Look, if you want us at our best, you have to give us the entire picture instead of this piecemeal bullshit.

"What's the cause?"

"The power behind what's happening is too much for a single gifted human, so our intelligence has compiled a list of all non-human persons in the area," Miette said, her voice shifting in tone and volume like a wayward wind. "Our superiors believe the only one of sufficient skill and power to cause such phenomena is a former Ministry Agent.

"His name is Reginald Kellogg; the last remaining subject of the Familiar Project."

Lola whistled through her teeth. *Well, this is going to be a fucking nightmare.*

"Is that bad?" Thad asked as the boat's pilot tied the mooring lines in place.

"Reggie can accumulate gifts," Lola said, bouncing nervously on the balls of her feet, "based on the people that he's closest to. If memory serves, he had a few nasty ones under his belt when the Ministry kicked him to the kerb well over a decade ago."

"Like what?" Thad said as he helped her step on to the jetty, nodding in thanks to the pilot as he did so.

"A limited form of telekinesis, short range wormholes, full-blown teleportation, and some kind of crude echolocation; the last one was gained from working closely with Hillgreen." She sighed heavily, breathing in the free air as she walked towards the mainland. "Fuck knows what he has now."

"Agent Kellogg's disavowal was not, uh, as *comprehensive* as it was made to appear," Miette said, seeming flustered for the first time. Lola arched an eyebrow and gestured for the Sylph to continue. "He was contracted to carry out off-the-books work for both the Director and Deputy Director, reporting to them personally."

Lola saw Thad's eyes widen as she burst into snide, derisive laughter.

"Does the current situation amuse you, Agent Oriole?"

"You..." Lola continued to laugh, almost doubling over as she teetered on the edge of hysterics. "You stupid fucking cunts! You allowed him to bond with both a Rakshasa and, worse, *Harper Cherry*!?

"You do realise what he has in his blood, don't you?" Lola asked rhetorically as Thad placed a gentle hand on her shoulder, his face a mask of confusion and barely contained terror. "You've not met Harper yet, have you, darling?"

"I've only heard about her in passing," he said nervously. He turned to stare down Miette. "What kind of gift could he gain from the two of them?"

Silence, except for Lola's laughter, which now threatened to collapse into horrified sobbing.

"Tell me, Miette!" Thad snapped, his voice as hard and sharp as flint, and Lola felt his power flare like an electrical surge. The Sylph flickered slightly, as if she was about to vanish into the sea breeze, but her pale eyes turned to the ground as shame coloured her pallid face.

"I'll be the first to admit that it was a short sighted mistake," she muttered softly, "but the Director gets what he wants, and Harper... well, she's more of a monster than any of us."

"I remember reading that Rakshasas could reshape reality on a mere whim," Thad said, digging his fingers into Lola's flesh hard enough to curb her laughter in a yelp of pain. He let go suddenly, and she felt his supernatural hunger recede back to its background level. "Sorry, Lo."

"No harm, no foul," she said with a smile. "I've never been totally sold on the reality shaping, myself; I think some kind of complex illusion is much more likely. Harper, on the other hand, can unleash a person's fullest potential, for better or worse."

Not to mention her other, far more powerful talent.

"If Reggie can gain gifts based on the person he's close to..." Thad muttered, and Miette nodded solemnly.

"Then putting him near Harper and Mohinder means that he now has obscene amounts of power." The Sylph finally raised her face from the ground. "Our intelligence suggests that he has developed some kind of limited wish granting ability."

"Limited and Wish don't really belong together," Lola said, making a point of getting underway once again, "but that isn't actually what worries me."

"What could possibly be worse than that?" Thad asked, his large stride easily keeping pace with her hurried gait. She did not respond immediately, instead leading the others to a small maisonette built over a garage. Thad looked surprised when she unlocked a hidden key safe and opened the front door. "Is *this* your safe house?"

"Not all safety comes from armoured windows and glyphs of protection, Thane," she said snarkily. "Sometimes it's much better to hide in plain sight; a wolf in the herd, as it were."

"As much as it pains me to say it," Miette said breezily as they went inside, "Agent Oriole has the truth of it. Remember our raison d'etre; we exist to protect the world from the unseen horrors and hidden threats.

"How else to do that, but fight in the shadows?"

I might actually come to like you, Lola thought with a smile.

"Regarding Reggie," she said, flinging open a wardrobe filled with her preferred street clothes and pulling out a selection to take on the road, "he can't really function without someone to bond with, so if he is the cause of all this, there's someone else pulling the strings behind the scenes.

"In short, he's the lapdog to a much more dangerous master."

"I must admit," Miette said, her voice suddenly quiet and fearful, "I had not even considered that."

Rookie error, Lola thought, but decided that cohesion within their team was more important than the joy she would get from gloating.

"We'll have plenty of time to discuss our theories and formulate a plan once we're on the road." Lola tossed Thaddeus the set of keys with a grin. "Why don't you have a look in the garage to see what you'll be driving?"

"Colour me intrigued," he said with a smile. "Is it

something special?"

"She's my pride and joy." His smile widened into a grin, and he trotted down the stairs as she slipped off the clothes she'd worn on the journey from Betony Island. Lola reached into the back of the wardrobe and extracted her specially embroidered Race Day boilersuit, relishing the faint petrol scent of the fabric as she held it close to her face.

Thank god, she thought gleefully, *I finally get to be myself for the first time in years.*

At long fucking last.

Chapter Nine – Unsettled Skies

Gavin

Gavin pulled his coat tight about his chest; the temperature had dropped rapidly in the last few days and a small squall had blown in from the Channel, drenching the Devonshire coast and battering the Hotel Montresor with stormy winds.

Coral was wearing an oversized black waterproof coat which flapped and fluttered in the breeze as she struggled to keep pace with the druid; her bad leg often troubled her in inclement weather, and today was a particularly unpleasant day.

"Gavin," she panted as he hobbled after him, "would you please slow down just a little bit?"

"Sorry, Coral," he said easing his stride to match her steps. "I always get a bit speedy when I'm out in the rain."

"I understand," she said slapping him firmly on the back, "I don't want to be out in this any longer than necessary. At least this weather feels like an ordinary summer storm, rather than something more ominous."

"I'd still prefer the sunshine," Gav replied. He slipped back into moody silence as they continued onward, heading in the direction of the Styles' family home. He began to think of the worry on Jacinth's face, which in turn led him into the black pit of despair that held all of his memories of Lucy.

She used to love the rain.

"You know, you never did tell me how the two of you met," Coral said after a few minutes. Gavin glanced at her, suddenly afraid that she could read his mind, but she just chuckled in response. "You get this particular faraway look on your face when you think about her, Gav."

"Not one of your *Sensitive* powers?" he asked with a smile, and she shook her head. "I'm sure you know the broad strokes, Coral."

"I don't want a historical account; I want details and emotions! Come on, Gavin," Coral said, almost sadly, "tell a story about her with a smile for once; I don't think she'd want you to wallow like this."

"It was raining on the night we met," he said, "just like it is now. I was a much younger man back then, and I had only just realised my knack for druid-craft, so being an active participant in this world was all rather new to me.

"I knew it all existed, of course; Flora and I have been best friends since we were children, but I always expected to be an outsider looking in." He couldn't help but smile at just how naïve and inexperienced he'd been back then. "Anyway, Flo had heard about a party at a hotel on the seafront, so we strode through the rain to get there; her makeup was a wreck by the time we arrived, but she still looked like a supermodel."

"Was the hotel the Monty?" Coral asked.

"Yes; Lucy's parents had left it to her, and business was booming. The first person I met that evening was actually Leroy."

"Really?"

"Yeah, he'd been friends with Luce a few years by that point. I spent the first couple of hours just listening to him; his stories about growing up in Hawaii, becoming a Ghoul, and then his time in the Second World War were fascinating." He turned to look at his travelling companion. "Did you know that the Bureau of the Weird and Eerie marked him as Killed in Action, so he wasn't able to return home?"

"Is that the only reason he stuck around here?"

"That, and he missed being by the water. It's a different ocean, but it still felt enough like home for him. Anyway, after several joints and more than a few tins of beer, this woman comes over to me, dressed up to the nines; I mean it, Coral, she looked like a fucking angel walking through the rabble.

"I think the first words out of my mouth were to that effect, and she found that very funny. She told me her name and pulled me up to dance with her; I was worried sick that my moves would be shown up, but she was such a terrible fucking dancer that it made me fall for her on the spot."

"Because she couldn't dance?" Coral asked incredulously.

"Because she didn't give a fuck," Gav said, his face beaming in the rain. "It was her party, in a hotel full of people, but she danced like she was the only woman in that room; hell, to me, she was. Once we were done with the dancing, we went upstairs and just fell into her bed.

"We didn't get back out for three days, save to use the loo or refill the teapot."

"You're a dark horse," Coral said with a chuckle. "You didn't need to sleep?"

"She was a Walker," Gavin replied coyly. "Sleep for her was just more time to play."

Coral nodded approvingly, and he went on, wiping the rain from his brow.

"When we finally climbed out of that bed, it was only for enough time for me to get my things to move in." His voice faltered a little. "That night was the one and only time she went into any detail about her troubled childhood, just so I knew what I was getting into.

"She mentioned the terrible things that had happened then, and that she'd only had one friend for the entire time she was going through all that; a mad little girl who was forced to wear a mask every single day." He shook his head angrily. "When she was through I told her that I'd never let anyone drag her back to that point in her life; I promised that I would keep her safe. We were married less than a month later, and then she shut down the Monty as a professional hotel; she already had enough money to last us the rest of our lives, and she wanted Flora and me to help her set up the Railroad operation.

"It was stressful, harbouring fugitives from the Ministry, but we still made sure to dance every single day for at least an hour." He sighed sadly. "I haven't danced since she died; it would feel like a betrayal."

"I'm sure she'd want you to be happy," Coral whispered, placing a hand on Gav's shoulder.

"I know she would, but she's still the only woman in the room, Coral," he said with a mournful smile. "I often ask myself what would she do in my position, but then I remember that we were such different people; Lucy Havelock was the light of my life, and I was the tree that turned to follow her, dawn to dusk, only to dream of her at night.

"She stole the sunshine from my life when she died, but only because no-one can possibly come close to how much she meant to me." His lip began to quiver as he spoke. "She was incomparable, Coral, and I should've taken better care of her."

"You couldn't have saved her, Gavin," Coral said softly. "Sometimes people just die, and it can't be helped."

"I know that," he said, his words barely audible over the pouring rain, "but it doesn't make me feel any better; I'd rather be incandescent with anger over my own failure than drowning and inconsolable in my grief."

And yet I still manage both, every minute of every day.

"Maybe living at the Montresor isn't doing you any good," Coral said. "Have you thought about moving somewhere else, even for a little while?"

"Wild horses couldn't drag me away from the Monty," Gav said, his voice hardening. "Besides, I don't live in the hotel."

"You don't?" she asked, perplexed.

"No," he said as they neared their destination. "I haunt it."

"Do you want me to do the talking?" Coral asked, and Gavin shook his head. "Are you gonna do this as a school welfare visit?"

"I'm gonna paint this more like a community support kind of thing. People know that I'm quite active in the local area, with food banks and the like, so that's our way in."

"Do you think they'll go for it?" Coral asked as he knocked sharply on the peeling paint of the front door.

"Nope," Gavin admitted, "but I told Jacinth that I would try."

Gavin was about to knock again when the hair on the back of his neck stood on end, prickling his skin into goose flesh. *Someone's watching us.* He turned to slowly look over his shoulder, hoping that he would be able to catch a glimpse of their observer.

Across the street, huddled beneath an old umbrella and clad in a threadbare grey hoodie with well-chewed cuffs, stood Alice Mann, his sixth form student. *She looks exhausted,* Gavin thought as he nodded slowly at her. She haltingly raised a hand in greeting, but her eyes were focussed on the house.

"Who is that?" Coral asked softly. Alice took a few uncertain steps towards the pair before her nerve gave out entirely, sending her trotting down the street, splashing through puddles as she went. Gavin went to call out to her, but decided against it as he realised the feeling of dread that had settled over him did not leave with the tired looking teenager.

"We're too late," Gavin muttered, before knocking more firmly on the door. He bent down to call through the letterbox. "Mrs Styles, are you in there?"

"Gavin, who the fuck was that!?" Coral said, pulling him upright.

"Her name is Alice," Gavin said. "She's one of my students."

"What was she doing here? Did she follow us?"

"No, but her presence is a bad fucking omen." He sighed heavily. "I fear that she's destined for the scene, Coral."

"Oh, shit," Coral replied. "Poor kid. What's her deal?"

"Seer, I think," Gavin said, knocking on the door once again. "She mentioned the whales before it happened, and the fact that she's here..."

He let his words drift off to replaced by the clink and patter of the rain as it poured on to roofs and gurgled through gutters. *I hope they haven't left already.*

"Oi, what are you two doing?" yelled a woman from across the street, stood in her doorway to avoid the worst of the rain.

"We were hoping to speak to Mrs Styles," Gavin replied, hurrying across the road so that he did not have to hold the entire conversation at the top of his lungs. The woman scowled at him as she shivered slightly in the chilly afternoon air; she was not dressed for such unpleasant weather. "Do you know where she is, please, or if her husband is around?"

"Who wants to know?" the woman snapped.

"I'm her daughter's science teacher," Gavin said, "and I work with a number of community organisations; I've heard from several sources that Libby hasn't been seen in some time. I wanted to stop by and see if there was anything I could do to support the family."

"I see," the woman replied, not sounding entirely convinced. "Can I ask your name?"

"Gavin Strangeways," he said, reaching out a hand that the woman briefly shook. "And you are?"

"Jane Billingham," the woman replied. "I've heard the name Strangeways before; do you know my brother?"

"You're Jacinth's aunt?" Gavin replied with a chuckle. *What are the chances?* "I knew your sister-in-law quite well; she was on the same cancer ward as my wife, Lucy. Have you seen any of the Styles family today?"

"She's gone to stay with her sister, somewhere up on Exmoor," Jane said, her voice softening slightly. "First her daughter vanishes, and then her husband dies only a week or so later; she's been through so much this summer already."

"He died?" Coral asked, and Jane nodded. "Do you know what of?"

"I can't say for sure," Jane replied, lowering her voice to an almost conspiratorial whisper, "but he was looking really terrible in the days before he died; bags under his eyes, ashen skin, the works. According to the obituary in the paper, he passed away in his sleep, but a part of me wonders if something else happened.

"He wasn't the best man, after all, and it was no secret that he had enemies." Jane sighed before standing up straight once again. "Still, it doesn't do anyone any good to gossip."

"Thank you for your time," Gav said, taking a step back from the threshold. "I appreciate being brought up to speed."

"I hope you find Libby, Mr Strangeways," Jane said, before closing the door. As they walked down the street, Gav's mind was already beginning to spin with ideas and possibilities.

"Sleep?" Coral said after a while. "Wasn't that what the lady by the beach said?"

"Yes," Gavin muttered. "Something out there is killing these people in their beds."

"That doesn't give us a lot to go on," Coral said sadly. "I at least hope that Flora and Reggie have better luck with their contacts that we've had."

"Me too, Coral," Gavin said, his mind still lingering on Alice's fearful expression for a moment. "If they can't turn up any leads, we're almost out of ideas."

"Almost?"

"Yes," Gavin said, "although the ones left open to us are going to be trouble."

And I'd rather not bring Alice into this if I can help it, he thought, *although there might come a point where we don't have any other choice.*

Whatever happens, though, I don't want Flora going anywhere near Digby and his Warlocks.

Chapter Ten – Designer Shirts, Knee Length Skirts

Flora

Flora had a slight bounce in her step as she walked up the driveway towards The Place; the chief meeting place and official clubhouse of the local Warlock Chapter. The spring in her step was not due to joy, however; she was deeply nervous about the whole affair, and her skin crawled every time she was even remotely aware of what she was wearing.

"This place looks like some kind of institution," Reggie said as they drew ever closer to the run down building before them.

"It was a private school, once upon a time," Flora said, "and it's still run like one, at least in terms of aesthetic and social hierarchy."

"Is that why we're dressed like this?" Reggie asked, gesturing to the grey shorts, white shirt, and ill-fitting blazer that he wore. Flora nodded, and pulled out a small golden badge, affixing it to the front of her own jacket, which was immaculately fitted to her seductive form. "Do I get a badge?"

"No," Flora said sharply. "I'm a Senior Prefect and this is my badge of office. You aren't a member, so you don't get a tie either; the striping indicates which house you belong to."

"There are *houses*?" Reggie asked with an incredulous snicker. "Flora, is this a sex thing?"

"For most of them, yes, but for some it's a prestige thing; non-human supremacy and all that." She sighed heavily as she deftly tied her black and ochre tie, leaving it fashionably loose. The colours placed her in Tamerlane, which was regarded as one of the more prestigious houses; the others were Victorine, Prospero, and Napoleon. "The Place has a blood quantum requirement of at least one half, unless you're a Legacy Candidate."

"Are you, uh, comfortable with all this?" Reggie asked nervously.

"Absolutely not," Flora said, rounding on him, "but my parents insisted that I join and I actually have quite a lot of influence here, so it's in everyone's best interest if I keep up appearances."

"What's a blood quantum?" Reggie continued after a moment of silence.

"A purity requirement," Flora spat, the words souring in her mouth. "You need to have at least one full-blooded non-human parent to apply, so you could technically join if you wanted to. You'll need to check any weapons at the door, just to warn you."

Flora gritted her teeth, took a deep breath, and forced her face into a pleasant smile as she approached the front door of The Place. *Such a pretentious fucking name,* she thought as she pulled on the bell chain. Warlocks all over the world were known for being cliquey and aloof, but the members of The Place were legendary even amongst their own kind.

The large wooden door opened with an audible creak, revealing one of Flora's less objectionable friends, Amelia, who immediately let out a loud squeal and pulled the Faun into a tight, excitable hug. Flora's friend was a Victorine Senior Prefect, with an outfit that differed only in the acid green striping of her tie.

"Oh, Sweetie, it's so good to see you!" Amelia

planted a quick kiss on Flora's lips before wrapping a powerful arm around her neck, looking over the Faun's shoulder as she ran her fingers through Flora's dark hair. "Now, do introduce me to this devilish morsel that you've brought to our little playhouse."

"This is Reginald..." Her voice trailed off as Amelia slipped her long, slimy tongue into Flora's ear, making her stomach churn with the invasive intimacy of the action, but she quickly got her revulsion under control. "This is Reginald Kellogg; he's boarding at the Montresor with us.

"Reggie, this is Amelia Kalish; she's the daughter of a Vodyanoy, and one of my oldest, uh, friends here." Flora stopped once again as she felt Amelia's sticky fingertips slip under her skirt to rest on the waistband of her underwear.

I do wish the Founders hadn't insisted on all the aspects of a public school, she thought with a shudder. Part of joining the membership roll of The Place was the implied consent given to any and all other students, with little option to say no to anyone higher up in the social structure, and Flora utterly despised it. *If only I'd known then, what I know now.*

"So, how did you meet Sweetie, Reg?" Amelia asked, her amphibian's eyes bulging wetly from her otherwise attractive face.

"I'd rather not go into it," he said, frowning uncomfortably. "Why do you call Flora that?"

"It's her nickname, from back in the day," Amelia said with a giggle. "Short for 'Sweet Spot'; our Flora has the most fuckable little arse The Place has ever seen! Oh, she was a favourite for all the boys and half of the girls too."

"Amelia -" Flora began but the Vodyanoy continued

speaking; whether she was merely oblivious to Flora's discomfort or actively enjoying it, the Faun could not tell.

"There was this one time where she was blitzed out of her head on Ambrosia and practically passed out in the Prefect's Common Room and we all took turns railing her; it really made me envious of the boys, but I still got my turn!" Amelia laughed at the memory as a sharp ringing began to creep in at the edge of Flora's hearing. She blinked rapidly in a futile attempt to clear her head, barely aware of Amelia's words. "Sometimes I wonder what she would be like if she were a *proper* girl, you know?

"Oh, darling, what a perfect honey-sweet cunt you could've had!" Amelia let out a dramatic sigh before giving Reggie a wicked grin. "Still, the Ambrosia heats the blood, regardless of gender, so I still got to have a play with Sweetie's special boy parts when she was off her perfect tits!

"We do have fun, don't we?"

Flora did not answer; in fact, she could barely move as the memories of the various parties came flooding back in a relentless tide of sights, sounds, and physical sensation.

"We're here to talk to Digby," Reggie said forcefully, both cutting off Amelia mid-flow and waking Flora from her stupor. "Can you ask him to come out and speak to us, please?"

"Digby takes callers up in his private office," Amelia said snottily. "You'll have to head up there; I assume you still remember the way?"

"Yes," Flora said, finally finding her courage once again, "I remember. I doubt he'll be pleased to see me, but this is important."

Flora went to step into the dimly lit foyer, but Amelia barred the way.

"I'm not armed, Amelia," Flora said, her patience wearing thin. "And I doubt Reggie is either."

"I'm not carrying," he said matter-of-factly.

"That's not the point, Sweetie," Amelia said, her eyes glinting nastily. "You still need to pay the entry fee."

"I'm here for business, not play," Flora said, but the Vodyanoy did not move her arm. "Amelia, I am not drinking any fucking Ambrosia; I have work to do."

"Digby asked me to make sure that you did," Amelia said in a saccharin voice. "After all, he is Head Boy, so he gets what he wants."

I need better friends, Flora thought, but her shoulders slumped and she closed her eyes and opened her mouth to receive the cloyingly sweet narcotic liquid. She retched as it touched her tongue, but persevered; Ambrosia was said to taste different to each person, but for Flora it simply had the bitter tang of betrayed trust and half-forgotten nightmares.

"Good girl," Amelia said, her hand moving inside Flora's underwear to close around her rapidly stiffening penis. The Victorine leant in close and whispered her next words as the Ambrosia began to muddle Flora's thoughts as the other woman began to stroke her sticky hand over the Faun's painful erection. "Digby can wait, so why don't you let me put that pretty girl cock of yours in my mouth for a while, for old times' sake?"

I should have listened to Gavin and avoided this place, she thought hazily.

"Just let me go, Amelia," Flora panted, and Amelia removed her hand with a pout. Flora glared at the

Senior Prefect as she moved towards Reggie, ewer of Ambrosia in hand. "He's not a member, and guests aren't required to drink."

"He might want to," Amelia said playfully, but Reggie immediately shook his head. "Spoilsport!"

"Come on, Reggie," Flora said, pulling him into the building, "let's get this over and done with."

Flora staggered up the stairs of The Place, barely able to think straight as the Ambrosia continued to work on her mind and body. She leant forwards as she went, desperate to hide her arousal, but her standard issue skirt did little to conceal her erection. The eyes of the portraits on the walls seem to follow her as she made her way down the corridors and hallways, almost accusatory in their stares.

Fucking hell, she thought tearfully, *I forgot just how horrible this stuff is.*

"Flora, are you alright?" Reggie asked as she lost her footing and fell to the wooden floor, knocking the wind from her lungs.

"I can't even stand," she muttered as he hauled her upright. She spied a familiar door just down the corridor, to her right. "Stay here, Reggie, and don't take anything anyone tries to give you. I won't be long."

She half ran, half stumbled to the door, crashing through it as soon as she had one hand on the handle. She snapped the lock closed behind her and dropped to her knees on the white and black tiled bathroom floor. Flora managed to get out of her underwear in a few fraught seconds before taking her swollen cock in her hand.

"Please, please, let this fucking stop it," she begged

tearfully as she began to furiously masturbate, her cheeks glowing red with shame and disgust; she hadn't been under the influence of the Ambrosia for years and had forgotten just how sexually compulsive it made her.

Whilst Amelia's words about the arousing effects of the Ambrosia had not been wrong, she had neglected to mention that the Tamerlane Senior Prefect's dual heritage made her uniquely susceptible to its aphrodisiac component.

Simply put, the combined Faun and Rusałka blood in her veins meant that she was doomed.

Flora started to sob as she entirely lost control of her body, giving in to her base biological urges as she clawed at her breasts through her thin shirt in a desperate attempt to expedite the orgasm that would free her from her torment.

Precum oozed from the glistening tip of her cock and the sight of it drove her into a frenzy, leading her to abandon her breasts and instead sprawl forwards as she pushed her fingers into her eager throbbing arsehole. She crammed in as many fingers as she could manage without any lube, pushing and rubbing her prostate as she continued to violently wank her cock. Her tears now pattered against the tiles of the floor as her sobs mixed with animalistic grunts as she frantically pursued her climax.

If only I could fuck myself, she thought deliriously, *or if I could suck myself off!*

Her orgasm hit her with all the force of a train crash and she thrashed and twitched on the bathroom floor as spurt after spurt of semen pulsed from her penis, the pleasure radiating from both her cock and from deep within her arse.

She screamed and cried out as a second orgasm took her, still frantically jerking her cock in a wild attempt to flush the poison from her body. She ejaculated all the while, pushing her hand deeper and deeper into her body with each emission.

Finally the flow subsided and she pulled her hand free of her behind, flipping around to greedily lick the cum from the bathroom floor, even as her stomach churned in revulsion. Once control of her body finally returned, she slumped on to the tiles, weeping amidst the tears and semen that still shone wetly on the floor.

I hate it here, she thought as her tears finally subsided, before setting about cleaning herself up enough to meet with Digby Coltrane, Head Boy of The Place. Once she was tidy enough to conceal her shameful act, she washed her hands and then returned to Reggie, who was waiting outside the bathroom door.

If he had heard anything, he did not mention it, and he nodded at her as she led him wordlessly through the remaining corridors and staircases towards the Head Boy's office.

The sooner this is done, the sooner we can leave.

Flora strode in without knocking, determined to make sure at least part of their interaction was on her terms. Digby was perched on his desk, clearly waiting for her. He gave her a wink, but frowned when he saw Reggie.

"I thought you were coming alone, Sweetie," he said, getting to his feet so that he towered over her. Digby was a Legacy Member, only one quarter Fomorian, but his heritage still showed in his formidable physical presence. "Who the fuck is this?"

"My name is Reginald Kellogg," Reggie said,

stepping forwards and shutting the office door behind him. "We've come to ask you about the strange occurrences that have been plaguing this area in recent weeks. We would appreciate it if you could share any information you happened to possess."

Was this what he was like as a Ministry Agent? Flora wondered, and Digby turned a dark shade of red; it had been a long time since anyone had dared to speak to him in such a manner. He took two steps towards the Familiar, but stopped short when Reggie produced a handgun seemingly out of thin air.

"You are required to surrender your weapons at the door!" Digby yelled.

"I didn't have it then," Reggie replied as he aimed the boxy firearm at Digby's chest. "Teleportation and wormholes have such a wide variety of uses, you know. By the way, this Maxim 9 is loaded with Black Salt rounds, so it will not only kill you, but hurt like a bastard the whole time."

"What do you want?" he growled, staring at Flora once again.

"I want to know if any of our people are causing this, or if they know who is," Flora demanded, but Digby just shook his head.

"They're just as frightened as the provincials," he replied, trembling slightly; clearly he was as fearful as the rest. "People just want to get the fuck out of dodge, at least until whatever is about to happen is over."

Damn. Another dead end.

"Satisfied, Sweetie?" Digby sneered, and Flora nodded. Reggie lowered the weapon, bringing the tension down a notch. Still, the Head Boy was furious and he held out his hand. "Give me your fucking badge, bitch."

"I earned it, fair and square!" Flora said, placing one hand defensively over her Superior Prefect's badge, but she quickly realised that she was just going through the motions; these people somehow held no sway over her any longer. "Am I being expelled from The Place?"

"I would kick you out of the National Convocation if I could," Digby said, his open hand still held out, but the faint tremor was enough to bring a triumphant smile to Flora's face. "What are you grinning at?"

"Take it," she said, tossing her badge and tie in his face, "and go fucking hang yourself with it, Digby."

She placed one hand on Reggie's shoulder and gave him a smile.

"I think we're done here, Reg," she said. "Would you be kind enough to see us out?"

"You don't get to just walk away from-"

Digby's words were cut off as Reggie collapsed the world around them into a whirling void, only to have it reassemble on the driveway of The Place. Flora's stomach churned slightly, but she managed to avoid vomiting on her already soiled uniform. *So that's what a wormhole is,* she thought. *I wonder what true teleportation is like?*

"Nice moves," she said with a shaky smile. "Thanks for helping out in there; you're a good fella."

"Thanks again for taking me in," he replied. "I'm sorry they treated you like that, but I am glad you chose to walk away from it all."

"Sometimes all it takes is one bad day to see something for just how rotten it really is."

"I know that feeling," Reggie said, shivering in the late afternoon gloom. "Come on, Flo; let's go home before the heavens open once again. I'll tell you all about my time at the Ministry on the way; it's a hell of a tale."

She nodded and they got underway.

"One day," Flora muttered darkly as they walked away from The Place, "I'm going to burn that fucking building to the ground, and bring a reckoning down on anyone that argues otherwise."

"When that day comes," Reggie said, taking her hand in his, "I'll be right beside you to help."

Chapter Eleven – Westbound and Down

Lola

"Woohoo!" Lola yelled as Thad churned through the gears and their vehicle, a dusty blue chopped and rodded Deuce coupe, roared along the A35. "Go, Thad, go!"

"This is a hell of a machine, Lo," Thad replied, grinning like a madman. "Did you work on her yourself?"

"From the wheels up," Lola said gleefully. "I'm glad you've got an excuse to open her up properly; she's not been able to fully clear her throat and stretch her legs for years now. I'll give her a tune-up when we get to Torquay.

"Gotta keep my baby running sweet as a nut and smooth as butter."

"You seem much more..." Thad hesitated for a moment, "I don't know; genuine, I guess."

"This is who I've always been, and now I don't have to fulfil the social niche of a Ravenblade, I can just be me, without adornment." She turned her head to grin at Miette. "Are you having fun?"

"I am not a fan of cars," the Sylph said, trying to conceal her nervousness. "Whilst a crash might not be fatal for me, this still feels rather unsafe."

"Try to loosen up a little," Lola said, "and you might start to enjoy yourself."

"You are still technically a prisoner," Miette warned, but Thad just laughed.

"Well, here's to the first Ministry Penal Legion!" he yelled, revving the engine joyfully. Lola laughed along with him, partly at the ludicrous situation they were in, and also at Miette's obvious discomfort.

She caught sight of herself in the mirror and smiled even wider; gone were the needlessly complicated outfits and chaotic hairstyles, replaced by a back-rolled rockabilly ponytail, a pair of sturdy work boots, a faded band tee, and her embroidered boilersuit.

All roads lead to home, she thought, *and I've never been dressed more aptly for the journey.*

Miette had closed her eyes and was snoring softly in the back seat; Lola wasn't surprised, as the Sylph had been flitting about for two solid days trying to organise things for their outing. She decided to enjoy the peace and quiet, returning to contemplating her reflection.

I'm still not sold on Michelle, but there might be a hint of a Shelly in there somewhere.

Maybe there's a different path for me after all?

"Penny for your thoughts?" Thad asked after a few more minutes of driving.

"I was just musing on names and the like," Lola said with an idle wave of her hand. "I've had some great screen names over the years, Thad."

"Such as?" he asked, drumming his fingers on the steering wheel.

"HotRodHarlot, Romeosexual_Beauty, and EdgarAllenPwned, to name a few."

"I don't believe that last one," he replied, laughing so hard that tears were in the corners of his eyes. "Not for a fucking moment."

"Yeah, no, that one was a lie," she said with a smile, "although as a teenager I did find it a lot easier to hide behind a male facade online; it made it easier for people to take me seriously."

"I can believe that," he replied, "but I'm glad that you can be yourself around me."

"You know, Thad, I've actually really enjoyed having a friend these past few months. I know that we didn't meet in ideal circumstances, but I've really grown fond of your company."

"Likewise, Lo," he replied. "So, what's the car called?"

"She doesn't have a name," Lola admitted. "Gideon used to drive her, and he thought it was stupid to name a vehicle. Maybe you should give her a name, especially as you'll be the one driving her."

Thaddeus thought for a moment.

"Bluebell," he announced. "That's the only name that seems right to me."

"Good choice," Miette murmured from the back seat, before drifting back to sleep.

"There's hope for her yet," Lola whispered. "Maybe she'll be more like a mentor than a jailer once we've proven ourselves trustworthy."

"Are we?" Thad asked, raising an eyebrow.

"Yes," Lola replied firmly. "We toe the line, Thad or else they'll kill us. I would actually like to get out of this with a modicum of freedom returned to us, but we'll have to earn it."

Thad opened his mouth, almost certainly to protest, but Lola held up a hand to silence him.

"I know you didn't do anything wrong, Thad, but..." she paused for a second, "but in their eyes, you *allowed* yourself to become a Famine, which is a transgression. I know you didn't ask for it, but-"

"I did," Thad said firmly. "I asked a monster I didn't fully understand to make me more than I was. I chose my fate, Lola, as did you, even if the circumstances forced our hands. I've made my peace with that now, and I was going to agree with you.

"What I wanted to ask was if you knew how long it would take before I could message Mallory and Jess." He sighed heavily. "I wish I could see them."

"You can call them whenever you like," Miette said, and Lola turned to look at her.

"I thought you were asleep."

"I was, but I don't sleep in the same way you do; think of it more like a restful trance where I'm still aware of my surroundings." Miette kept her eyes closed but gave Lola a smile. "I'll issue you with smartphones and laptops when we get to Torquay. I know you've missed your internet friends, and you deserve a chance to speak to them."

"Huh," Lola uttered, surprised.

"I'm not all stick, you know." Miette snuggled down in her seat. "And it really is a lovely car, Lola; I just hope Thane doesn't crash in his hurry to get to our destination."

"I'll be careful," he said, but Lola could already feel their speed increasing in his eagerness to talk to his lovers.

I understand, Thad, she thought with a sad smile. *I can scarcely wait to be online once again.*

Thad carried their bags into the little house the Ministry had rented on Marcombe Road as Lola walked around the building, trying to work out where would be the most sensible place to set up her digital command post. She dithered between the living room and one of the upstairs bedrooms, before settling on the former.

Next on her list was the most important task of any

field operation; she did a quick search on her brand new smartphone of all the local takeaways, making sure to read the reviews thoroughly instead of relying purely on numerical ratings.

"Miette, do you eat?" Lola asked as the Sylph breezed into the room.

"I do, although I can go for many weeks without eating whilst suffering no ill effects. I do enjoy food, however; what were you thinking of getting?" She peered over Lola's shoulder, looking through the options.

"Thad," Lola asked as he brought in the fourth bag of her computer equipment, "what do you fancy for dinner?"

"Lots," he said with a chuckle. "I don't care what we have, as long as it's much."

"There's a fairly well rated Mexican place, or if you want something greasy there's Fatboy's Chicken Shack; any preference?"

"Chicken," Miette said, almost immediately. "I don't often get to enjoy fried foods when I'm in the office."

"Is Desai still maintaining his ridiculous *healthy eating* policy?" Lola asked, and the Sylph nodded. "Ugh! Sometimes I wonder how many good Agents we lost to the Amberlight Agency because of that policy alone."

"My loyalty is not so easily bought," Miette replied haughtily, but a smile played on her insubstantial lips, "but a nice greasy meal would earn you some serious brownie points."

"Lola," Thad said after bringing in her fifth case, "what is all this for?"

"Those three are all my computer gear; screens, electronics workstation, and various gadgets. The other two are various tools and weapons." She gave him a wink. "Thanks for doing all the heavy lifting, Thad.

"Tell me, have you ever piloted a drone?"

"Can't say I have."

"Would you like to?" she asked, patting one of the boxes, and he nodded eagerly. "This one is fitted with the entire array of Jacobi filters for the cameras to allow us to spot any ghostly action from the air.

"I didn't invent the filters, but they're mainly used on plate cameras, so I worked out how to apply them digitally to our eye in the sky."

"That's..." Thad blinked in surprise. "That's actually brilliant, Lo."

"Thank you." She handed her phone to Miette. "Order whatever you want; I'm going to get set up."

She opened the largest of her boxes and pulled out the two powerful desktop computer towers; they would be used to filter through the internet for any clues and leads, following ever more precise algorithms to find patterns, victims, and much more. It was a high throughput approach that didn't always work, but it automated a lot of the grunt work and freed up the Agents to follow up any promising leads.

As long as my servers are still up, she thought, *but I don't see a reason why they wouldn't be, unless they got to my offshore accounts.* Through various shady dealings, Lola had managed to set up an international cloud computing service, simply called Regency, that allowed her to both make unfathomable amounts of money and scrape huge sections of the internet for data.

The entire thing had been pulled off under the Ministry's radar, accomplished with seed capital from

Constance Walpole in exchange for Amberlight having access to her services. She'd accepted this happily; the door went both ways, after all.

Still, my arrest might've been enough for Connie to pull the plug, she worried, but decided to focus on the investigation at hand.

In Lola's experience, most of the first signs and symptoms of a supernatural event or crisis were not found in news articles or police reports, but in blogs, especially short-form micro-blogs; Twitter and its various siblings were an absolute goldmine for early warning signs.

Quick, simple, and easy to do on the move, she thought with a smile, *as well as being highly reactive to unfolding events.*

She set things up so that her phone would receive constant updates on the massive data trawl as it progressed, feeding them live information that they could use on the ground. That, along with a piece of complicated pattern recognition software that she'd written specifically for mapping supernatural occurrences, would not only allow them to act on events that had happened, but also potentially get ahead of them.

Lola's predictive model wasn't perfect, but it was getting better with each operation she undertook. A smile crept on to her face when she connected to her many powerful servers without a hitch; the Ministry clearly had not found all of her hidden assets, and it seemed her relationship with the Amberlight Agency still remained intact.

Her algorithm, combined with the Ministry database of names, speciation, and locations of all known Ceps in the vicinity of the phenomena, truly allowed her to hit the ground running within hours of being on the scene. By the time they woke up the following morning, Lola's combined digital research operation, which she had dubbed Bright Eyes, would have generated several leads for them to chase up.

Her final case contained her tools of the more lethal variety; custom pistols, concealable knives, and poisons by the dozen. As much as she preferred life behind the screen, the part of her that had been forged in the fires of Lamplight itched to be in combat once again.

"What are our rules of engagement for this assignment?" Lola asked Miette when the Sylph handed her phone back.

"Try to limit civilian casualties, but anyone associated with Kellogg is a fair target; in short, weapons free, but exercise some self-control." Miette gave her a grin. "My missions are rarely anything other than wet work; leave the spying to the Ghosts and the killing to the killers."

"Fantastic," Lola said with a grin. "Any ideas on how to kill Reginald; his mixed bloodline will make him resistant to most methods."

"Hopefully Thaddeus will be able to consume him," Miette replied, and Thad gave Lola an excited thumbs up, "but if not, we've been given access to this to use against him."

Lola took the palm-sized tablet that Miette removed from her small rucksack and scrolled through it, her eyes growing wider with each passing moment. *Is this really what I think it is!?*

"You look surprised, Lola," Miette said playfully. "Did you think we'd risk two such skilled assets without ensuring that you were properly prepared for what you might be facing?"

"Hey, Lo," Thad asked, strolling over, "what is that?"

"It's a digital copy of The White Book," she said, her voice quiet and reverential. *I need to make a personal copy of this when no-one is looking,* Lola thought. *This will be impossibly valuable, almost priceless, on the black market.*

"Not just any copy, but an *unredacted* copy of The White Book," Miette corrected, and turned to face Thad. "It came with a message for you, specifically."

"Which is?" Thad said.

"Commander Holloway sends her love," Miette said with a sly wink, "and wishes you happy hunting."

Chapter Twelve – A Three-Pointed Circle

Gavin

"You went to The Place?" Gav said, barely containing his anger at Flora when she arrived back at the Montresor with Reggie. "Why the fuck would you go there, of all places? Good god, Flora, you know better than anyone just how badly they treat everyone that passes through the doors of that fucked up school!"

"I realise that now," Flora said sharply, "and it turned out to be a fucking dead end anyway. Still, I thought the situation was bad enough to chance it."

"I..." Gavin took a deep breath and wrestled his emotions to the bottom of his soul. He looked at Flora and saw her properly for the first time since she had come home; her clothes were soiled and damaged, and she had clearly been crying. "Are you alright, Flora? Did they hurt you?"

Flora just stared at the ground, her lip quivering.

"If you want us to go up there and teach them a lesson," Leroy said quietly, "I'm sure we can get the gang together to royally fuck them up."

"There's no need," she whispered. "I've been expelled, so I'm never going back."

She looked up to face Gavin, and her azure eyes burned with icy fire.

"Besides," Flora continued, "if anyone is gonna bring that place crashing down around them, it's gonna be me."

"We're with you when you do," Coral said, placing a hand on Flora's trembling arm.

"I'm not sure it would be a fair fight for you, Coral," Flora said quietly, "but your support is appreciated."

"Don't dismiss me so quickly," the woman said, leaning heavily on her cane. "A nail bomb is a nail bomb, regardless of who you are, Warlock or otherwise."

"A few good earth rites combined with an unseasonal rain would drown the entire place in a mudslide," Gavin said, "but this is a conversation for another time. My initial question still remains unanswered, Flo; do you need any medical treatment?"

"Nothing lasting," she said with a meek smile, "but I could use a little something to clear the last of the Ambrosia out of my system. That mix you gave me last time certainly brought me back down to earth, admittedly after a few hours of absolutely blissful oblivion."

That's because it was mostly heroin, Gav thought guiltily. *Although when compared to Ambrosia, it seemed like the lesser evil at the time.*

"I've not got any of that to hand, I'm afraid, but I could mix you up a tincture of Sweet Breath if you like?"

"What's in that?" Reggie asked suspiciously.

Lavender, rosehip, sugar syrup, and a shit load of codeine. Not for the first time he wondered if he'd accidentally addicted Flora to opiates, but he put the thought out of his mind. Reggie was still staring at him, but his patient came to his rescue.

"He can't tell you his Druidic secrets," Flora said, suddenly keen as punch, "but Sweet Breath is fantastic shit. I have a bit of it as often as I can; it helps me feel right as rain when I'm feeling blue."

Gav tried to give her a smile, but it faltered at her next words.

"Sometimes I wonder if I'd survive without your ministrations, Gav; when I can't get my Druidic medicines I feel absolutely wretched." She gave him a broad, grateful grin. "You're an absolute life saver, Mr Strangeways."

I am a terrible fucking person, he thought, but he still went to unlock his medicine cabinet and fetched her another bottle of the herbal codeine syrup. Gav felt his stomach tie in knots as Flora popped the top off the bottle and took several deep gulps, sighing in satisfaction when she was done.

"This shit is magic," Flora said to Reggie as she resealed the bottle and popped it into her bag. "Gav started making it for Lucy to help her with some of her... troubles... and she kept taking it right up until she died; she swore by it as a cure-all, and he was good enough to make it for me when I asked him to.

"Like I said, a life saver."

"I do my best," Gavin said quietly, barely trusting himself to speak without screaming.

"Well, I'm off to bed," Flora announced, already slurring her words slightly. "We can resume our planning in the morning. Goodnight, all!"

One by one the residents of the Montresor retired to bed, until Gavin was left alone with his thoughts. He wrapped his fingers tightly around the locket at his neck as he stared into the middle distance, anxiety and shame eating at his insides.

He'd never told Lucy about the contents of his tincture; he'd been so focussed on her well-being that he didn't want to risk her relapsing into her old ways just because she didn't want to take pills for her deteriorating condition. He knew that it was a shitty excuse, but it was a load-bearing one; without it, he would never get out of bed again.

It's a surprisingly fine line between love and abuse, he thought as he remembered the glazed look she would get in her eyes after consuming his 'medicine'. *Still, it's impossible to see the border until you've already crossed it.*

With that second load-bearing lie propping up the first, Gavin decided to call it a night, and went to bed.

"Where are you skulking off to at this time of the morning?" Coral said accusingly as Gavin crept through the foyer of the Hotel Montresor, backpack over his shoulder and a mistletoe covered staff in his right hand.

"I was thinking about our particular situation last night," Gav said sheepishly, "so I've called a meeting of the entire Circle to see if anyone else has any ideas about what the fuck is going on. I'm gonna try and catch the train up to Newton Abbot so I hitch my way up to-"

"For fuck's sake, Gavin," Coral said, shaking her head dismissively, "why didn't you just ask me to drive you?"

"The true meeting place of the Dartmoor Circle is a closely guarded secret-"

"It's a set of standing stones in the middle of Brockhill Mire, up on the moor," Coral said, drumming her fingers on the handle of her cane. Gavin stared at her in shock. "You told me the location when you got back from your last meeting; you fell in the mud and would not stop complaining about it."

"That I did," Gav said sheepishly. "But the meeting is just for true Druids..."

Coral raised a stern eyebrow.

"... which I now recall that I made you in exchange for the last Snickers in the fridge a few months back."

"Yes, you did." She looked his staff up and down. "You were gonna get on the train with that?"

"That's not a crime," Gavin replied defensively.

"True, but someone will get a rash," Coral smiled as she pulled her keys from her pocket. "Mistletoe is poisonous, you know."

"It's also a key ingredient in powerful protection spells," Gavin said as they made their way out to Coral's beat-up and rusted Nissan Micra. "Do you have anything like that on you?"

"I have a butterfly knife in my boot and I can do some damage with my cane," Coral said, "but nothing supernatural. Do you think I'll need it?"

"I have no idea," Gav admitted as he put his Arch-Druid's staff of office on the back seat of the car. "I'm hoping that we'll get some useful answers today."

"And if we don't?" Coral asked, and Gav just shrugged.

"Then maybe we wait for the problem to come to us." He sighed heavily as he settled in the worn passenger seat. "It's not much of a plan, but it's all we have left."

"Fair enough," Coral replied, switching the engine on. "By the way, you need to start weaning Flora off that shit you're giving her; I don't know what it is, but it isn't helping her in the long term."

"I know," Gav whispered. "I just hate to see her so upset, though."

"Maybe actually feeling upset for a while will help

her figure out what she wants in life." Coral swore loudly as the car stalled as soon as she started to pull away. "Fuck! Piece of shit car!"

"Need a bump?"

"Nah, it'll be fine once it's warmed up." They sat in silence for a few seconds. "Anyway, I'll stop dispensing bartender's therapy and we can focus on today; what's likely to occur when we get to the stones?"

"Vane and Borage will lead the proceedings, and there will be a bunch of mumbling in Cornish followed by the opportunity to ask questions and report any *incidents* that might've been observed. That's when we'll speak up."

"We?" Coral asked, successfully pulling away this time as she spoke. "I'm not *actually* a proper Druid, Gavin!"

"Of course you are," he replied, leaning back in his chair and closing his eyes. "I said you were. Truth be told, it's good to have you along. Druids can be a lot like Mormons where witnesses are concerned; it takes at least two to convince them of anything, even if it's obvious."

"Like those trees?" Coral said, and Gavin opened his eyes to follow her gaze. Dozens of trees up on the nearby hill were withered and wilted, with their leaves faded to a pale grey and their trunks shrivelled and bent towards the ground.

"Those were fine last night," Gavin said, "weren't they?"

"They were," Coral confirmed. "Is it worth bringing that up to the Circle?"

"Absolutely." His eyes drifted beyond the trees to the murmurations of starlings that moved through the air like erratic black clouds. His brow furrowed and his smile faded to a frown as something uncomfortable stirred in his soul. *This is worse than I thought.*

"Gavin?" Coral asked, also looking at the birds. "I've never seen them like that at this time of year; is that normal?"

"It most certainly is not." He tore his gaze away from the mesmerising flock to look at Coral. "The whales were bad, but this... this is something else. We need to hurry."

Coral nodded and stepped hard on the accelerator, sending the little car speeding down the road in the direction of Dartmoor.

"Fucking hell," Coral gasped as Gavin helped her along the final little stretch of the hidden pathway that wound its way through the mire, "this journey is punishing! No wonder you collapsed into the mud."

"It's only about twenty metres now, Coral," he said, letting her steady herself on his arm. "Do you need to rest, or can we push on?"

"Will there be places to sit when we reach the stones?"

"Yes, and there should be food and drink too."

"Then let's get this over with," Coral said, forging onwards with a pained grunt. Luckily for her, the path widened after a particularly dense patch of gorse, revealing a small hill in the centre of the mire, topped with eleven standing stones; eight were a little shorter than the height of a man, but the other three loomed over fifteen feet tall.

Coral whistled softly as she laid eyes on them, and Gavin couldn't help but grin. *There's nothing quite like seeing the Three-Pointed Circle for the first time.* He helped her to one of the roughly carved wooden benches that were placed inside the stone ring for the Druids to use during meetings or in times of quiet contemplation.

"Get your breath back," Gavin said kindly, "and I'll see about weaving you a crown. Any requests?"

"Anything without thorns," Coral said with a breathless chuckle, and Gavin quickly gathered some ivy and marsh marigolds; protection and friendship, which would help her integrate into the Circle. He took a seat beside her and began to braid the plants with practised hands. "How long have you been a Druid, Gavin?"

"Since I was old enough to forage on my own," he said with a smile, "so about thirty years."

"Damn, that's a long time!" He handed Coral the roughly woven headpiece and she popped it on, grinning at him. "How do I look?"

"Smashing," he replied, before glancing around the little clearing in the middle of the stones. They were the first ones there, which was odd; Druids weren't known for being punctual, but Vane and Borage lived nearby.

Something's wrong.

"Coral," he said lowering his voice to a whisper, "if anything happens, do you remember the route through the mire well enough to get back to the car?"

"Yes," she replied in equally hushed tones. "Why?"

"The others should be here by now, and there's something out there in the fog, watching us." He slowly reached into his backpack without taking his eyes off the misty mire. "Get out your knife."

"Do you want it?" she asked, but he was already

pulling an old Berretta from the bag.

"I don't fuck around," Gavin whispered before standing up, pointing the pistol into the gloom, and addressing the unseen observer. "I know you're there, so let's not have any funny business! Come into the clearing, nice and slowly."

There was a slight rustle as a wizened old man, dressed in a faded green robe, slowly walked across the stone barrier with his hands raised above his head. Gavin sighed in exasperation and lowered the pistol, clicking on the safety as he did so.

"For fuck's sake, Peter!" Gavin stowed the gun in his bag and the old man took a seat across from them. "I might've shot you!"

"I was fully expecting you to," Borage said in a deep voice, mellowed by years of pipe smoke and blackberry wine. "Who is this lady that comes with you?"

"I'm Coral Grosse," she replied, "an Initiate of the Circle. Gavin inducted me a few months ago."

"I see," Borage replied, still eyeing Gav with suspicion.

"Where is everyone?" Gavin asked. "I called a bloody meeting!"

"And why did you do that?" Peter asked, leaning forward and glaring at them both. "What motive can you possibly have to summon us all together, on today of all days!?"

"I wanted to talk about the fucking omens that are appearing all over town!" Gavin yelled, getting to his feet once again. "I was hoping that we could put our heads together and solve this thing, but apparently you and Elmyra went over my head, *yet again*, to cancel the meeting!

"And what the fuck do you mean by 'today of all days'? It's a normal fucking Thursday, Peter!"

"Good heavens," Peter replied softly, placing a hand over his mouth in shock. "You really don't know, do you?"

"Know what?" Gavin said, his anger leaving him in an instant as he saw the horror on the old man's face.

"Elmyra headed into town to meet with you, the day after the moon mirages were seen. She hoped that you would have some information on the occurrence, but she clearly never made it to you." Peter shook his head sadly. "Nobody heard from her after she left, so there was a certain level of suspicion surrounding you, Gavin; a suspicion that was obviously misplaced!"

"Has anyone been to the police?" Coral asked.

"It was the police who found what was left of her in Primley Woods late yesterday afternoon." He choked back a sob. "She had been murdered, Gavin, and that's not the worst of it!

"Whoever had killed her had cannibalised her; eaten every scrap of her flesh, right down to the bone!"

Chapter Thirteen – A Bite in the Morning

Lola

"Cannibalism!?" Thad said, horrified, and Lola nodded sadly. He peered over her shoulder at the computer screen as the morning sunlight streamed through the living room window. Miette was still snoozing upstairs somewhere, so it was just the two disgraced Agents alone at the computer. "What could do such a thing? Werewolves?"

"These bones were left arranged in a ritual pattern," Lola said, pointing to the exceptionally gruesome photos that were plastered all over Twitter and Facebook. "Werewolves will normally hide a kill, unless they're in the middle of a blood frenzy, but this doesn't have any of the hallmarks of that.

"This smacks of magic, but there have been no other signs of such things in the area. All the weird omens we've seen here are not typical of human spell casting, nor is the confluence of factors needed for an Awakening present here." Lola sat back in her chair. "If I didn't know better, I'd say that this looks like someone *playing* magic."

She tapped the arrangement of bones on the screen.

"This particular ritual pattern appears in occult literature all over the world," she explained, "but the important thing is that this *doesn't actually do anything*. It just looks creepy; nothing more, nothing less. Still, someone thinks this is either important or powerful enough to send a message to everyone nearby.

"Maybe this isn't related at all, Thad," Lola said

rubbing her eyes. *I should remember to put my glasses on right away.* "This just could be some fucking lunatic who fancied an old lady for dinner. Honestly, it's too early to tell."

"Did you manage to get any hits on our man?" Thad said, taking a sip of the strong coffee he'd brewed for them.

"Reginald Kellogg?" Lola asked, stifling a yawn. *Travel always makes me fucking exhausted, but this is far better than anything with Gideon ever was.* She caught a glimpse of Thad's reflection in the mirror and smiled. *No more tearful boot knocking and black eyes for me.*

"That's the one," Thad said. "Did he pick that name for himself?"

"All the Familiars were named after famous inventors or industrialists," Miette said from the doorway, before drifting over. Lola turned to face her, but immediately spun back around when she realised the Sylph was undressed. "What's the matter, Lola?"

"You're in the nude," Lola said quietly. "It's a little off-putting, truth be told."

"I am?" Miette looked down awkwardly. "I do apologise."

There was a faint breeze and she was suddenly garbed in a diaphanous sky blue dress.

"Much appreciated," Lola said, before summing up the morning's leads. "We've got a cannibalised body, dozens of dead trees, unusual bird activity, and we also know where our target is staying."

"Already?" Miette asked, eagerly leaning in to look at the screen. Her hair touched Lola's bare shoulder, chilling her to the bone. *Is everyone but me short sighted or something?*

"One of the many surveillance cameras in the town picked him up, and I was able to follow him here." Lola pointed to a run down, bordering on derelict, building on the seafront. "The Hotel Montresor.

"I've set the drone to watch the place to see if he leaves, and I've already found a floor plan in case we need to go in and get him. Unfortunately, it's a little bit out of date and there's limited information on who lives there." She rattled off a command on her keyboard. "The property is owned by Gavin Strangeways; a local science teacher by day, and Arch-Druid by night."

"What on earth would Kellogg be doing with the Druids?" Miette asked. "Could the cannibalised corpse be part of a Druidic ritual?"

"Unlikely," Lola replied, bringing up the victim profile from the police records. "Our vic was Professor Elmyra Vane, a wealthy retired botanist with ties to Kew Gardens, along with the Eden Project down in Cornwall."

"Let me guess," Thad said, "she's also a Druid?"

"An Arch-Druid, from the same Circle as Mr Strangeways." Lola sat back in her chair once again. "I don't think this is some sort of internal power struggle, though."

"Why not?" Thaddeus took another sip of his coffee. "Maybe he was sick of waiting for Vane to die."

"Druids are a bureaucratic mess at the best of times," Miette confirmed. "Killing to advance an agenda is unheard of."

"Not to mention that they tend to be a bit more subtle than this," Lola added. "Yes, their practices can be a touch neolithic at times, but what happened to Professor Vane was barbaric; this is far too monstrous for them to even conceive of, let alone carry out."

"So where does that leave us?" Thad said, clearly eager to act.

"We know where Kellogg is, so we observe the building until we have enough information to go in and grab him." Miette reached over and picked up Lola's half-finished cup of coffee, draining it in a single gulp. "We'll keep an eye on the cannibalism, but I don't think it's connected.

"Coincidences happen more often than not."

"That's a thing dead people tend to say," Lola said, echoing her Lamplight trainers. Miette did not respond to her words, instead drifting to the kitchen in search of more coffee. Lola sighed and turned to look at Thaddeus. "You heard the boss, Thad; hurry up and wait, just like always."

"I thought working off-grid would be more exciting," he said sadly.

"Oh, it will be," she said with a grin. "You just have to wait until the shooting starts, that's all."

"So, Thad," Lola asked as he practised his unarmed combat in the living room, "what excuse did you give to Marsh?"

"What do you mean?" Thad asked, pausing mid punch to stare at her.

"You obviously didn't tell him who you were working with, so-"

"Yes, I did," Thad said firmly, his face suddenly stony. "I'll admit that he wasn't best pleased, but he was relieved to hear from me. It was good to hear his voice, although he's apparently been through a hell of a time in the past few months."

"But why would you tell him if you knew it would

make him angry at you?" Lola asked, deeply confused.

"He wasn't angry at me, Lola," Thad said slowly, walking over to her. He squatted down so that he was level with her, much as one would when speaking to a child. "I said he wasn't pleased, but that's only because he would rather I was home with him, instead of running cases down here."

"But why did you tell him at all?" Lola murmured, feeling like a scolded child, although she could not understand why.

"Because we tell each other things, Lo," Thad replied, "especially the uncomfortable things; that way we can help each other through the hard times."

Lola said nothing, blinking back shameful tears that she had no explanation for.

"It's about trust, Lola, and I'd tell you the hard things too; how else are we going to get through this alive?" He took her hands in his. "I need you to tell me the truth about things, even if you think they'll upset me; can you promise to do that for me, please?"

"I'm sorry," Lola said, more as a reflex than anything else.

"You don't need to apologise," he said kindly. "I understand that you've not had any healthy relationships to learn from, so I'm trying to help you understand what should've been taught to you when you were growing up."

"Thank you," Lola whispered. She contemplated ending the conversation there, but something compelled her to go on. "People have tried to speak to me about this before, but I never let them get this far; I just didn't want to think about what was taken from me, so I hurt them to stop them talking.

"You're only the second person I've ever been close to in my life, Thad."

"Was Gideon the first?" he asked, and she shook her head.

"Gideon was a mistake that I kept making, day after day," she said, wiping the tears from her eyes. "I know I should've been upset when he was killed, but all I felt was relief. Some nightmares are ones we make for ourselves, Thad, and those are the hardest to wake up from."

"So who was your first friend?" She smiled sadly at his question, and he quickly continued. "You don't have to tell me if you don't want to."

"We were in Lamplight together," Lola said, "but we weren't in the same group. We'd come together at night and just chat, like friends should. She could ask me anything she wanted or be as honest with me as I needed her to be, because I couldn't hurt her.

"The place where we met wasn't real, you see."

"I'm not quite sure I understand," Thad said, "but thank you for telling me. It's an honour to be your second ever friend."

"*Close* friend," she clarified. "I still count Charity amongst my friends, even if she did send me back to Betony, although I will admit that I'm still a little bit angry about that."

"Have you ever been in love?" Thad asked, surprising her into silence. It took her a moment to recover before she answered.

"No," Lola lied. There was a soft ding from her computer, mercifully giving her an exit from the conversation and she went to check on the information that had been flagged up. A smile crept on to her face when she saw that it was a list of residents at the Hotel

Montresor. "Go wake Miette; we've got the information we've been waiting for."

A few minutes later all three were gathered around the computer once again. Lola looked at Miette, expecting her to give the briefing, but she gestured for the Juliet to speak instead.

"Right," Lola said, thrilled to be giving a tactical assessment in the field once again, "There are six residents at the Hotel, with varying amounts of detail, along with a floor plan.

"Firstly, there is Arch-Druid Gavin Strangeways. He's a school teacher and is in tense standing with his Circle. Most Druids are dreamers and stargazers, so I wouldn't rate him as any sort of threat."

Thad nodded.

"Next we have Leroy Kapule; a Ghoul who was stranded here after the end of the Second World War. The addition of a Ghoul brings our cannibalised corpse back into play." She smiled at Thad. "Like most Ghouls, however, he's likely to be little more than a rabid animal; easy to outmatch and therefore no threat.

"We've already covered Reginald Kellogg, so there's no need to recap here." She brought up the next set of pictures. "This is Coral Grosse, who has surprisingly little to her digital footprint. She does appear to be a human, however, and is physically disabled, so we don't need to worry about her."

Finally, she put a picture of two startlingly attractive siblings on the screen.

"Here are our main problems; Flora and Paris Cain. Both are Fauns, and the former is an accomplished Warlock. Whilst we'll both be immune to their charms, Thad, they might pose a risk to you, Miette, and it seems that they are physically capable too.

"However, if we strike after dinner, in the early evening, both should be in a state of torpor, so they won't be able to put up much resistance. I'd recommend hitting these two first, and then Kellogg; we can mop up the rest with relative ease.

"Thoughts?"

"That sounds like a good plan, Lo," Thad said warmly. "That also gives us a few hours to prepare."

"Very good, Agent Oriole," Miette said, placing a chilly hand proudly on Lola's shoulder. "This should be a nice, quick operation. Simple and by-the-book; you certainly live up to your reputation. We'll strike at half-past nine this evening, right when the Fauns will be weakest.

"Arm yourselves appropriately before then," Miette continued. "We will not be leaving any witnesses."

Chapter Fourteen – From the Air and the Land

Flora

"Gavin!" Flora yelped as a white seabird slammed into the picture window of the Monty's decaying seafront lounge. She took a few nervous steps towards the glass, peering at the ground to see if the poor creature was injured, when several more birds crashed into the window, pounding in an irregular pattern like feathery hail.

Flora let out a deafening scream as she scrabbled away from the window. *This is some fucking Hitchcock bullshit,* she thought wildly as she hid behind a chair, *and I am too pretty to be killed by birds!*

Gavin was by her side in a flash, aided by Reggie who teleported in alongside him. The Druid placed one hand reassuringly on Flora's leg as he looked on in horror as even more birds thrashed against the windows, smashing their delicate skulls and snapping their slender necks as they did so.

"Are you doing this?" he asked Reggie directly. When the Familiar did not answer, he asked him again, more gently this time. "Reggie, are you in any way responsible for this? It's okay if you are; we'll find a way to help you."

"He isn't, Gav," she said shakily. "He's already told me pretty much everything about his time in the Ministry, and it doesn't add up."

"Reggie?" Gavin asked, clearly seeking

confirmation from the Familiar.

"I'm not doing this," he replied after a tense moment. "I didn't even know any of this was happening until I came here, Gavin; I promise."

"I believe you," he said softly. Gavin crouched down beside Flora, taking her face in his hands. "Are you hurt, Flora?"

"Just shaken up," she whispered, wrapping her arms around him. "Gavin, what the fuck is going on out there?"

"I'm not sure, but I'd be willing to bet that those are Roseate Terns," he said glancing at the damaged window. "In fact, I'd bet my life on it."

"Why?" Reggie asked, peering through the glass at the shattered bodies of the birds.

"One of my students read out an essay about them in school recently," he said getting to his feet to join Reggie, guiding Flora to go with him, "and I have a growing suspicion that she is somehow involved in all of this, although it's probably just tangential."

"Then we should go and speak to her!" Reggie said excitedly. Gavin went to reply, but Flora got there first.

"Absolutely not," she snapped. "We don't get children involved in anything like this, even as a last resort. We'll find her if we think she's in danger, but if that's not the case, then we'll leave her be.

"God only knows, teenagers have enough to fucking deal with nowadays, without all this horror added on top." She sighed sadly as she looked at the fragile black-faced birds whose bodies lie strewn on the terrace. "We should call the RSPB, Gavin; they'll want to know about this."

"I'll do it in a little bit." He sighed as he continued to

idly look out of the window, but Flora felt his hand stiffen in hers.

"What's the matter?" she whispered.

"Don't stare," he replied, barely moving his lips, "but there's a drone out there, hovering above the bay. It was there this afternoon, when Coral and I got home, and it's still there now. Someone is watching us."

"The Ministry?" Flora said in hushed tones, and Gavin nodded imperceptibly. "Do you think they'll attack us?"

"I hope not," Gavin replied, "but I've been weaving binding wreaths and stashing them all over the hotel in case they do."

Fuck. Flora had hoped that the people following Reggie had either lost him or had simply given up, but evidently his past had finally caught up with him.

"I should leave," Reggie said, but Gavin caught his arm. "They'll hurt you to get to me!"

"They can try," he replied quietly, "but we agreed to look after you. If you stay here, we can run interference long enough for you to escape, if the need arises.

"I think there's more to all this than meets the eye, though."

"If they come," Reggie said, his voice calm and even, "they'll come tonight. They'll attack after dinner in the hopes that you and Paris are lost to your torpor. They'll hit the two of you first, then come after me.

"I'm not sure who they'll send, but they'll be well trained." He nodded as he spoke. "There will be a team of three; no more, no less."

"Start stashing weapons," Gavin said, and Flora nodded. "I'll go warn the others, and then I'll get started on dinner; anything you fancy in particular?"

"I don't suppose you can eat those?" Reggie asked, gesturing at the dead birds with a chuckle.

"I'm sure Leroy could make a meal with them, but I would prefer something a little less ominous," Flora said with a smile. "How about we order from our usual Nepalese place?"

And I can see if they can take in Reggie if it all goes south, Flora thought. She winked at Gavin, who immediately understood. He nodded in agreement, and they all set about their tasks, the impending threat of the Ministry incursion hanging over them like the Sword of Damocles.

Let them come, Flora thought angrily, still bristling from her encounter with the Warlocks the previous day. *I could use someone to work out my rage and frustrations on.*

The attack came just after half past nine, as someone or something powerful smashed through the front door in three deafening kicks. Gavin was already lingering in the foyer with Leroy, whilst Coral, Flora, Paris, and Reggie were settled in the Silver Schooner, with Taylor Dayne playing on the jukebox.

Flora had been uncertain about Gavin's plan to evacuate Reggie immediately, but she had to agree that it would be useful to have someone else to check on them once the altercation was over, to whatever end. Paris had agreed to go with him; Flora had briefed him on the underground network she'd spent years building with Lucy, and he seemed to grasp the importance of what was about to happen.

At least they'll both be somewhere relatively safe, Flora thought, *even if it does kneecap our defensive capabilities somewhat.*

She snatched up her hockey stick as the loud commotion continued in the foyer and looked at her friends that were gathered in the bar.

"Reggie, run!" Flora yelled glancing at the Familiar, who seemed to be completely paralysed. "Paris, get him out of here, now!"

Paris grabbed Reggie and the two of them vanished as the Familiar teleported to the pre-arranged safehouse, putting both men out of harm's reach. Coral, energised by the sounds of violence in the next room, snatched up an empty champagne bottle and rushed towards the door just as a woman in a black coat burst into the Schooner, staggering as she went.

Just as the mysterious woman regained her balance, ensuring that her blue eyeglasses were correctly seated on her face, Coral brought the bottle down on the back of her head. The tough glass broke with a loud smash and the Ministry Agent toppled to the ground like a sack of potatoes, grunting in pain as she did so.

Flora dashed forward, hockey stick in hand, and quickly swept away the Agent's fallen glasses; she wasn't sure what they were, but they definitely looked important. Coral went to say something but a pale woman dashed into the room with them, faster than a roaring wind.

This strange newcomer dealt a savage punch to Coral's face and gestured in Flora's direction with the questing fingers of her other hand. The Faun felt the air leave her lungs and she suddenly realised that they were up against a Sylph.

This is going to end very quickly if we don't deal with her, she thought as she gasped and clutched uselessly at her throat. Coral began to recover from the blow to her face, but the Sylph raised her hand to suffocate the young bartender. Flora knew that she was too far away to harm the elemental and Coral wouldn't know how, so this would likely be the death of them both.

A strange thing happened, however, and an invisible force hurled the Sylph across the room, slamming her into chairs and tables, freeing the two women from her grasp at the same time. Flora let out a loud gasp as the air flooded back into her lungs. She pointed past Coral to the collection of wreaths that Gavin had stashed by the door.

"Bergamot and blackthorn!" Flora croaked, and Coral snatched up the wreath and tossed it to the Faun in one swift motion.

She caught it just as the invisible entity slammed the Sylph to the floor before her. She placed the wreath around the elemental's neck and pulled it tight, locking her powers away. Before the Sylph could remove the binding wreath, Flora brought her spiked hockey stick down on the elemental's hands, pinning them to the wooden floor of the bar.

"Go and help Gavin!" Flora yelled as the Sylph howled in frustrated agony. Coral dashed out of the room as the stunned Agent began to get to her feet. She stared at Flora with her violet eyes, and the Faun's face broke into a broad grin.

She's a Juliet! She has no power over me!

Her smile faltered as the woman pulled a pair of knives from her belt and took several unsteady steps towards Flora. She glanced at her hockey stick, but it was keeping the Sylph out of the fight, so she decided to leave it there.

The Agent reached out for the sporting implement,

only for an arc of green lightning to send her hand reeling backward in pain.

"Nobody touches my toys but me, bitch," Flora said smugly, not once taking her eyes off the woman's knives. "Come on, if you think you're hard enough!"

Flora tucked her hands behind her back, hiding her extending Rusałka claws from her opponent. *Let's see how pretty you are when I'm done with you.* The Juliet dashed forward, throwing one of her blades as she did so.

Flora dropped to her knees, letting the knife whizz overhead; she had no way of knowing if it was poisoned and she wasn't planning on finding out the hard way. The Juliet seized the opportunity and drove the other blade down towards Flora's heart.

She didn't count on the Faun's lightning reflexes, however, nor the tough horns on her head. Flora lurched forward, away from the weapon, and slammed her horns into the Juliet's ribs, breaking several of them with an audible crack. She cried out in pain, which only increased as Flora rammed her own venomous claws into the Agent's forearm, causing her to drop the knife.

Now we're playing on my terms, she thought, and rolled backwards, throwing the Juliet through the glass of the French doors that led into the courtyard. *I wonder how long it will take for the paralysis to take effect?*

She knew that a Juliet would boast a tremendous resilience to toxins of all kinds, but they weren't Hydras; the woman would succumb eventually. *The faster her heart beats*, Flora reasoned, *the faster she'll drop.*

The Ministry assassin rolled through the broken

glass and managed to regain her footing swiftly enough to redirect Flora's next lunge, throwing her into the ornamental fountain that stood in the centre of the courtyard.

She's had some training in redirecting momentum, Flora thought, but she was struck completely speechless by the Juliet's next action; she shoved the Faun-Rusałka hybrid beneath the surface of the water. *Is... Is she trying to drown me!?*

Flora's mouth opened wide in what must've looked like a scream of terror, but she was actually laughing at the Juliet's futile attempt to murder her.

Bitch, you didn't do your fucking homework, did you?

After a few seconds of frantic splashing, however, with the floodlights of the courtyard glittering on the surface of the water, she felt the Juliet's grip loosen as her gaze drifted out of focus. Flora had done enough accessibility research for her videos to recognise a photosensitive absence seizure when she saw one, and she pressed her advantage, erupting from the water like a demon from the deep.

She knocked the Ministry Agent to the ground and aimed a vicious striker's kick at her head. The Juliet came to her senses just in time for her to scrabble out of the way of a blow that would've snapped her neck had it connected.

Even then, Flora adjusted her aim and managed to snap the bones in the woman's left leg. The Faun was about to suggest a truce when the Juliet pulled a derringer pistol from her boot, causing Flora to bring out her most powerful skill in order to end the conflict.

She extended her fingers, locked eyes with the

Juliet, and let out an unearthly warbling whistle that echoed around the courtyard before worming its way into the Agent's brain. Although her opponent had clearly had some training in resisting such gifts, Flora's dual heritage quickly wore her down until she only had two choices; pass out, or suffer a seizure strong enough to kill her.

A satisfied smile crept on to Flora's face as the Juliet's eyelids flickered shut and she fell into a deep, hypnotic trance that only the Faun could wake her from.

Nighty night, babes.

After deftly binding the hands of the hypnotised Ministry Agent with a cable tie she'd kept handy for this exact purpose, she dashed back into the Montresor to help her friends.

The fight isn't won yet, she thought as she went, *but we've dealt with two thirds of their force.*

We might actually have a chance to survive this.

Chapter Fifteen – If I Can Shoot Rabbits

Gavin

Put your humanity aside, he thought as the front door burst open. *These are the same bastards that tortured Lucy for years on end; you said that you would've saved her if you could have.*

Time to keep your promise.

He drew the Berretta and aimed it squarely at the heart of the bearded man who barrelled towards him, but a quick glance at his face made Gavin hesitate; in spite of his imposing size, the man was barely older than a teenager.

"Fuck," he swore under his breath as he tossed the gun aside, letting it slide underneath a nearby dresser. The man smiled at this, interpreting it as a prelude to surrender.

It was just a distraction, however, and the man was sent crashing to the floor by the wire that was strung across the foyer. Gavin allowed himself a small satisfied smile; Leroy had been sceptical of such a 'Looney Tunes' plan.

His pause meant that he was caught by surprise as a woman in blue glasses leapt over the wire and closed the distance with all the speed she could muster. She crashed into him and pressed her mouth to his, allowing her saliva to pour through his lips in a nightmarish parody of a kiss.

Gavin felt the power flow into him; seductive, compelling, addictive. Before it could take hold, however, it came up against a far greater opponent than the Druid's own willpower, and was swiftly washed away by the relentless tsunami of grief and guilt that still lingered in the wake of Lucy's death, bolstered by his unwavering hatred of those that harmed her.

My heart is already taken, he thought as he shoved her away from him and slammed the sock full of pennies into her stomach, causing her to double over. She took an unsteady step away from Gavin, right into Leroy's reach.

The Ghoul picked her up, one hand on her collar and the other on her belt, and slammed her face first through the closed doors to the Schooner. He looked at Gavin, who gave him a shaky thumbs up. There was a smashing sound from the bar and Gav couldn't help but smile; he was certain that the woman had been further incapacitated by Coral.

A swift breeze rushed past him into the bar, but he didn't have a chance to react to that as the large man had gotten back to his feet and was bearing down on him. Gavin ducked two heavy punches, leading the man towards the stairs where he could use his size against him.

Instead of advancing with him, the large agent turned towards Leroy and pulled a long glove off of his right hand, revealing a terrifying skeletal arm. The Hawaiian Ghoul was momentarily surprised when the man seized him by the wrist with a look of triumph on his face. Instead of injuring Leroy, the man suddenly went weak at the knees and began to slump to the floor.

"You misread that one, brother," Leroy said sadly. He shook the man off and shoved him against the opposite wall with a deafening thud. Before the Agent could react, Coral burst into the foyer, unfolding her butterfly knife with panache as she went.

She stabbed the large man at least six times in the stomach before he punched her in the chest, hard, sending her sprawling. Gavin rushed forward to see if she was still alive just as the man closed in to finish the job.

"Why don't you pick on someone your own size, bro?" Leroy said, placing his considerable bulk between the Agent and the injured woman. He immediately began a ritual that Gavin had only seen him perform once before; the traditional ha'a warrior dance, complete with all the strutting, chanting, and roaring that ritual demanded.

Oh, you're fucked now, sunshine, Gavin thought as Coral groaned in his arms.

The man swung at Leroy before his dance was over, which only angered the Ghoul even further. He caught the skeletal hand in his own massive fist and twisted the Agent's arm, forcing him to expose his ribs or break his wrist. As soon as he had a clear shot, Leroy slammed his free hand into the man's chest, his fist landing again and again with all the force of a runaway train.

"I've got that undead strength, bro," Leroy said angrily, "so how about you just fucking give up now, okay?"

"Fuck you," the man hissed through his pain, and a nebulous limb of shadow flicked out from his body and curled around an ornate vase that nestled in an alcove beneath a small portrait of Lucy.

Don't you dare.

The shadow hand brought the vase whipping through the air to smash into the back of Leroy's head. The Ghoul was staggered by the force of the blow and he let the Ministry Agent go, who turned his attention back towards Coral and Gavin.

The latter was already advancing on the Agent, fire blazing in his heart as he held Coral's taser in his hand. His other twirled his sock of pennies, and he feigned left as he closed in on the looming man, who immediately took a large stride to block him; exactly what Gavin had hoped for.

"Lucy made that vase for me," he growled as he slammed the pennies into the man's testicles, causing him to yelp in pain. As soon as his mouth was open, Gavin stuffed the taser between his lips and into his gums, shocking him again and again, until he was a twitching, blubbering wreck on the ground.

"Jesus, Gavin," Leroy said as he regained his senses. "I know that vase was important to you, but-"

Leroy's words faltered as Gavin swung the pennies into the man's crotch again, and then one more time for good measure. The Ghoul winced sympathetically with each impact, but Gav could only feel cold rage towards the incapacitated man.

"Do you want me to do him, Gav?" Coral asked spinning the butterfly knife in her hand as she walked over to where the man lay on the ground. "I'll make it quick."

"No," Gavin replied, handing her the taser, "but make sure he stays down whilst I tend to his wounds."

"You're going to treat him?" she asked incredulously, but she did as he asked.

"He's worth more to us alive," he said, "for now."

The Agent groaned in pain and Coral reflexively lunged towards him as Leroy shook his head in pity at the wounded man's plight.

"I've dealt with the Juliet," Flora said, running into

the Foyer as Coral stunned the man with the taser once again. "The Sylph is nailed to the floor in the bar, and I'm sure you could whip up a better binding to hold her in place, if not destroy her outright."

"We'll tie them up, I'll treat their wounds, and then we can all have a civil discussion," Gavin said, wiping a smear of the man's blood from the corner of his mouth. "I would like to hear their side of the story before we decide what to do next.

"Let's find out what our guests really want."

The man with the skeleton arm was the first to awaken. Gavin had rifled through their captives' pockets and had found only one set of identifying documents; a driver's license for the man, naming him as Thaddeus Thane. The woman and the Sylph were unknown, but the tattoo on the woman's left wrist was familiar; he remembered that Lucy had one just like it, although she would never speak about it, save that it was a lingering reminder of her time in the Ministry.

They're about the same age, he thought. *I wonder if they knew each other in a former life?*

The woman drooled slightly in her catatonic state, and he shook his head disdainfully. Whatever this woman was, she had tried to ensnare him in some kind of enchantment, and Gavin did not appreciate such underhanded tricks in the slightest.

"Flora," he said, looking over his shoulder at the Faun, "wake her up."

"Who are you people?" Thaddeus asked thickly, his mouth clearly still injured. Flora stopped short as she saw Thad flexing his skeletal hand.

"Just ordinary folks, going about their ordinary business," Coral said, holding an ice pack up to her eye. "You've no reason to barge into our home and attack us like this; we have rights, you know!"

"I wouldn't call any of you ordinary," Thad said darkly, looking at Leroy with an angry gaze. "I know that you're a Cep, so why couldn't I consume you?"

"You can't eat a black hole, brother," Leroy said softly. "You might be a Famine, but I'm a Ghoul; nothing to take, and nothing to kill."

"How do you know that I'm a Famine?"

"I've been around the block a few times," the large man replied. "I've seen a couple of your kind; I've never seen it end well for any of you, though."

"Why don't you untie me and we'll see who ends up worst off?" Thad growled, and Leroy sighed heavily.

"Look, if you wanna dance again, Pretty Boy, that's entirely up to you, but you gotta clear it with him first," Leroy said, gesturing to Gavin. "I'm serious, bro; he's the one you should be worried about."

"Flora," Gavin said sharply, already tired of the circus before him, "wake her up!"

Flora nodded and let out a low whistle that rose into a raucous cacophony that startled the woman awake. She gasped and looked around, immediately straining against her bonds. She glanced at Thaddeus, and then at the Sylph, who was still held in stasis by Gavin's binding wreath. Her eyes widened in terror as she stared at the group assembled before her.

"How did this happen?" Her voice trembled as she looked at the bound Sylph. "Miette? Miette, what did they do to you?"

"So that's two names," Gavin said softly, squatting down so that he was at eye level with the woman. "I'm still short one, however, so what do I call you?"

"How did you resist me?" she asked, thrashing

violently in her chair. "HOW!?"

"My heart is too broken for anyone to steal," Gavin replied gently, " and my hate for the Ministry is deeper than anything you could possibly comprehend. So, stranger, what do I call you?"

"Get us out of here," the woman said, staring at the Famine. "Eat them, or-"

"Don't look at Mr Thane," Gavin said, tilting her face back towards him. "I'm talking now, and I want an answer; who are you people, and why are you here?"

The woman closed her eyes and shook her head. Gavin sighed heavily before he continued, trying to keep his emotions in check.

"Please, miss, work with me on this. I've got a lot going on right now, and you are a complication that I don't need." He placed a hand on her shoulder, trying to will some sense into her. "This is your last chance; let's do this the nice way."

"Fuck off, human!" the woman spat, and Gav stood up, his shoulders slumping in defeat. *Fuck it,* he thought, *we'll take these pieces off the board and continue with the problem at hand.* He walked over to Flora and Leroy, making sure to keep his voice low.

"What do you think?" he asked.

"This whole thing reeks of a deniable op," Leroy whispered. "I doubt anyone will come looking for them if they don't come home."

"I was thinking the same," Flora said. "I haven't heard anything about Ravenblades or other Agents in the area; this is either a rogue team or something so off-the-books that it won't even register if they disappear.

"I'd say that our hands are full enough with what's

happening here, and they're just gonna get in our way." Flora sighed. "We might not get so lucky the next time they come for us."

"For sure," Leroy said as Gavin nodded. "They're a powerful team, and they won't come in so haphazardly again. If we can't make them see sense-"

"We don't have time for that," Gavin said sharply. "There's too much at stake."

He looked over at the bound captives.

"This ends tonight."

Interlude One – Awaken, My Love

The first of the twitching emaciated creatures looked out across the bay as the totems of bone, sinew, and feather jangled noisily around its neck. It jabbered excitedly slapping a misshapen hand on the side of the cave, signalling the others to join it at the entrance to their lair.

"Why do you make such a noise?" Sister demanded as she joined Brother, who was still excitedly chittering as he pointed towards the darkening horizon. She huffed and grabbed at his hand, but he quickly folded into the shadows, emerging a few feet away with a mad cackle. Sister growled in frustration at Brother's antics, but he was clearly excited about something.

"New!" he cried out, gesturing out across the water. "New coming soon! Nearly ready!"

Sister sighed and shook her head; even though Brother was older than her, his grasp of language was almost non-existent. She stretched her dirty fingers before placing them on the side of her head in an attempt to cut through the chaos in his mind.

She saw the thousands of points of light that moved throughout the entire bay area, with some much brighter than others. One, however, was a whirling column of prismatic brilliance that almost hurt to look at, and she finally understood.

There will be another of our number soon.

She relayed these thoughts to the rest of her family as they approached from deeper in the cave system.

"Settle down, Brother," she said, trying to be kind to the jabbering idiot as he moved from shadow to shadow, unbound by the laws of space. "If you don't calm down, Mumsy will make you forget again."

Sister loved her family dearly, but she lived in constant terror of Mumsy and her long, crooked fingers; it would only take a chance word or clumsy action for her to reach out and steal her children's memories away. Even though Sister had managed to sneakily steal back some of what had been stolen from her, she feared being made to forget just how special she truly was.

More than anything, she feared being forgotten.

"I'm here!" Babby yelled as she pattered joyfully through the cave. Whilst the others were clad in macabre totems and crude clothing, Babby wore no garments or trinkets; her burned flesh was all the adornment she would ever need.

"Babby fire!" Brother demanded, clapping his hands like a chimpanzee. "Babby fire now!"

"Abracadabra!" Babby cried out, producing a ball of bluebell fire in the palm of her outstretched hand. The smell of burning flesh filled the cave, which only served to excite Brother further.

"More, more!"

He was about to reach out and grab the flames when another, much older voice echoed through the red sandstone formation.

"Settle down, my loves," Mumsy said as she shuffled towards her children. Sister kept a wary eye on Mumsy's nightmarish hands, which were currently concealed within her robe. "Even though another darling comes to us on swift wings, we must be patient and careful."

She revealed her oversized left hand and wagged her index finger in a chastising manner.

"Naughty children get the Forgetting, after all." She looked at the gathered members of her family, her grey eyes alert and keen, despite the tinge of jaundice that coloured their edges. "Now, tell me, which of you made a magic spell in the woods?"

Only silence met her question.

"Come, my loves; Mumsy will find out eventually, so be good children and tell the truth." Still, no-one spoke. "I will have to tell Aunty if you have been naughty, and lying to your Mumsy is the worst naughtiness of all."

The children looked down at their feet, and Sister took the opportunity to play her hand. She placed her stained fingertips to her temples, as if she was using her magic spells, and decided to lay the blame for her actions on her innocent sibling.

"Brother did it!" Sister lied, pointing at him in an accusatory manner. "I can hear him thinking about it!"

"Are you telling the truth, Sister?" Mumsy asked, raising a filthy eyebrow, and Sister nodded, hiding her thoughts away in a deep dark place. There was a nervous pause, and then Mumsy nodded. "Very well."

"No!" Brother cried out, suddenly terrified. "Sister lying! Lying!"

"Aunty!" Mumsy called out, and her cry was answered with a rumbling growl from deep within the cave. "Brother has been telling lies! He must be punished!"

"No, Mumsy, no!"

A wicked grin crossed Sister's face as the dark, terrible shape of Aunty entered the firelight, and the coastal caves that were home to the Forever Family were filled with blood curdling screams.

Part Two: Something Wicked in the Bay

Chapter Sixteen – Trick Shot

Lola

Lola watched as the man in the tie-dye tunic stalked out of the room, muttering to himself. She tried to ignore the pain in her leg and looked on, seeing the Faun, Flora, exchange a nervous look with the obese Ghoul. *Oh, is there division in the ranks?* Lola wondered. *Maybe we can use this to our advantage.*

"Where's your friend going?" she asked, almost snidely. "Doesn't he have the stamina to question us?"

"He's gone to get his focus for a banishing ritual," Flora said, "so if you don't want this to get any worse for you, I'd start fucking talking."

"A *banishing ritual*!?" Thaddeus said, almost bursting into laughter. "Good luck with that! Magic doesn't work on me, Druidic or otherwise!"

"You don't seem to understand, bro," the Ghoul said, almost grey with worry as he took Thad's skeletal hand in his own, "Gavin isn't like other Druids; he's dangerously practical, almost to a fault, and he's still grieving his late wife.

"This was her home, man, and you broke in and trashed the place." The Ghoul shook his head sadly. "Gavin is not happy with you at all, and he's, uh, not exactly playing with the full deck tonight, bro. You should probably apologise when he comes back."

Thaddeus's grin faded, and a glimmer of worry crossed his face.

"What do you mean, *dangerously* practical?" the Famine asked, and Flora answered.

"He's gonna hit you in the head with a brick," she

said, matter-of-factly. "He'll keep going until you're dead, however long it takes, and then he'll do her next."

"A *brick*?" Thad asked, and the Ghoul nodded. "But, that's insane!"

"You attacked us, bro," the large man said, shrugging slightly. "All's fair, as it were."

"But you can't just hit someone with a fucking brick!" Thad yelled, wriggling in his chair once again. "That's murder!"

"Technically it would be self-defence in this instance," Flora said, checking her perfect cuticles as she spoke. "Besides, this is absolutely a black op, so it's not like they're gonna send anyone else down here to find you.

"If there's one thing I know about the Ministry, it's that its Agents are *expendable.*" Flora glanced at the imprisoned Sylph. "Also, that thing is definitely there to keep an eye on you both, so you're on some kind of prison release, aren't you?"

Oh, we are so fucked, Lola realised, and Thad began to scream and beg for his life as Gavin strode back into the room, half a house brick clutched in his hand. He barely broke his stride as he raised it up to slam into Thad's skull.

Lola's eyes widened as she saw one of the wooden charms on Gavin's bracelet; a small redwood moon that she hadn't seen in over three decades. Gavin was bringing the brick down as she yelled out to him, taking the only shot she had.

"Are you Lucy Havelock's husband?" she asked, and Gavin halted, mid-swing. The brick trembled in his hand as he turned to look at her. "She had a tattoo just like mine, right?"

"What number?" he growled.

"Eighty four," Lola answered. "Zero Eight Four, if you want to call it out like they used to on the Island. I... I'm sorry to hear that she's dead; she was a truly beautiful soul, with the kindest heart you could possibly imagine."

"Who are you?" Gavin said, and the rage in his eyes made it clear that the danger had not yet passed.

"My name is Lola Oriole," she said, "and Lucy was my only friend growing up."

"Prove it."

"I don't know if this is going to make any fucking sense to you," Lola said softly, hoping that her words would save their lives, "but she used to come to me in my dreams. She called me 'The Girl in the Mask'."

There was a heartbeat of tension as the Druid locked eyes with her, searching for a hint of a lie, but then he relaxed with an explosive sigh, lowering the brick before slumping into a nearby chair. The brick clattered to the floor of the bar, the sharp sound causing Thaddeus to twitch violently in his seat.

"What the fuck do you people want with us?" Gavin asked, running a hand through his dishevelled hair; most of it had escaped his ponytail during the fight. "And don't you fucking dare lie to us, or else I promise I will visit horrors upon you worse than anything you can imagine."

"Worse than Lamplight?" Lola muttered, and Gavin nodded.

"All that government sanctioned torture was designed to keep you alive and functional, and it will not be a patch on the hillbilly shit I will unleash on you." He gestured at Miette. "Did you know that you can trap a Sylph inside a specially charmed airtight jar? It takes them a couple of months to slowly suffocate, but it happens eventually, and then all you're left with is a fine residue called Sylph Sparkle. It ain't a pinch on Mummy Dust, but it's real powerful shit."

Lola blinked, horrified at the threat.

"Yeah, a Sylph will pretty much eat themselves alive to fight the suffocation. It's pretty low effort too." He pointed at Thad next. "Now, you might be immune to any supernatural shit, but I can still flood a room with Devil's Trumpet smoke and toss you in until you go completely insane. Might take you a few days before you start chewing your own fingers off, but trust me, boy, it'll take."

There was a beat of silence as his gaze returned to Lola.

"Now, you, Ms Oriole, I owe a debt of kindness to as you were kind to my Lucy, but if you choose to make your bed, Flora will ensure that you lie in it until you rot. She'll put you in a trance so deep that not even death will wake you from it."

He tapped his fingers idly on the arm of his chair, seemingly waiting for their response.

"Those are some fairytale level punishments," Lola said, almost admiring his inventiveness, "so I guess we have a deal, Mr Wizard."

"That's what I like to hear," Gavin replied, leaning forwards in his chair, suddenly ready to listen. "So, Ms Oriole, spokesperson for the Ministry, what the fuck are you doing here?"

"We're investigating the strange phenomena that are occurring in the local area," she said flatly, no longer attempting to do anything other than get out of the room alive. "We think it's linked to a former Ministry asset, Reginald Kellogg, and we tracked him to this place."

"He's not involved," Flora said with certainty. "I had a long talk with him about his gifts and his time with you folks; he doesn't have anything that could cause this."

"He worked with the Director," Lola retorted, "and a woman named-"

"Harper Cherry, who had hoped that she could induce a form of limited wish fulfilment in him," Flora said sharply, silencing Lola.

Do they actually know more than we do?

"The issue with the approach of both Cherry and Desai, is that they forgot the most important rule of a Familiar's ability to develop sympathetic gifts," she continued, smirking as she spoke. "The Familiar has to actually bond with you, and that won't happen if they don't like you."

"You guys run a fucking clown-shoes operation," quipped the woman with a black eye. "Although you did take that blow to the head like a fucking champion; I'll give you that."

"So," Gavin said, taking charge of the conversation once again with the practised ease that only a teacher could muster, "it's clear it isn't Reggie, so you can leave him the fuck alone. Aside from that, what other leads do you have?"

Lola swallowed awkwardly and shuffled in her seat, suddenly afraid.

We have nothing left to bargain with, unless...

"We don't have any more information than you do," she admitted but quickly added an offer that would be too good to refuse, "but we do have an unredacted copy of The White Book; if you let us walk out of here alive, you can have it."

Gavin smiled at her, nodding as he did so.

"Ms Oriole," he said cheerfully, "you have yourself a deal."

It took almost an hour for Reggie and Paris to return with The White Book, but when they did and Gavin had verified its authenticity, he had turned them loose, true to his word. Admittedly, he had liberated her and Thaddeus from their bonds first and taken them aside for a quiet word.

"I know what it's like," he said softly, "to have to march to the beat of someone else's drum. It's no fun, and your friend, Miette, seems like she might be a bit of a vicious taskmaster. Hopefully this will help to keep her in line when she asks too much of you."

He gave Lola a small ceramic jar filled with a glittery silver powder.

"Sylph Sparkle, as I mentioned, is made through an arduous ritual and it is rather repellent to the creatures it comes from; a quick sprinkle of this will sanctify a room, or a pinch to the face will send her running for the hills for a while." He smiled at the awe on Thad's face. "Use it sparingly, though, as I'm not going to give you any more."

"Why are you giving us any at all?" Thad asked, suspicious of the Druid's motives. "Are you trying to get us to fight each other?"

"I know the signs of a forced hand, and I don't care for it. You're too young to live in bondage to the Ministry, kid, and you, Lola, have had to endure it for far too long." Gavin sighed heavily. "I'm just doing what I think is right.

"Now let's get your friend untied, and then you can

fuck off out of my home."

Miette was freed without any fuss, and the three Ministry operatives were turfed out on to the street without ceremony or even a goodbye. As they began their slow journey back to their safehouse, the location now compromised to the Montresor cohort, Lola contemplated voicing her theories about what was happening in the bay.

One of the others, however, beat her to the punch.

"I could feel the power in Reggie," Thad said, finally breaking the defeated silence that held them all in thrall, "and they're telling the truth about him. He's not strong enough to do any of this, not by a country mile."

"This would be easier if you hadn't given them the fucking book," Miette grumbled. "But I *suppose* I should thank you for at least getting us out of that monumental fuck up alive. I still can't believe what a strong resistance they put up.

"I also can't figure out what was throwing me around," she went on. "It didn't feel like a Shunt or Fulcrum; this was up close and personal. If I didn't know any better, I'd say that the hotel is-"

"Haunted?" Thad suggested, and she nodded. "I felt something too, even though I didn't see anything concrete."

"It's still a shame we didn't get to bag our man," Miette said sadly. "Bringing Reggie back into the Ministry's sphere of influence would've been incredibly useful."

"I'm glad he wasn't there," Thad admitted as Lola continued to mull over possibilities. "I said that he wasn't powerful enough to cause the phenomena we're here to deal with, but he was definitely strong enough to kill us, even three on one.

"There's something about him that feels *imminent*," he said darkly, "like a star that's about to explode."

"Why don't we focus on what's still to do, rather than what we've lost?" Lola suggested. "We know that Kellogg was a false lead, but the premise still stands; there are other non-humans capable of doing this, such as Demons, Djinni, and a whole host of other creatures."

"Most of them fly under the Ministry's radar," Miette replied testily and Lola nodded.

"That they do," she agreed, "but they also have needs that can lead to semi-human offspring. There's a Warlock Convocation in the local area, so we could try and trace these creatures back from their spawn."

"That's not a terrible idea," Miette said, nodding in approval. "We'll head there first thing in the morning."

"Good plan," Lola said, shielding her exposed eyes as a police car tore past them, lights flashing, "but I will need to get my glasses repaired as a matter of urgency. Can you please organise that when we get back to the house, Miette?"

"Of course," the Sylph replied as they neared their destination. "What are you going to do?"

"I'm going to make a hot chocolate, take my pills," Lola said, "and then sleep for as long as you'll let me."

Thad nodded in agreement, and Miette did not object, filling Lola with relief.

Thank fuck, she thought. *This has been a hell of a fucking day.*

Even as she drifted off to sleep that night, her thoughts kept drifting back to the Faun, Flora.

She has such stark blue eyes, especially when she's underwater. Such beautiful eyes.

<u>Chapter Seventeen</u> – An Attempted Release

Gavin

"Would you really have killed him with that brick, or done those terrible things that you threatened?" Flora asked quietly as Gavin continued to stare blankly at the empty seats in the lounge. "Or was it all talk?"

"I didn't shoot him when he came through the door," he said slowly, his fingers tightly interlaced. "I had a clear shot and could've put him down for good, but he was still half a child, so I tossed the gun away.

"When he spoke, though, I could see that there was something wrong in him; something rotten and violent. He had the eyes of a true believer." Gavin nodded gently. "So, yeah, I was absolutely gonna kill him; all of them, actually.

"I'm still not sure that letting them walk away was the right choice, but I meant what I said; if we cross paths again, it's not gonna end so well for them."

"It might end a lot worse for us."

"It might, but I want to think that they can do better; *be* better." He sighed heavily and put his head in his hands.

"You're a good man, Gav," Flora said, and he immediately sat up shaking his head.

"No, Flora. No, I'm not." He stared at her, the stress of the past few days finally catching up with him. "The Sweet Breath, I've been giving you, it has-"

"Opiates?" Flora replied, one eyebrow raised. "I'm trans, Gav; I get a lot of blood tests and shit like that tends to show up. I've known for a long time, and I'm okay with that. Anything to make my day a little easier.

"Thank you for telling me, though." She smiled sadly at him. "Do you think they'll come back tonight?"

"No," he said, every ounce of his energy seemingly spent. "They'll regroup and reassess; it's what they're trained to do. Also, the woman, Lola, seemed to understand just how fucking angry I was at them for daring to come here; she'll counsel caution, I think."

"So, what now?" Flora asked, twirling her hockey stick as she stifled a yawn.

"I don't know how you can act so normally," he said. "Even though I feel dead on my feet, I'm still wound as tight as a watch spring."

"That's the adrenaline of the fight," Flora replied knowingly. "You won't sleep until you get it out of your system. I tend to go for a swim or a run, but tonight that feels foolish."

She smiled at him sheepishly.

"In my younger days I'd go and get into another fight; one I could get my release from, though." The Faun sighed heavily and brushed her hair from her eyes, revealing a small cut above one perfect eyebrow. "Also not an option in this situation, unless you'd like to have a scrap?"

Gavin did not reply; his gaze was fixed on her face, laser focussed on the cut and the little smear of dried blood that accompanied it. On anyone else it would be just an inconsequential scrape, but that one tiny flaw somehow changed Flora's entire face, making her seem imperfect and approachable; human, even.

Oh fuck, he realised, *I finally get it.*

"Gavin?" Flora's eyes were full of concern.
Such beautiful blue eyes.

"Gavin, why are you looking at me like that?" she asked bashfully, awkwardly looking down at the ground. He hadn't seen her do that in decades; not since her first early attempts at womanhood when they were much younger and he was nowhere near as brave as he was now.

He took a few slow steps towards her, and her eyes widened in realisation as she rose to meet him, wrapping one powerful leg around him as he seized her, pulling their bodies close together. She kissed him deeply and he could taste the lingering blood in her mouth, but it only strengthened his resolve.

"Gavin," she said softly, pulling away slightly so she could gently stroke his bloodied tunic with one delicate hand, "you don't have to do this just for me."

"This is for both of us. I've spent too many sleepless nights wondering what this would be like," he admitted. "Until now, though, it was purely abstract, but tonight... anything feels possible, so let's just see what happens, okay?"

"Okay." Flora smiled as she rested her forehead against his shoulder. "Promise me that you won't hold back?"

"What do you mean?"

"You don't need to be gentle with me," she answered, her words tinged with a lustful growl. "I'm not some delicate flower, Gavin, so you don't have to worry about breaking me."

"Is that so?" He kissed her again, and could feel her smile against his lips.

"Yes," she replied nipping at his lip. "If we only have this moment, then I want you to do it properly. I want you to fuck me like you mean it."

"I can do that," he said as a lascivious grin crept on to his face. "My room or yours?"

"Mine," she said, leading him towards the stairs. "More space to play, and my bed is made for shagging in."

I don't doubt it, he thought as they trotted upstairs as quietly as they could manage. Flora led the way, pulling him eagerly into her lavishly furnished boudoir before pushing him down on to the bed with one powerful shove from her freakish foot.

Gavin immediately reached out and grabbed the soft, supple flesh of her thigh and started to knead it in his strong scarred hands, groaning with delight at just how wonderful Flora felt. *I could spend a lifetime just on her legs,* he thought giddily, *but there's so much more of her to enjoy.*

She quickly shed her t-shirt and bra, letting her breasts hang free in the cool night air. Gav reached towards them, but she leant back, grinning, and waved a chastising finger in his bemused face.

"You don't get me that easily, darling," Flora said in a playful, sultry tone. "If I've had to wait all these years, you're going to fucking earn it."

"Don't be a fucking tease, Flora!" Gavin said, trying to seize her with a chuckle, put she pushed him back on to the bed. He squirmed and struggled but still she held him fast, leaning down to whisper in his ear.

"You have to do one thing for me," she said huskily, "and then you can fuck me as hard as you want."

"What do I have to do?" he asked, straining against her, his lust and arousal frustrated by both clothing and restraint.

"Tell me you love me," she whispered, her breath

warming the gentle curves of his ear. Her eyes met his as she pulled back, but her smile faltered as she saw his eyes reflexively flick to the corner of the room; some part of him was expecting to see a disapproving phantom, but there was only the mottled wallpaper.

Still, he felt a chill run down his spine and he gently shook his head, even though his body ached for Flora's touch. *I'm not ready,* he realised, *and not with her.*

"I... I'm sorry, Flora," he said, barely audibly. "I can't say that to you, not in the way you want, and I can't do this. I'm so sorry."

Flora didn't say anything, but she did slump on to the bed beside him, a slightly glazed look in her eyes. He reached out to comfort her, but she pulled away.

"I think you'd better go, Gav," she whispered, and he nodded, getting slowly to his feet. He wanted to turn around and apologise again, but she had asked him to leave and that was what he did.

"Goodnight, Flora," he said quietly as he crossed the threshold of her bedroom.

"Goodnight, Gavin," she replied, and he pulled the door closed behind him.

He got less than half a dozen paces down the hallway before he heard her begin to sob.

Gavin took one of Lucy's old dresses from the wardrobe and carried it to the bed, where he laid it out lovingly as tears streamed down his face. He tenderly stroked the simple patterned cotton and wished with all his heart that he had the love of his life back in his arms, instead of mere haunted relics.

"I wish you were here, Luce," he said tearfully. "I miss you all the time."

He sighed heavily and crumpled on to the ground as

he gave way to his grief and guilt.

"I'm sorry I couldn't save you."

When Lucy Strangeways had started getting sick, Gavin had immediately turned to his Druidic Magic to protect her from malign influences and malicious intent. As her illness worsened and her condition grew ever graver, he pored over volume after volume of supernatural dangers in order to work out what was wrong with her.

When Arch-Druid Borage finally convinced the half-mad Gavin to take Lucy to a conventional doctor, it was already too late; the pancreatic cancer that was eating her from the inside was terminal.

She had died less than a year later, in the very room where he now wept.

"I fucked up, Luce," he whimpered, snot dangling from his nose and saliva dripping on to the carpet as his sobbing escalated. "I fucked up so badly and I fucking let you die because of it!

"I fucking killed you!"

"What would you give to make things right?" asked a soft voice from across the room. Gavin looked up through his tears and saw that his balcony door was open, with a dark figure leaning against the worn stone balustrade.

"Who are you?" Gavin asked, his sobs dying down as he shakily got to his feet, wiping his face clean with his trembling hands. "Why are you here?"

"I'm here to help you, Gavin," the figure said, a smile in its voice. His eyes finally focussed and he realised that the person was a man seemingly spun out of the night sky. The man, although made of star speckled blackness at first glance, glowed with a faint internal light that spilled into the room. "I come to you to light up the darkness, Gavin, so I will ask you once more.

"What would you give to make things right?"

"I don't make deals with people I don't know," Gavin said, his voice trembling, "much less creatures that I don't understand. Besides, why should I believe you? Why not give me something for free, just to prove your power?"

"Ah, the negotiator!" The Illuminated Man laughed heartily as he leant against the door frame. "I have heard stories about you, Mr Strangeways, and how pleasing it is to see that you live up to the myth; quick witted and clever with words, yet so *ruthlessly* practical.

"Yet, you still let your wife die a horrible death, by your own admission."

Gavin took a step forwards, reflexively clenching his fists in rage.

"Come now, Gavin; you can no more hurt me than you can chase the moon from the sky." The smugness in the Man's voice was unbearable, but there was a hint of something familiar to it. "You're just a human, after all, and I have more power than anyone could possibly understand; in fact, I am raw power *incarnate*!

"So, I will ask you, one third and final time; what will you give me in exchange for the life of your wife?" The offer hung in the air like a noose; both lethal and impossibly inviting, all at once.

Maybe I could have her back, he thought, *even if it's just for a little while.*

"How much time can you give me with her?" he asked, wavering slightly.

"A lifetime of lifetimes," the Illuminated Man

purred, "for the right price, that is."

The predatory tone gave him pause and he took an uncertain step back, almost as if he was coming to his senses after waking from a particularly deep dream.

"I can't stand this indecision, Gavin!" The Man's voice was sharper now, with a second layer beneath it that he was so sure he'd heard before. "This behaviour is what drove your wife into the ground!"

It is, he agreed in his mind, *and she would not have it claim my life too.*

"I won't give you anything," he said resolutely. "Lucy would never want me to make that decision for her."

"As you wish," the Illuminated Man said, bowing slightly. "I'm afraid that I must cut our conversation short; the night is young and there are many more dreams to fulfil. I'm sure I'll see you soon enough, Mr Strangeways."

With a sudden flap of the curtains in the sea breeze, the starry visitor was gone.

This just keeps getting stranger and stranger, Gavin thought as he closed the balcony door and climbed into the bed. After a few moments of uncomfortable stillness, he rose once again and locked the balcony door and windows, just in case, before returning to bed and drifting off into a fitful, haunted sleep.

Chapter Eighteen – Seeing the Wood for the Trees

Flora

Flora began to sob as soon as she heard Gavin walk away, thrashing violently on her bed and tearing at the bedclothes with her venomous claws.

I am so fucking stupid, she thought angrily. *Why do I always have to fuck everything up!?*

"I had him," she mumbled into her pillow as her tears soaked into the material. "He was in my bed and I fucking had him!"

She had been close to Gavin her entire life, even before her transition, and now she had poisoned the longest standing friendship she'd ever had. *He'll hate me forever after tonight,* she thought anxiously as she rose from the bed and began to pace nervously across the floor. A few Peepers scattered at the corner of her vision, but she paid the pests no mind.

Gavin had supported her through thick and thin, and had always been there for her, far more than her family ever had; even though they meant well, they'd still pushed her to join The Place, to make a name for herself amongst the local Warlocks. Gavin, on the other hand, had immediately realised just how much damage the strange, almost fetishistic, customs of The Place were doing to her, and had tried to get her to see it for what it was.

She'd ignored him, of course, and had struck out on her own; headstrong as ever. Still the truth of his warning had always lurked in the bottom of her heart, along with other, darker secrets. Flora chewed on her fingertips as she paced, the soporific venom that flowed through them helping to slow her racing mind a little, at least enough to think clearly.

"Why tonight?" she asked the empty room. "There have been so many other points where we've been alone and wound up, so what made tonight different?"

In truth, she had been a little startled when Gavin had started flirting with her, although she could not put her finger on the exact reason behind it. Something about their interactions had felt wrong, even taboo, and when they had made their way upstairs every creak of a floorboard or whisper of a curtain in the sea breeze had set her nerves on edge.

"There's nothing wrong with it!" Flora said to the mirror she stood before, her words defiant and sharp, however the nausea that settled into her stomach made her think otherwise. "His wife is long gone, and we have a natural chemistry; where's the harm?

"Where's the fucking crime in that!?" She shook her head angrily as she glared at her reflection. "For fuck's sake, it's not like I was kissing Paris!"

But it felt like that, didn't it? The little voice in the back of her head had a nasty habit of asking pertinent questions, but she didn't have the energy to force it back into the darkness this time. Flora nodded sadly at her reflection; something about kissing the man she'd longed for felt almost perverse; incestuous, even.

"I love him," she said weakly. "He's always been the one, ever since we were small boys together."

Thick as thieves?

"Yes."

Brothers in arms?

"I..." Flora hesitated. "He's not my brother, though!"

True, he isn't your blood, the voice conceded. *Still, that isn't what counts, though, is it, Flora?*

She remained silent, but her hands were starting to shake slightly.

He's as much your brother as Paris, if not more so.

"But I love him..."

There are different kinds of love, Flora, whispered her mind, not unkindly. *You want him around and close, but you're not used to having family you can depend on. After all, you were raised to think that the only person who could have such a bond with you was a romantic partner.*

"I've ruined it now, though," she whispered, tearing up once again. "I didn't know what I wanted or what I needed and now-"

Do you really think so little of him? The voice was angry now. *Or so little of yourself, for that matter?*

You are more than just children at a teenage party. It will be awkward for a few days, but you will move past it; stronger than ever, in fact, as the air is finally clear between the two of you.

"Thank fuck for that," Flora said with an exhalation that was half-sob and half a chuckle of relief. She went to turn away from the mirror, but the voice spoke again.

We aren't done yet.

"Isn't this enough?" she said, almost pleading with the whispers in her mind; voices that her mother had assured her were the true tongues of the water, and would never lead her astray.

Your enemy is deadly, Flora, and to survive what is to come, you must know yourself completely.

"What else is there to explore?" Flora asked angrily, gesturing to herself. "I've done the introspection, and I know what I am."

Why are you so worked up tonight, Flora? What has bestirred you so?

"No," she said, bitter tears stinging the corners of her eyes as she stepped close enough to the mirror for her breath to fog the surface. "You don't get to ask me that. It's not fair!"

Tell me the truth, Flora, the voice said, kind and gentle once again. *You don't really enjoy it when you fill your bed with men, do you?*

"I..." She faltered as she placed her forehead on the cool glass. "I fucking hate it. I hate the way they look at me, the way they touch me, and... it just feels wrong. I thought it would be different with Gavin, but it was the worst of all."

Then why do it at all?

"I have needs," she said, "and urges that I can't hold back. I need people to touch me, to fuck me, even if I hate it."

Silence.

"Still," Flora went on, "it's easier to just pretend I like it, even if it makes me sick to my stomach. It's better than admitting what I really am."

Which is?

"A sissy straight boy just playing at being a fag," she hissed, repeating the words Digby had said so many years ago after finding out that she had a fledgling crush on Amelia. "I'm a disgusting disgrace."

You're not a boy, Flora.

"And I can't get Lola's eyes out of my head," Flora wailed, unable to keep her voice down any longer. "She had such perfect eyes, and I can't stop thinking about her! I've never seen someone so beautiful before, and I just want to kiss her, even though it's wrong!"

Why is that so wrong? Something in the voice had shifted, and Flora realised that she was almost there, but the hardest part was about to happen.

"Kissing girls is something boys do," she said through gritted teeth.

But look at yourself, Flora! The voice was strangely compelling and she took several shaky steps away from the mirror, her eyes fixed on her reflection. *You spend your life online and your mind has been poisoned by fetish content and transphobic discourse; you are anything but a boy, Flora Cain.*

She looked at herself, not through the lens of a camera or any other social filter; Flora gazed into her heart and found the simple truth that she'd fought to suppress her entire life. As soon as the words left her lips and she uttered them aloud, she felt freer than ever before, and she collapsed back on to the bed in a wave of giggles, instead of tears, giddy as a dream.

"I'm not a boy," she repeated through her laughter. "I'm a lesbian."

"Gavin," she said, catching up with her best friend as he made his way down for breakfast in the Montresor's dining hall. "Gavin, I need to talk to you, before we see the others."

"Flora, I'm sorry about last night-" he began, but she cut him off before he could finish.

"That's okay, Gav," she said warmly, almost bouncing with excitement as she spoke. "It never would've worked between us; I love you, but not in the way that I thought. You're my second brother, Gav, my *favourite* brother, and I'll always be by your side, but that's all.

"I'm sorry it took me so long to realise that, but what happened last night was the catalyst for some serious soul searching on my part." She saw him smile with relief. "Are we good?"

"Yeah, we're good, Flo." He chuckled and pulled her into a tight hug. "We had a weird night after a bunch of people broke into our home and tried to murder us; I think we're allowed a bit of slack. I'm really glad that you're more settled with who you are and where we stand, Flo.

"Hopefully this will help you find happiness and meet someone, if that's what you want."

"I've, uh, actually got a bit of an announcement to make over breakfast, so you'll get an idea of what I want after that's all done." She gave him a peck on the cheek. "Thanks for always being there for me, Gav; you're the best."

"I try," he said, and they continued down the stairs to the dining hall together. Leroy had been cooking up a storm, and everyone else was already seated when Gav and Flora arrived. The Druid took a seat, but Flora remained standing as she drummed her fingers eagerly on the back of her chair.

"Good morning, chat," she said, grinning from ear to ear. She'd got up extra early and had applied a touch of makeup along with her favourite dress to round out her flawlessly feminine look. "I've got a bit of an announcement to make, if you'll permit me?"

"Go ahead, Flo," Gav said, a wry smile on his face.

"Well, I did a lot of soul searching and introspection last night, and I have come to the realisation that I... am a lesbian!"

Her words were met with an initial beat of silence, followed by a chorus of cheering and whooping from her friends. Gavin banged his cutlery on the table in celebration, but Paris looked a touch confused by the whole ordeal. Flora also noticed sly winks between Coral and Leroy, which caused her to raise a suspicious eyebrow.

"Am I the last one to find this out?" she asked, and there were several awkward nods.

"Flo, honey," Coral said as kindly as she could whilst attempting to stifle her laughter, "you pay a hot woman to come in several times a month to pretend to drown you, not to mention that you are the textbook image of a lipstick lesbian.

"Still, congrats on finally coming out, and welcome to the Girl's Club." She raised a glass of orange juice in Flora's direction.

I can't believe it, she thought as she took her seat, face reddening with each passing second. *I'm always the last one to know everything.*

Hell, I didn't even know that Coral was gay!

"Tell me, Flo," Coral asked her around a mouth of Eggs Leroy, "was it the Sylph or Violet-Eyes that got you?"

"The latter," Flora admitted. "I've never seen anyone quite like her. Which one got you?"

"Oh, neither," Coral said, waving a dismissive hand. "I like my girls a bit rougher than that, which is why I only really go for werewolves nowadays."

"Respect," Leroy said, leaning across the table to fist bump the young bartender. "Has anyone else got any more announcements to make, or can I read my paper in peace?"

"I saw what's causing all this last night," Gavin said matter-of-factly. "It was in my room when I went to bed."

Everyone stared at him in shock.

"Flora's news was more important," he said firmly, "but my encounter did confirm my suspicion about what was happening."

"Which was?" Coral asked eagerly.

"Whoever is behind this is doing so remotely; I know a psychic projection when I see one." He filled a plate with kippers, bacon, and hash browns before continuing. "This is an extremely powerful Exception, but it's a gifted human, for sure.

"There's something about this that feels weirdly familiar, but I can't quite put my finger on it."

"Gavin," Flora asked quietly, her news all but forgotten, "is it worth paying Malcolm a visit?"

He groaned and leant back in his chair, but nodded as he did so.

"I think you're right, Flo," he said, grimacing. "I think you're right."

Chapter Nineteen – Wrong Place, Wrong Time

Lola

Lola and Thaddeus swaggered up the drive to the building that had once been Edenbridge School for Boys, but now was simply known as 'The Place'. The leaden sky hung heavy over the Juliet as she couldn't help but frown at the sheer affectation of it all; she'd known many Warlocks in her time, but this Convocation was especially up its own arse.

Still, hopefully they'll play nicely even though we're showing up uninvited. A smile crossed her lips. *But if they do decide to put up a fight, however, that's just fine with me.*

Lola drummed her fingers on the handles of the Taylor & Bullock Buccas that were holstered at her hips. Thaddeus carried a standard issue Jack in one hand, with a heavy drum-fed shotgun resting on the opposite shoulder. Lola took a moment to carefully drink in Thad's appearance, paying special attention to his boots.

Yeah, she confirmed, nodding softly, *he's definitely getting taller.*

"What?" Thad asked, grinning at her. "You've got that look on your face again."

"How tall are you, Thad?" she asked, all sweetness and innocence.

"I'm not a hundred percent sure, but six foot one, I think."

And the rest, Thad, Lola thought. *You're six foot six,*

easy.

"Why do you ask?" he said, raising an eyebrow. "You've been living with me for months now; are you not used to me being taller than you?"

"I guess watching you smash through the Hotel Montresor's front door really hammered it home for me," Lola replied with a smile, "if you'll forgive the pun."

"I have felt a lot stronger recently," Thad admitted. "I'm starting to wonder if there's something to Charlotte's theory about my gift."

"Who's Charlotte?" Lola asked, but Thad awkwardly skirted around the question.

"She thought that I might be able to pick up residual skills and traces of gifts when I consume Ceps. Seeing as the first one I ever went to town on was a full-blooded Fomorian, that might explain the strength."

"I see," Lola replied, but she was still thinking about the elusive Charlotte. *Maybe an old flame of his? He certainly seems reluctant to talk about her.* She decided to change the topic; no sense in getting him unnecessarily flustered before she needed him to knock some heads together. "Will you tell me about the vampires again, Thad?"

"The Master?" he asked with a chuckle. "Again, Lola?"

"It sounded like a hell of an adventure, and I'm a little annoyed that I missed it," she admitted. "Not to mention that Charity practically threw the fact that she got to fight vampires in my face."

"I'm sure she didn't say it to be cruel."

"It's okay if she did." Lola sighed heavily, stopping in her tracks as guilt weighed on her heart, sudden and heavy. "I didn't do a very good job of being her friend,

Thaddeus, and my whole affectation of hiding behind Gideon drove us apart. I was needlessly unpleasant to her, as was Joseph, and she deserved better.

"I wish I could make it up to her." Lola sniffled slightly and blinked away the stinging droplets that were threatening to spill over at the edges of her eyes. Her corrosive black acid tears were another hallmark of being a Juliet, although they only noticeably appeared with the most heartfelt sorrow or vicious pain; most of the time they were dilute enough to go unnoticed. "Still, what's done is done; all roads lead to home."

"Why do you keep saying that?" Thad asked.

"It's just a thing I say," she lied, but it was a half-hearted deception at best.

"Lola, please be honest with me."

"I don't know what to tell you, Thad," she whispered, swaying slightly in the summer breeze as her eyes slipped out of focus. "I've lived with the shadow of my destiny looming over me ever since I was a little child, and no matter what I do, I'll never get out from underneath it.

"My story is already written and there's nothing I can do, except apologise for the horror that's to come." She idly stroked the tattoo on her left wrist. "I envy you, Thad; you're unbound by any of it and you can live any way you want.

"Your choices actually matter."

She expected Thaddeus to laugh at her, but he reached out with one bearish arm and pulled her into a tight hug. Lola continued to stare into the middle distance, almost drowning in the inevitability of her own life.

"If my choices matter," he said softly, "and I can still

change things, I'm going to stick by you until you're free of the destiny you think you have. I will meddle in fate and stick my oar in until time has no alternative but to set you free."

"I don't think it works like that," she whispered fearfully.

"Well, why don't we stick together and find out?" His kindness made her want to fall to the ground and weep, but she managed to stay upright, giving Thad a weak nod. "Tell me, Lo, where does the finale of your story play out?"

I can't tell him, she thought as her insides were twisted by the anxiety that had gripped her for as long as she could remember. *I'm not supposed to tell anyone.*

"Lo?"

"I'm not supposed to say," she said sadly, but then, almost impulsively, whispered a single word to him. "Prague."

"Thank you for telling me," he replied, holding her tight.

"What do we do now?" Lola asked, feeling suddenly untethered from the plan that had held her entire life together.

"We make sure that we keep you away from Prague at all costs. Regarding our immediate concern, however," he said looking up the hill at the ageing building that loomed over them, "why don't we go and ask the Warlocks what they know."

"They won't tell us willingly," Lola replied, feeling a little of her old self creeping back in at the edges. "We'll have to be very persuasive."

"Oh," Thad chuckled, looking at the shotgun as the first fat drops of rain began to fall, "I think we can manage that."

"We don't take visitors," snipped the bespectacled man at the door, "especially ones from the Ministry, so why don't you both just fuck off home?"

Before Lola or Thad could respond, the man, who wore an acid green striped tie and had the look of a Strix about him, slammed the door closed in their face, leaving them standing alone in the pouring rain. Thad reached out and hammered on the door once again, only to be rewarded with the sound of a heavy lock sliding into place. Lola frowned and nodded at Thad, who flicked the safety off the automatic shotgun and aimed it at the aged wood of the door.

"Oh little pigs," Lola trilled playfully, "won't you let us in?"

"Or else we'll huff and puff and blow your door down," Thad continued with a smile, although this quickly faltered as a rattle emanated from the other side of the entrance. He turned to Lola, a look of shock on his face. "Was that an armoured shutter?"

"Sounded like it." She peered over the top of her glasses at the rough wood of the door; it had clearly seen many conflicts and she wondered if it was reinforced with sorcery as well as steel. *This might not be as easy as we thought.*

I wish we had a Tracer.

"Maybe if we..." Lola's words trailed off as she felt a deep sense of unease stirring in her stomach. Thaddeus was still staring at the door, apparently oblivious to the vibes that had struck Lola so suddenly. She reached out, tapped his arm sharply, and shook her head as she gestured for them to move.

"What's wrong, Lo?" he asked as she led him away

from the building, heading uphill through the dense trees that lined the western border of The Place's estate. She didn't answer, her attention drawn instead by the strange bubbling of the mud at the base of a dead poplar tree. She knelt down and touched the soupy mess, but immediately snatched her hand away with a hiss of pain.

"Fuck me, that's either acidic as all hell or boiling hot." She sniffed the air above the mud and gagged slightly. "Sulphur! If I didn't know any better, I'd swear this place was volcanic."

There it is again, she thought as the wave of unease swept through her once more, threatening to turn her bowels to water at any moment. Her mind raced back to a previous case; a suspected haunting in a factory that had turned out to be a faulty oil pump. Unfortunately, it had burst into flames and burned down several buildings, killing dozens of innocent people.

The strange sensations she'd felt in that building had followed her for years, however, and she had researched industrial accidents and other disasters with an almost obsessive zeal.

Infrasound, Lola realised, and the strange movements in the earth confirmed her suspicion. *There's going to be a landslide!*

Not a second after the thought entered her mind, there was a deafening rumble as a section of the hillside above The Place gave way, sending a huge volume of wet earth cascading down on the former school. Lola looked on in horror as several cars, trees, and an entire wing of the building were buried almost instantly by the thick muddy tide.

"Fucking hell," she muttered, before turning to look

at Thaddeus, raising her voice to be heard over a second landslide. "Come on, Thad; we have to help them!"

"What can we even do?" he asked, slumping against a tree as the vibrations loosened the earth beneath his feet. "Lo, if we go down there, we are going to be buried alive!"

"I don't care!" Lola screamed, practically dragging Thaddeus to his feet. Water dripped down her nose and the rain had plastered her hair to the side of her face, giving her an unhinged look. "We have to do something, or else they are going to die! Can't you fucking hear them?"

Lola gestured to the wrecked building, from which emanated distant screams and faint cries of pain.

"We aren't going to leave them, Thad," she said, already striding down the slippery hillside, clutching at spindly trees as she went. Lola glanced over her shoulder, hoping that the large man was following her.

Oh, thank god, she thought when she saw him half-running half-sliding down the hill to catch up with her. Her blood turned to ice water in her veins when she reached the slide, however; the entire front of the school had been torn away, and a pale hand was sticking out of the mud, twitching and thrashing rapidly.

Lola immediately began to wade through the thick mud and debris, her eyes focussed on the hand as the movement began to slow.

If I only save one, she thought frantically, *it will be enough.*

She wrapped her fingers around the pale wrist and began to dig through the heavy slime with her other hand, pulling with all her might as she did so. Less than two seconds later Thaddeus was by her side, and they managed to haul the half-Strix from the mud with a wet slurp. He flopped back on to the ground and Lola wiped the wet earth from his face, clearing his airways. Thad laid the limp man on a section of door that was large enough to serve as a makeshift stretcher.

"You'll have to resuscitate him, Thad," Lola said, pushing the Famine towards the Warlock. "I'll kill him if I do it."

Thaddeus did not hesitate and immediately blew five breaths into the man's mouth before beginning rapid chest compressions. His face was hard and focussed; he was clearly holding back his powers in order to save the wounded man.

Lola left him to his work and began to search for more survivors. Simply moving through the mire was hard going and the threat of the rest of the hillside coming down on them loomed large in her mind. Behind her, she heard the man on the board gasp as Thad coaxed him back into the world of the living.

That's one, she thought with a grim smile. *Come on, now, Lola; keep at it.*

Fate, as far as she was concerned, was on her side, and she quickened her pace when she saw another limp form in the mud.

Be good to me, she pleaded with any god listening, *and let me save another.*

<u>Chapter Twenty</u> – The Stopped Clock

Gavin

Gavin's face was set in a hard frown as the first heavy drops of rain landed on the windscreen of Coral's ratty old Micra. The journey to Dawlish Warren wasn't a long one but Gavin didn't care for it, despite the scenic coast that ran alongside the road in places.

"I've not seen Malcolm since Lucy's funeral," he said quietly, and Coral nodded. "It feels like a lifetime ago, but I'm so fucking angry at him; he had no right to say what he did."

"I'm sure he didn't mean you any ill will, Gavin," Coral said quietly. "He's just a bit... odd, is all; things don't always come out as we intend them to."

"I'm sure you did your best," Gavin said bitterly, quoting the old man's words. "He just patted me on the shoulder and gave me a forced smile, like I was supposed to thank him for his comforting words.

"He's a selfish lunatic, always babbling on about the fucking stars and lights in the sky." Gavin tried to halt his words, but there was no stopping them now. "I want to hate him more than anything in the world, but the most I can ever muster is anger and even that decays into pity the moment I see him.

"He's all alone in the world, with only his radio and telescopes to keep him company. As much as he keeps insisting that one day *they* will come back for him, I think he knows just how bleak his life has become." Gavin drummed his fingers anxiously on the dashboard as they entered the small town. "I know that I should make an effort to see him from time to time, but I can't be around him, Coral; not after everything that's happened."

"You don't have to explain it to me," she replied softly. "He's your dad; your relationship with him is nothing to do with me."

"But you think I was too harsh on him at the funeral?" Gavin asked, his anger flaring once again.

"You put him in the hospital, Gavin," Coral said evenly, keeping her eyes on the road. "He made a comment that could've been meant in several different ways and you flew off the handle at him; he ended up with three broken ribs and a dislocated shoulder.

"Flora had to knock you out in order to get you to stop."

"I..." Gavin hesitated for a second as the campsite came into view, "I don't remember it being that bad."

"It was." Her voice wavered for a moment, and Gavin thought he could hear a hint of fear in her tone. "I thought you were going to kill him, Gav. I know you loved her, more than anything, but you can't keep going apeshit every single time someone does something that *might* be construed as an insult to her memory.

"One of these days you're going to hurt someone who really doesn't deserve it, and they're going to lock you away for the rest of your life." Coral sighed heavily. "I wouldn't have let you kill those Ministry Agents, Gav; at least, I would've tried to stop you. That's not who you are."

"You don't know me," he spat angrily.

"Yes, I do!" Coral stepped on the brakes, glaring at him. "I have lived with you for fucking years, and you were *never* like this when she was alive! It's been two years, Gavin; you have to let her go."

"No," he said tearfully, shaking his head in defiance. "I won't. I *can't!*"

"You're not well, Gavin," Coral said, placing a trembling hand on his shoulder. "I think you should see a doctor, or a grief counsellor at the very least."

He was silent.

"We're all worried about you, Gav," she went on. "What happens if this side of you comes out when you're at work? What if you end up hurting one of the children?"

I would never do that, he thought, but deep in his heart he knew it wasn't true. He'd already had instances of students making snide comments about his friends and housemates, which had pushed his temper to the limit, but if any of them had dared to utter a word about Lucy...

"You're right," he said softly as he looked over at the campsite, "and I will speak to someone when this is all put to bed, but right now I need that anger to keep me going; I've got nothing else left."

"I understand, Gav," Coral replied, giving him a swift peck on the cheek. "Thank you for agreeing to see someone. I wish I could say that the first step is always the hardest, but that just isn't true. Still, you'll be amongst friends the whole time."

"Yeah," Gavin said, wiping his eyes and nose on his sleeve. "Come on, Coral, let's get this done."

"I fucking hate this place," Gavin muttered as he exited the car, turning his collar to the rain that still fell from the steel coloured sky. "I've always hated this place."

Gavin had been bullied relentlessly in his youth,

both for growing up in grinding poverty and for having parents who were, at best, deeply unconventional. Both Bethany and Malcolm Strangeways were fascinated with the occult; whilst the former focussed her time on mysticism and the magic of nature, Malcolm had turned his gaze to the stars.

Unfortunately, it meant that neither really had the time to raise Gavin as parents should. He could easily recall the names of every herb and flower needed for a fifth circle protection spell, but had no memory of Bethany ever telling him that she loved him.

Her death had little impact on Gavin, a boy of sixteen at the time, but it had driven Malcolm completely mad. Every conversation was about Bethany, or the creatures on the radio, or the lights in the sky that one day would come to take them both away. Grief had pushed him into obsession, and it was only at Lucy's funeral that Gavin realised just how alike the two men actually were.

Like father, like son, he mused sadly. *Maybe that's why I can't bear to be around him?*

A vision of what's to come?

He shook his head at the thought and strode directly towards Malcolm's caravan. It was covered in antennae and satellite dishes, along with a poorly constructed ham radio tower that loomed over the site like some crude metal deity, complete with occult banners and strange totems attached to the struts.

"Are you ready for this?" Coral asked kindly as they neared the door.

"No," Gavin replied, but he knocked anyway. There was a minor commotion from inside, and then the door opened a crack and Malcolm yelled three words before slamming it shut again.

"Get a warrant!"

Gavin groaned and knocked once again, raising his voice to be heard over the radio broadcasts that he was certain Malcolm would be listening to.

"Dad!" He began to shiver slightly; the rain was unseasonably cold. "Dad, it's Gavin! Will you please let me in? I need to talk to you!"

The door opened once again, revealing a man with long grey hair, thick glasses, a tie-dye headband, and several day's worth of stubble. He blinked a few times, as if he was seeing a ghost, and then spoke.

"Oh. Hello, son." Another pause of a few seconds. "You're all wet."

"Yes," Gavin said, already exhausted, "it's raining."

"So it is," Malcolm confirmed. He looked past Gavin, seeing Coral for the first time. "She's not a policeman, uh, I mean, uh, a lady policeman-"

"Gods give me fucking strength," Gavin muttered, and Malcolm sighed angrily before addressing Coral directly.

"I'm sorry, Miss, but you're not a pig, are you?"

"No," Coral replied, smiling slightly. "I'm definitely not a cop, Malcolm. We've met before; I'm Coral. I live with Gavin at the Monty."

"Oh, yes, now I remember." He returned her smile. "My memory isn't what it used to be, especially today."

"Old age?" Gavin asked.

"Nah, I'm just smacked off my tits," Malcolm said with a giggle. "Come in, both of you."

Gavin and Coral made their way inside the cramped caravan; whilst it had actually been quite roomy in Gavin's youth, Malcolm had filled it with a wealth of electrical equipment, ageing books, and other esoterica. The Druid took special care to help Coral avoid the two overstuffed suitcases that were just inside the door.

"Are you going away, Malcolm?" Coral asked.

"Oh, yes, they'll be coming to get me any day now," Malcolm said excitedly.

"The psych nurses?" Gavin quipped.

"There's no need to be unpleasant, Gavin," Malcolm chided, before answering Coral's question. "The people in the lights; they'll be coming for me soon, I'm certain. See, if you look at my predictions..."

Malcolm began to gesture at a complex star chart, covered in post-it notes and marker pen, but Gavin quickly cut him off.

"I'm sorry, Dad, but we don't have time for aliens and light people today." He sighed sadly. "Something has taken one of my students, and I need your help to work out what it was."

"Oh," Malcolm replied, suddenly serious. "You better sit down then, and I'll put on a pot of tea. Is jasmine green agreeable?"

"Yes, thank you." Gavin and Coral settled on to an uncomfortably small sofa. "Dad, when we're done here, I want you to go and stay with one of your friends for a while, okay?"

"Why?" Malcolm asked, raising a concerned eyebrow. "Are you in some kind of trouble, Gavin?"

"Not exactly," he replied, choosing his words carefully, "but the Ministry came knocking yesterday, and I don't want you tangling with them."

"I've dealt with the Ministry before," Malcolm said dismissively. "They've never been more than I could handle."

"This is a black ops team," Coral said. "Something bad is going down, and they smashed through our front door with the distinct aim of harming us. Gavin's right, Malcolm; you should make yourself scarce."

"Why don't you go and stay with the Rev?" Gavin suggested, and Malcolm seemed amenable to the idea. "Norfolk is far enough out of the way to be safe."

"The Rev?" Coral asked.

"Reverend Geoffrey de la Cruz," Malcolm said with a grin. "We used to be part of an interfaith group focussed on the occult, back when he was still practising and I was still a Rabbi. Admittedly, I fell out with my higher ups years before he did, but now we're both just normal folks."

"What caused you to lose your faith?" Coral asked, and Malcolm pointed upwards.

"I realised that there are far deeper mysteries in this world," the old man said with a grin. "The Rev, however, dropped out of our little group because he shacked up with the most beautiful invisible woman you've ever seen.

"Sometimes I think he got the better end of the deal." He filled the teapot and carried it over to a cluttered table. "So, Gavin, tell me about your missing child."

Gavin summarised the situation as briefly as he could without missing any important details, and Malcolm nodded along the whole time, pausing only to pour the tea. When he was finished and each of them was sat down with a cup of tea in hand, Malcolm spoke.

"Tell me, do either of you know anything about Mithras?"

"Godzilla's friend?" Gav said with a smile.

"Don't try to be funny, Gavin," Malcolm said, but he couldn't help a cheeky little grin. "No, I'm talking about the Roman God of Mysteries."

"Never heard of him," Coral said, and Gavin had to agree.

"Well then," Malcolm said, rubbing his hands together, "settle in; this is a hell of a story, and not one the Druids would ever dream of telling you."

"And you think this holds the key to what's going on here?" Gavin asked sceptically.

"Oh, yes," Malcolm said with an excitable bounce. "It explains not only this, but it's the key to everything that's happened in this country for the last two millennia."

I find that hard to believe, Gavin thought, but as he sat and listened to his father and the afternoon wore on into early evening, he began to realise that he was slowly being won over by the old man's words. Once Malcolm was finished, Gavin just stared into the middle distance as the information percolated through his brain.

If this is true, Gavin thought after almost five minutes of stony silence, *then we are fucked beyond belief.*

<u>Chapter Twenty One</u> – Hungry for Truth

Flora

Flora and Leroy walked along the pier, huddled beneath their umbrella as the last vestiges of the rain fell from the sky. She had been pacing around the Schooner for over an hour when Leroy had suggested a walk in the rain.

"But Gavin isn't home yet," she'd said anxiously. "I thought he would be back by now."

"I'm sure he's fine," Leroy replied. "You know how Malcolm likes to talk, and I'm sure that Coral is coaxing every little story out of him."

"You really think he's okay?"

"Yeah, I do, and I think it's good for him to spend some time reconnecting with his father." Leroy's face darkened as he frowned. "The years go by faster than you'd believe, Flora, and people are gone all too soon.

"Gavin will miss Malcolm when he's gone, even if he doesn't see that right now."

"I wish he would go to the doctor," she whispered. "He's not been right ever since Lucy got sick; he's like a man possessed, seeing ghosts of her in every little thing. I worry that living here isn't good for him."

I worry that it's not good for all of us.

She sighed sadly and Leroy had placed a kind arm around her, before telling her to put her fancy shoes on, and that they were heading out for the evening. Now here they were, dressed to the nines and walking through the wet weather along a nearly deserted pier, but despite the inclement conditions, Flora was already starting to feel a little better.

"Gavin and I nearly had sex last night," she blurted out as she looked out over the stormy sea, the glow of the arcade making the water shine with an eerie half-light.

"Are you serious?" Leroy asked with a chuckle. "How far did you get?"

"I had my tits out and everything," she replied sheepishly. "I... I said something stupid, and it kinda put the kybosh on the whole thing. I was upset at first, but after a good cry I was finally able to see the real me for the first time ever."

"Sometimes you need a good nudge in order for you to see that you were on the path the whole time," Leroy said with a knowing smile. "Have I ever told you about when I first became a Ghoul?"

"You mentioned something about the Nightmarchers," Flora replied, "but not much more after that. Why do you ask?"

"When the hunger first takes you, it's like nothing else you can possibly imagine." Leroy leant forward and the safety railing creaked underneath his considerable weight. "It's not just in your stomach, Flora, but it's in your very soul; every part of you, flesh and spirit, is starving. It just isn't something you can ignore, but it does show you what kind of person you are, for better or worse."

Flora nodded, but didn't say anything; what Leroy was telling her was clearly important.

"Now, most Ghouls are corpse eaters, which was something that just didn't sit right with me." He shook his head sadly. "All those graveyard lurkers, they had problems before they joined the ranks of the undead; it's not my business, of course, but I'm just saying it like it is.

"If you feel that hunger and the first thing you think of is human flesh, then you were already a fucking monster."

"Have you ever eaten a body?" Flora asked, and Leroy shook his head.

"No, and that's the point, Flo; as soon as I felt the hunger, I knew that I could never touch the meat of another human, no matter how much it hurt me. I never would've known the resolve I truly possessed had I not been tested like that." He chuckled softly. "Besides, the *flesh of the dead* covers hot dogs and cheeseburgers in my opinion.

"I won't say it's been easy, though. There were a few days during Market Garden where we were low on supplies and I was surrounded by my dead brothers..." His face hardened at the memory, but his smile returned quickly enough. "Like I said, the pain of the hunger is nearly unbearable, but eating my fellow soldiers; that was a bridge too far for me.

"Sometimes you've got to walk right up to the ledge just to prove to yourself that you aren't gonna jump."

There were a few minutes of silence as they both watched the lazy sway of the surf as it rumbled on to the deserted beach. The wound above Flora's eyebrow throbbed slightly, but she tried to put it out of her mind.

"So you're saying that being gay is a lot like cannibalism?" she asked, and Leroy nudged her playfully.

"No, but lying to yourself is." He gave her a wink. "Hiding the truth will just eat you up inside, and that can only end in bloodshed, one way or another."

"I guess deep down I always thought that I could live a double life," Flora admitted. "Play the respectable straight woman by day and be the sapphic fetish influencer by night, but all that ever served to do was cause a rift in who I was.

"So much mental turmoil because I couldn't accept the truth..." she trailed off as she looked out over the water; a piece of the puzzle had fallen into place in her mind. She turned to Leroy, her eyes wide.

"What's up?"

"What if whoever is causing all this doesn't know that they're doing it?" Her brain was gathering speed now, as the mystery began to unravel before her very eyes. "Gavin mentioned a psychic projection, but not all of those are deliberate; in fact, most start occurring accidentally. What if the, uh, what did Gavin call it?"

"The Illuminated Man?" Leroy suggested.

"Yeah, that sounds right. What if our Illuminated Man isn't fulfilling wishes in general, but one wish specifically?"

"I wish that someone else was doing this," Leroy said, and Flora nodded. "Holy shit, Flora, you're a genius."

"Thank you, but I've not earned that accolade just yet," she replied with a grin, "but I will. Next question; why did the Illuminated Man offer to bring Lucy back to life?"

"He thought Gavin would agree to his terms?" Leroy frowned. "Wait, Gavin wasn't even offered any terms; it was an open question. In fact, why even ask in the first place? Why not just take whatever it was he needed?"

"Consent!" Flora said, speaking the word with the force of a lightning strike. "There are certain Ceps that *must* ask permission before they use their gift on you. Preachers, for example, can't use their mind control unless you speak to them first, so we can use that to narrow down what we're looking for."

"Nice, very nice, Flora!" He chuckled and pulled her into a tight one-armed hug. "Whilst I hate to interrupt your flow, I must insist that we get something to eat; I'm wasting away over here."

"Fatboy's?" Flora suggested, her own stomach growling.

"Fatboy's," Leroy agreed. "Let's eat every fucking chicken in that place."

"This is why we're such good friends, Leroy," Flora said as they strolled down the pier. "When it comes to dinner, you can actually keep up."

The two Ceps were sat in a booth in the corner of the chicken shack as the worsening downpour drummed on the window. They had their third sharing platter on the table between them, already half finished. Flora was watching the rain snake its way down the glass when she felt her phone ring in her pocket.

"Hello?" she asked, not even looking to see who was calling.

"Hi, Flo," Gavin said. "We've had some luck with Malcolm, but I'm worried about him being on his own tonight. Coral and I are gonna stay here, drive him up to his friend's place in the morning, and then head back down afterwards."

"That burns a lot of time," Flora said, frowning slightly, "but you do whatever you need in order to keep him safe. We'll reconvene tomorrow night and we can all go through what we've learned."

"Good plan." Gavin hesitated for a moment. "Malcolm mentioned that there's been a mass die off of local honeybees, which is not a good sign. I still have no idea what kind of Cep could possibly be causing this, but it seems like its power is increasing. Flora-"

His voice faltered slightly.

"Flora, I don't know if you've heard any news today, but there's been an accident at The Place."

"What!?"

"There was a mudslide brought on by the rain, and it destroyed a portion of the school."

"Is anyone hurt?"

"Yes, and some deaths too; I'm not sure how many. I'm sorry I don't have more information for you."

"That's alright, Gav. Thank you for telling me." Flora was speaking on autopilot as the news about The Place started to sink in. "I'll speak to you tomorrow."

"Look after yourself, Flo. Much love." There was a click as the call disconnected.

"Flora," Leroy said, reaching across the table to take her greasy hand in his, "you look like you've seen a ghost. Are you alright?"

"There was a landslide up at The Place," she said softly. "People died. Also, Gavin and Coral won't be back until tomorrow night."

"A *landslide*? That's fucking awful." His grip tightened to a comforting squeeze. "Do you want to go home?"

"I wonder who died?" she murmured. Her emotions threatened to overwhelm her as the memory of Gavin's muttered threat drifted to the surface, so she decided to laser focus on the task at hand. She blinked a few times to clear her head and took a long sip of her cola before addressing Leroy. "Why are they afraid to go to sleep?"

"What?"

"The victims of the Illuminated Man," she clarified. "Why do they all stay awake until they die?"

"Flora, we don't need to-"

"Yes," she said sharply, "we do. I can't process anything else, Leroy, so we're talking about this now. So, why do they fear going to sleep?"

"Maybe they can't?" Leroy said. "Or their sleep isn't good for them?"

"Good suggestions," she replied. "They could also be having nightmares that are scaring them to death. There's so much that we don't know, Leroy, and we don't have anyone we can ask to help us, unless you happen to know a neurologist who specialises in sleep and dreams."

There was a pause.

"You don't know someone like that, do you?" she said, raising an eyebrow.

"Unfortunately not," Leroy said sadly. "I've got a lot of education under my belt, but I've not got around to neurology yet. I'm sorry, Flora; I wish I had the answers you were looking for, but sometimes the dead have no more tales to tell."

The dead, she thought, sitting upright as her heart began to race.

"You know who would've known, though?" Flora asked excitedly.

"Lucy?"

"Lucy." Flora got to her feet, energised. "Gavin kept all of her things exactly as they were, including all of her books."

"He's not gonna be happy about-"

"He's not going to be back until tomorrow night," Flora reminded him. "Besides, he'll understand; this is his mission, after all."

"When should we start?"

"As soon as we can," she said eagerly. "I know she was a prolific writer, so this might take all night."

"I'll get us some chicken to take home," Leroy said, getting to his feet. "I've got a good feeling about this, Flora; hopefully we'll start to get some answers before too long."

They began to gather up their things as, unbeknownst to them, a withered twitching man watched them from the dark shadows beneath the pier. He lingered for a few seconds as they exited Fatboy's Chicken Shack, but by the time Flora turned to look towards the coast, he was gone.

<u>Chapter Twenty Two</u> – Armchair Politics

Lola

Lola, Thaddeus, and Miette picked their way carefully along the coast path as the rain continued to lash the Devonshire coast. Unexpectedly, the Sylph seemed to be faring the worst out of the three of them; a fact that Lola couldn't help but mention.

"Are you doing alright there, Miette?" she asked, raising her voice over the weather.

"I have been better, Agent Oriole," the Sylph snapped.

"That surprises me," Lola replied, a grin creeping on to her face. "Given all the wind, I would've thought you would be in your elem-"

"You have had a trying day," Miette said, rounding on the Juliet, "so I will spare you this once, but I swear if you make any more jokes about my species, I will kill you on the spot!"

I thought it was funny, Lola thought before ducking down to avoid a face full of spray as a wave broke on the nearby rocks.

"Do I make myself clear?" Miette asked, leaning in so that her face was barely an inch from hers.

"Yes, boss," Lola replied sulkily, which seemed to be enough to mollify the Sylph. *She clearly doesn't want to be out here any longer than necessary.*

"Are you sure this is the right way?" Thad called out, and Lola nodded. It had taken several hours to pull the surviving Warlocks from the tragic mudslide, but her efforts had not gone unrewarded; the Head

Boy of The Place, Digby, had given them several suitable leads to follow up on.

I would've helped them anyway, Lola thought. She was still devastated that several of the Ceps had perished in the disaster, but there was no time to mourn the innocent victims; there was much work to be done, and the site would be crawling with the press before too long.

Just keep moving, she thought as her mind filled with another of her lifelong mantras, *there will be time to scream at the horror when the work is done.*

It was a lie, though, and she knew it; there was never enough time to truly process any of it, and the work was never ending. Even two hours in the shower had not washed away the memory of the thick mud as it clung to her legs and hands, nor the mental images of shattered masonry and twisted asphyxiated bodies.

"It's always been this way," she murmured, "ever since the fire."

"Lo, are you alright?" Thad asked, placing his human hand on her shoulder.

"Of course," she said, faking an uncertain smile. "Why would you think I was otherwise?"

"You're crying, Lola," he said tenderly.

"It's just the rain, Thaddeus," she replied, wiping the acidic tears from her eyes. "Besides, there's too much to do now; no time for tears when we have so many leads."

"It would be easier if you let us split up," Thad said pointedly to Miette, who ardently shook her head. "We'd cover more ground-"

"I am not allowing either of you a moment alone with any kind of entity that can wield such power!" Miette's voice was shrill, even more so than the whistling wind.

"Because you want to keep us safe, or because you don't trust us?" Thad asked darkly.

"Whichever is more palatable to you," the Sylph retorted. She pointed past the Famine and the Juliet, towards a stone formation at the water's edge. "Is that it?"

Lola followed Miette's gaze and allowed her eyes to adjust to the darkness of the rain soaked night. Before them stood a deep cut in the cliff side where a former mine had once been; all that remained of that structure, however, was a curious hollow with a grim name.

"The Devil's Armchair," Thad said, almost awed. "Yeah, Miette, that's definitely it; we're almost there."

"Then let's push on," the Sylph ordered. "The sooner we're out of this weather, the better."

"What makes you think it'll be any drier at the Armchair?" Lola asked.

"I've met Devils and Demons before," she replied darkly. "They despise discomfort and this one will not want to treat in such unpleasant conditions; trust me, Oriole, if your information turns out to be correct, we will not be in this squall much longer."

"And if I'm wrong?" Lola asked, fearing the answer.

"Then I will throw you into the fucking sea!" Miette yelled, pointing at the churning foam and black waves of the turbulent waters, before smiling at the Juliet and sugar coating her next words, sweet as a viper. "So, Agent Oriole, don't be wrong."

The roar of the ocean faded as soon as they entered the curious rock formation and the falling rain ceased immediately. Lola's eyebrows raised in surprise when she noticed a door made of polished red wood nestled amongst the stony cliff and her curiosity was piqued when the glass of the wooden portal began to glow warmly, as if lit from within by some inviting fire.

"Maybe we shouldn't do this," Thaddeus said, hesitating at the edge of the Devil's Armchair. "We don't know what this thing will want from us."

"From you, Mr Thane," said a rich voice from behind them, "nothing at all."

They all turned to look at their host, who swaggered into the dim light with a wicked grin on his face. Lola had expected a suave man in an immaculately tailored suit, but what she saw was a spare framed shirtless man in ragged grey tracksuit bottoms with dirty straw coloured hair, red rimmed eyes, gold teeth, and countless track marks on his bare arms.

"My gift keeps you from manipulating me," Thad said firmly, and the man shook his head with a chuckle.

"I would never manipulate anyone," he said mirthfully. "I, along with the rest of my kind, am nothing but completely honest. Regarding you in particular, Mr Thane, I could bind you as tightly as any other, but I don't make deals with Fae."

"I'm not a Fae!" Thad hissed, and the Demon smiled sweetly.

"Is that so?" he asked, before turning to Miette. "I'm afraid Sylphs are also off the menu, sweetheart, so you'll have to wait outside."

"I will not!" Miette snarled, her voice powerful as a hurricane, but the man didn't so much as flinch.

"Fine," he said leaning on the door as he picked at his shiny teeth with a silver toothpick. "You can just fuck off, then; plenty of others to deal with, especially at this dark hour. I'm not short on company, you know.

"Or, Ms Oriole, you can step into my office, and we can talk. Don't worry; nothing is binding until you want it to be." He bowed graciously and extended a bony hand. "On this, you have my honest word, so why don't you step over the threshold and tell me why you're here?"

"What do you want from me?" Lola asked as she took an uncertain step towards the door. "Are you going to barter for my soul?"

"Absolutely not," he replied, taking her hand. "You're no good to me as an empty vessel, darling."

"You aren't going to drag me to hell?" She stepped through the door as he opened it, and was shocked by just how lavish the interior was; everything was beautifully upholstered and a table creaked under the weight of an exquisite feast, comprising every dish imaginable. The Demon steered her to the head of the table, and she took her place in the seat of an honoured guest.

"No, my love," he replied, laughing. "Gods above, the Angels' propaganda machine really is absolutely mint, isn't it?"

"So there isn't a hell?" Lola asked.

"No, babe, and I promised the truth, so here it is; the Gates of Paradise are always closed to mortals like you." He sprawled on a pink couch across the table from her. "Be it Heaven, Elysium, or whatever the Fae are calling their land now, your name isn't on the list, so you aren't coming in.

"Sorry to disappoint you, Lola." He reached out and poured himself a small glass of pale blue liquid that seemed to glow like a full moon. "Cheers, by the way; this one is on you."

What the fuck have I gotten myself into?

"What do I call you?" she asked after a moment. "Or do I have to work it out in order to leave here?"

"You can come and go as you please," he replied, "and my name is Speedball."

"Speedball?" Lola asked, barely able to believe his words.

"Indeed; we're named after what we love the most, and I do so crave the sharp sting of the needle." He grinned at her. "Who better to deal with the Kiss-Crazy Queen than the Prince of Painful Bliss?"

She went to reply, but he held up a hand to silence her, and then produced a small six-sided die made of black horn, with a single gold rivet on each surface, He placed it on the table between her, and the rivets wavered for a moment before shifting to sixes, and then almost immediately back to ones once again.

"Before we get down to brass tacks, Lola," Speedball said playfully, "I always like to offer a little freebie to my clients, if they agree to play a little game with me; consider this a top-up, an upswing of perfect pink blow that rounds out the most exquisite heroin."

"What is it?" she asked.

"A drop of pure luck," he replied with a golden smile. "You'll know how to use it, when the time is right, and it will swing fortune in your favour, but only if you can answer a little question for me."

"Go on," Lola said. She felt a smile creep on to her lips as she realised that she was actually beginning to enjoy herself.

"Who, what, where, and, most importantly, why is the Beggar King?" Speedball took another sip of his strange drink, and gestured for her to eat. "Please, indulge for as long as you'd like; the feast is on the house. You can give me your answer when our business is concluded."

"Can I have some of that?" she asked, gesturing at his glass.

"This is *of* you, Lola, not *for* you." He waved his free hand over the drinks before her. "Have any beverage, liquid, or libation that you desire, other than mine."

"I'd prefer a beverage to a libation," Lola quipped as she poured herself a glass of sparkling green soda. "The latter tends to come with an unadvertised side dish of rohypnol, at least in my experience."

"There won't be any forcing of hands here, Lo," Speedball said kindly. "The Angels do their best to twist arms and manufacture consent, whilst the Fae spin their lies and tricks into a binding web, but we Demons, dear Lola, are nothing but honest with you.

"In fact, we have a pointed rule that *you* must seek *us* out."

"Why?" she asked. She took a deep sip of her drink as she waited for an answer, and it was the greenest thing she'd ever consumed; mint, aniseed, apple, grass, and so much more, all at once. She blinked in surprise and delight.

"Good, isn't it?" Speedball said, and she nodded. "As for your question about our honesty, it's quite simple, really; we don't need to resort to tricks or strong-arming because we're winning. The status quo favours us by several country miles and that suits us just fine.

"In short, why break a perfectly functioning system?"

That actually makes a lot of sense.

"So, dear Lola, let us get down to brass tacks; what

are you here for?"

"Information."

"Don't lie to me!" Speedball hissed, and the room darkened for a moment as his eyes blazed a blinding white. The shadows soon receded, however, and he returned to his casual demeanour in a few short heartbeats. "Apologies, Lola, but I don't allow lying in my house; what you get from me is what I expect from you, you see."

"I was being honest," she said quietly, cowed by the sudden display of power.

"Nobody comes to a restaurant to just glance at the menu," he said playfully. "However, you might not realise just how hungry you really are, so why don't you just pay upfront and then you can take whatever you want."

"The price doesn't vary?" Lola asked nervously. She looked past him at a glass jar on a shelf; a jar that contained a scarred, still beating, heart. *That looks familiar.*

"Every cost is bespoke to the request, but it's a flat rate for you, darling." Speedball leant forward, knocking over several items on the overflowing table. "You've got those heroin lips, sweetheart, and I have a powerful need... not to mention a burning curiosity for just how perfect the rest of you is going to taste."

Lola was frozen in her seat.

"So, Agent Oriole, let me indulge in your poisoned flesh, and I will give you whatever you want." He leant lazily on one arm, smiling at her lovingly. "You have to fuck me, Lola, or you'll never get what you need."

"I don't want to," she said, her voice small and unsteady.

"I know you don't, darling," he whispered, "and that's why I want it so much. It has to hurt you, sweetheart, or else it's nothing to me."

The Juliet began to cry softly.

"Oh, yes," Speedball murmured, "that's exactly what I need."

"What happens if I just get up and leave?" she said, trembling tearfully in her seat.

"You end up in Prague, my dear girl."

"And if I do as you ask?"

"You still end up in that haunted city, but you'll have a ghost of a chance to get out alive." His smile widened into a vicious grin as the tears came hot and fast, stinging her eyes and burning her cheeks. "Oh, you are a thing of beauty, Lola; all poisoned lips and tears of black acid.

"Still, I do want you to try and enjoy this, if you can, so how about I mix a little sugar into the bitter medicine?" The Demon's visage wavered for a moment, before he transformed into the alluring form of Flora Cain, complete with the startling azure eyes that had stunned Lola so much the night before.

Disturbingly, the needle marks remained.

"So, Lola," purred the transformed Speedball as he crawled across the table towards her, "do we have a deal?"

Chapter Twenty Three – Playing Make-Believe

Flora

"Where are they?" Flora asked as she anxiously paced along the length of the bar in the Silver Schooner. Lucy's assorted notebooks and loose sheaves of paper were arrayed on the tables in the Montresor's private drinking establishment, roughly organised by topic. She glanced nervously at the window; there had been no further bird strikes, but being so close to the large expanse of glass made her jumpy.

"I'm sure they're just stuck in traffic or something, Flo," Leroy said, trying to soothe her. "The rain only stopped a few hours ago, so there could be flooding or-"

"They're here!" Flora yelled as she saw Coral's car pull into the Monty's overgrown car park. "Leroy, make sure that Paris and Reggie come down here at once."

"Sure thing, boss," he said with a smile and strolled out of the room, making sure to take his sizeable deli sandwich with him.

I have so much to tell them, Flora thought as she trotted towards the foyer of the hotel, but she stopped when a chill ran down her spine. She turned on her heel, expecting to catch sight of one of the Peepers as it scampered out of her eyeline, but there was nothing there.

Instead, one of the books gently slid off the nearest

table and landed on the wooden floor with a thud. The hair on the nape of her neck began to stand on end as she muttered a single word to the otherwise empty bar; a question that would inevitably go unanswered.

"Lucy?"

There was no response, but something about the fallen book drew her gaze; it was emblazoned with a lion-headed man emerging from a shattered rock. Something about the strange image felt oddly familiar, but she couldn't quite place it. She gingerly picked it up, still transfixed by the artwork on the book's cover.

Maybe I can-

"Flora?" Gavin's words cut her thought short. She whirled around to see him staring at Lucy's belongings in horror.

"Gavin, I thought it would-" she began, but he nodded blankly and half-sat half-slumped into the closest chair.

"Good idea, Flo," he mumbled numbly. "I'm sure Lucy would have some insight about this. Good work."

"Are you alright, Gavin?" Coral asked as she entered the Schooner, leaning awkwardly on her stick as she shouldered what could only be a backpack full of books.

"Flora was clever enough to get Lucy's writings out for us to use," he said, his voice barely a hoarse whisper. "I, uh, I just wasn't expecting to see them in here, so it's thrown me a bit. I see you've already found the book I was going to go and dig out."

"What?" Flora said, and then looked at the volume in her hands. "I... This one just jumped out at me; I only picked it up as you arrived back here. Is it important?"

"Malcolm gave it to her as a wedding present," he said, taking it from the Faun's trembling fingers. "He said that there was a map to what we're looking for, although it would be a bit of a bastard to find..."

Before Flora could respond, the rest of their little group entered the Schooner. Paris had his usual spring in his step, but Reggie was looking positively terrible; his skin was ashen, his hair was lank with sweat, and he wore a long coat comprised almost entirely of crudely stitched rags over an open shirt and a pair of tattered black britches.

What struck Flora hardest, however, was the ugly wound that glistened freshly on the Familiar's chest. He winced in pain with every step and he collapsed against the bar as soon as he was close enough, panting and groaning with the effort of remaining upright.

"Fucking hell, Reg!" Gavin said, pushing the book into Flora's hands as he reached for the little pouch of herbs at his hip. "What happened to you?"

"I'm dying," he replied with a dark chuckle. "When I first arrived here, I was late because I needed to see a friend and now I'm finally starting to feel the effects of his handiwork."

He pushed Gavin away before the Druid could administer any kind of medicine.

"Sorry, Gav, but this needs to happen." He gave the man a grin that was more grimace than anything else. "When the Ministry made me, they put a cage around my heart and a noose around my neck in case I ever defied them. My friend removed the cage, and now I'm falling from the gallows.

"If he was right, the rope will snap, instead of my neck."

"And if you're wrong?" Gav asked nervously. Reggie gave Gavin a pained grin before he replied.

"Oops."

"How long until we know?" Flora asked nervously, clutching the book against her chest in white knuckled hands. Reggie tried to respond, but let out another shuddering gasp of agony instead. "Reggie?"

"Pretty soon," he said breathlessly.

"What do we do?" Gavin asked as the Familiar slumped to the floor of the Schooner, but he was already too far gone. Reggie started to convulse rapidly, his limbs trembling as they repeatedly struck the polished wooden floor. "God damn it, Flora, what do we do?"

"I have no idea," she whispered as Coral went to protect the shaking man's head, but she was stopped in her tracks as he produced a piercing scream before falling still. Reggie let out a final death rattle, and his eyes stared lifelessly at the ceiling as his body lay limp on the bar floor.

"Fucking hell, man," Leroy said, crouching down beside Reggie and listening to his chest. "I think he's really dead, folks."

The Montresor gang stood around silently for a few minutes, wondering what to do next. Gavin seemed like he was about to make some kind of announcement when Reggie moved once again, his eyes momentarily burning with ghostly bluebell fire before simmering down to a faint blue glow. He sat up shakily, looking around at his compatriots with an unsteady smile.

"I, uh, I think I just died," Reggie said with a nervous giggle.

"How are you alive?" Flora asked, and the Familiar just shrugged.

"I have no idea," he admitted, "but I've never felt better."

He stared at the window for a moment, and then looked back at Flora.

"Whilst I was out, though, I think I encountered what was causing all this."

"What did you see?" Gavin asked, crouching by the revived man, his eyes wide and desperate.

"I saw something that seemed to be constructed of stars and the night sky," he said quietly. "I can't say for sure, but it seemed like a psychic projection that was formed entirely from-"

"Dreams?" Flora asked, and Reggie nodded. She placed a hand on Gavin's shoulder to prepare him for what she was about to tell him. "Gavin, I think I know who's doing this."

"It's Lucy's spirit, isn't it?" he asked, his lip trembling slightly, and she shook her head.

"No, Gavin; it's her child."

"No," Gavin said, for the twentieth time. "I won't believe it."

"Gavin, it's true," Leroy said quietly. "Lucy swore me to secrecy, but I knew her throughout the entire pregnancy. If you don't believe me, she writes about it at length in her journals-"

"NO!" Gavin roared, finally rising from the floor after hours of sitting slumped and docile. "Lucy did not want to have children, regardless of what I wanted, so we didn't have any! She would've told me if she already had a kid and she didn't, therefore you must be wrong."

"It's right here, Gav," Flora said, handing him a book, but he slapped it out of her hands. Her temper flared and she shoved him. "Why can't you see what's right in front of you!? Are you really going to be so fucking obtuse?"

"She would have told me!" Gavin said, shoving Flora back. "She told me everything!"

"Where did she get her tattoo?" Reggie asked quietly. Gavin spun around to face him and Flora was momentarily afraid that he would throw himself at the weakened Familiar.

"The Ministry gave it to her," the Druid said, but he suddenly seemed unsure of himself.

"Where?" Reggie repeated, more forcefully this time. "Come on, Gavin Strangeways; if she truly told you everything, why can't you give me an answer?"

There was silence in the Silver Schooner.

"I'm sorry she kept things from you, Gavin," Flora said, gently placing an arm around her best friend, "but everyone has secrets."

"She didn't want to have a family with me," he whispered sadly, his anger entirely gone. "Was I not good enough for her?"

"In her journal," Flora said, leading Gavin to one of the little sofas dotted around the bar, "she mentions that the child very quickly started to display dangerous powers; talents that would've killed both of them, had they been allowed to develop fully.

"She went back to the Ministry and had them put some sort of block in the child's head; something that would keep the gift from ever manifesting, no matter what. Once that was in place, she put her up for adoption."

"Her?" Gavin asked, his voice breaking slightly. "Lucy has a daughter?"

"Yeah," Flora said. "She'd be somewhere in her late

teens, and Lucy met you soon after the adoption was done. I think the pain of what happened, along with just how dangerous the child became is the reason that she never wanted any more.

"I'm sorry that you could never have the family you wanted, Gavin, but it wasn't because she thought you were inadequate in any way." Flora held the man as he began to weep. "It was because you were enough for her, and she was satisfied with her life."

Gavin nodded, sniffling and wiping at his tears as he did so.

"Tell me about the child, Flo," he said through his sobs. "What was her name?"

"Ariadne Havelock," Flora said.

"That's a shit name," he said, chuckling as the tears continued. "Was she a Walker, like her mother?"

"No, she wasn't," Leroy said, joining them. "She was the complete opposite. She was a Shaper; a weaver of reality and an eater of dreams. It's a monstrous gift, Gavin, and very few Ceps survive infancy when their powers develop."

"The child, Ariadne, what can she do?" Gavin asked, gradually coming back to himself.

"Pretty much anything she wants," Leroy said, "aside from sleep; Shapers are insomniacs, and they need to eat the dreams of others in order to survive. They can manifest almost anything from the remnants of the dreams they consume, but in their infancy they can only create echoes of what they've devoured.

"Dark reflections of people's dearest desires, most usually."

"Waking nightmares," Gavin said, and Flora nodded. "My student, Libby, she's gone forever, isn't she?"

"I think so," Flora replied sadly. "From what you

told me, it sounds like her father's dream was to be in a world without her. I'm so sorry."

"These dreams that they eat," Gavin said, his voice barely above a whisper, "I'm assuming they can't take them without asking?"

"They need consent," Leroy confirmed, "which is why Shapers tend to prey on the most vulnerable members of society."

"We think Ariadne doesn't even know what she is," Flora said softly, "so this manifestation might be completely subconscious."

"But she would feel a unconscious draw to these events?" Gavin asked.

"Perhaps, but she might also want to stay as far away from them as possible; a desperate urge to keep her hands clean, as it were. Still, it gives us a chance to find her before things get any worse."

"Flora," Reggie said from across the room, "this mental block, it wasn't called a Mindlock, was it?"

"I think so, yeah," she said. The look on Reggie's face made her blood run cold.

This is going to be bad.

"Fucking hell," Reggie said, his tail twitching fearfully. "If her Mindlock has failed, then we aren't just dealing with a Shaper in denial; we're up against a-"

"A Hag," Gavin said, cutting him off. "That's what Malcolm explained to us, and it's worse than that; there's a whole established Coven of them, right here in the bay area."

"Since when?" Leroy asked.

"Roman times, apparently," Gavin said with a heavy sigh, "and they must know that a new member is coming into her own."

"So we're up against a Hag Coven *and* a Ministry black ops team?" Reggie asked, chuckling madly. "Oh, man, we are so monumentally fucked."

"Gavin," Flora said, her voice trembling with terror as she raised a fearful eyebrow, "what the fuck is a Hag?"

"An ancient and unspeakable horror," Gavin said darkly. "I'll elaborate in the morning though; right now I'm dead on my feet, so all I need is sleep and a little space to process what you've told me."

He got to his feet, and planted a brotherly kiss on Flora's forehead before staggering in the direction of the foyer.

"Don't stay up too late," Gavin said to all of them as he headed to bed, "and, whatever else you do, don't make any deals with strange men made of stars."

The silence was deafening after Gavin's departure, going on for some time until it was finally broken by Flora's small terrified voice.

"We're going to die, aren't we?"

"Probably, Flo," Leroy said softly, taking her trembling hand in his as the shakes took hold of her.

God fucking damn you, Lucy!
Damn you to fucking hell!

Chapter Twenty Four – The Dot Connector

Gavin

The sun was creeping back over the eastern horizon as the inhabitants of the Hotel Montresor began to wake up; at least those of them who had managed to get to sleep in the first place.

Gavin Strangeways, however, had sat up all night with Lucy's silver locket clutched tightly in his hand. He'd left the balcony door wide open and had arranged his late wife's belongings on the bed in the hope of drawing the Illuminated Man back to the shadows of his bedroom, but it was all for naught.

"Fine," he said quietly as the sun was fully over the horizon and the day was truly upon them. "I'll come and find you myself."

He glanced at the handgun that he'd carefully loaded with custom bullets, tipped with silver and mistletoe; the only thing that Lucy was certain would be able to kill her, both in and out of a dream.

Well, that and cancer, he thought bitterly.

He stretched slightly and closed the balcony door before slipping out of his tunic and heading to the bathroom. He needed to have a shower before breakfast, and when his friends were sufficiently caught up with his plan, Gavin intended to walk the streets of the Torbay area until he managed to find Ariadne.

I'll spare her the pain of knowing what she's done, he thought. *One bullet for her, and then one for me;*

that'll be the last remnants of Lucy's legacy scrubbed from this place.

"At least I won't have to look very hard," he muttered, certain that Ariadne, or at least the Illuminated Man, would seek him out before too long. Whilst most Ceps viewed the Tangle as a source of power or a tool for investigation, the Druids saw it as a living tapestry, akin to the web of roots, mycelia, and burrows that filled the soil of a forest; it was the stuff of life, and it responded to the will of the living.

"She'll come to me soon enough," he murmured, slipping the gun underneath his pillow, "and I'll let her say her piece; she deserves that much."

The shower did little to improve his mood, but seeing the enthusiasm of his friends as they gathered around the breakfast table did lift his spirits somewhat. Leroy pulled him into a tight hug before he sat down, and Flora gave him a playful wink as he took his seat.

"How did everyone sleep?" Gav asked.

"I don't think anyone got any rest," Coral said with an exhausted smile, "or else we all decided to experiment with smudged eyeliner at the same time."

"Sleep or not, at least we can eat well," Reggie said as he loaded his plate with American style pancakes and maple bacon. "So, Gav, you were going to explain what a Hag was; care to pick up that thread?"

"Sure," Gavin said, taking a bite of the mushroom omelette that Leroy had made for him. "So, this links in with the book Flora was holding last night, but it requires a bit of a journey."

He sighed heavily, ate several more bites, and then launched into the explanation.

"Sometimes, albeit rarely, there are Exceptional children born to otherwise ordinary families. More often than not these children are identified early by other Ceps in the community, or their gifts manifest in a way that catches the attention of the Ministry; either way, they are taken under the wing of someone more knowledgable who can guide their development.

"There are rare cases, however, where this doesn't happen." He took a sip of his tea, preparing for what was to come. "These children fly under the radar and one of two things will happen; they'll perish, along with their families, or they will repress their gift. This repression can come in a wealth of ways, and the Mindlock that Lucy inflicted on Ariadne definitely comes under this category.

"A Cep can only ignore their gift for so long, however, and the more deeply they have repressed it, the more powerful it will become when it finally has its day in the sun. The cognitive dissonance this causes often drives the Cep completely mad, and many of them end up fleeing normal society because of this."

"So why call these repressed Ceps an awful name? Why *Hags,* of all things?" Flora asked.

"They still hold childish beliefs about the world, including a fixation with magic; they think their gifts are magic powers, brought about through spells, rituals, and other practices, including cannibalism and ritual sacrifice." Gavin's fork trembled in his hand as he fought to keep his anger at Lucy in check. "When Lucy locked Ariadne away from her gift and foisted her on to a normal family, she doomed the poor child to this fate."

"It's also worth pointing out that Hag Covens can trace their lineage back hundreds, if not thousands of years, and they are always looking for new recruits."

Gavin nodded at Reggie's words. "When one of these Ceps joins a Coven, all of the childish beliefs are deeply reinforced, perpetuating the dangerous behaviours Gavin just mentioned.

"Although Hags tend to live in secrecy, they can be extremely dangerous when confronted; this is never more true than when they have their eyes on a new member."

"But why hide?" Flora asked. "If they're so powerful, why don't they rule out in the open?"

"And this ties in to the book you found last night," Gavin said. "Hags are a holdover from the earliest days of the first ever iteration of the Ministry; before that, Ceps were reliably identified by the local Druidic Circles and such repression was avoided."

"So what happened?" Leroy asked.

"The Romans invaded," Gavin said, gesturing for Flora to pass him the book emblazoned with the lion-headed man, "and they brought the Cult of Mithras with them."

"Mithras," Gavin said as he helped Paris tidy the dirty plates away, "is the Roman God of Mysteries. Very little is known about the operations of the original cult, but they were definitely identifying Exceptions and training them to operate in the shadows.

"The Cult also pushed the persecution of the Druids, forcing us into the fringes of society and limiting our ability to guide Exceptional children through the early stages of their awakening." He shook his head angrily at the injustice of it all. "The Cult is solely responsible for why Ceps are marginalised today, but that's for another time. What is important to know now, however, is that the Cult collapsed with the Fall of Rome, and for the next several centuries, it was complete fucking anarchy wherever Exceptions were concerned.

"The traditions of the Cult continued, however, getting more and more diluted with each passing generation, until all that was left were the crude shapes of the rituals-"

"From which Hag Covens were formed?" Flora asked, and Gav gave her a thumbs up. "Wow. You weren't kidding when you said that this was a journey!"

"Yeah; it's a lot to take in, but I promise that we're nearly there. I do feel this is a decent point to have a bit of a tea break, though," Gavin said, stifling a yawn. *Maybe I should've tried to get a little bit of sleep last night.*

"I'll put the kettle on," Coral said. "I've already heard this bit from Malcolm, but you should finish, Gavin; the sooner we're done here, the sooner we can start looking for our emerging Hag."

That's what I'm afraid of, he thought, images of the old handgun filling his mind as he did so. Still, Coral had a point; there was no point prolonging the nightmare any more than necessary. *I just hope Libby and Jacinth will forgive me for my failure.*

"Fine," Gavin said, rubbing the exhaustion from his eyes. "So, when the Enlightenment occurred and the Ministry, at least as we know it, was officially formed, it was revived from the ashes of the long dead Cult of Mithras."

"What?" Reggie said, his eyes wide.

"Black coats, Ravenblades, the strange hierarchical structure, and the obsession with secrecy all stem from that one Roman era Cult," Gavin said. "Hell, even the Ministry's motto, *Pugnamus In Obumbratio*, is an old Cult pass phrase."

Reggie let out a dark chuckle.

"When you put it like that, it's hard to see the Ministry as anything other than a fringe group of fanatics with a shit load of political power," Leroy said. "Fucking hell, Gavin; I never realised the Ministry was so..."

"Insane? Derivative? Downright cringey?" Reggie offered, and Leroy laughed. "Tell me, Gavin, does the motif of a Lamp feature in the Cult's work at all?"

"Prominently," Gavin said. "I think Lucy's tattoo is what prompted Malcolm to give her the book in the first place."

"So how does this tie in with the Hags?" Flora asked, clearly trying to keep the conversation on track.

"The Ministry basically stole the Hags' entire series of rituals, motifs, and overall aesthetic," Gavin continued, "and this served to piss them off something awful, which in turn forced them deeper underground and made them even more dangerous.

"Remember, mentallly these Ceps are still children, so they are having an angry child's reaction to all this; nothing about it is going to be rational."

"I guess it would also help to hide the Hags further," Leroy said, and Gavin nodded, "and allow them to act under the radar, hidden by the supernatural noise generated by the Ministry."

"Exactly. The Ministry also buried every reference to Mithras it could find, which only makes our task of finding the Hags harder." Gavin sighed heavily.

"Why?" Paris asked, sweating with mental exertion as he tried to keep up.

"Malcolm seems to believe that the remaining Hag Covens dwell within Mithraeums hidden throughout the country. He mentioned that there were clues hidden throughout the Torbay area to find the concealed temple that our Coven is operating out of."

"And we need to find them why, exactly?" Flora asked, taking a drink gratefully from Coral.

"They might have a way to help Ariadne," Gavin said, frowning, "not to mention that you can be absolutely sure that the Ministry will be looking for them, and if they get there before we do, they will kill every last one of them.

"Enemy of my enemy, and all that." He stared into the middle distance for a while before going on. "I think the rest of you should try and follow the hidden trail to the Mithraeum whilst I find our blossoming Hag."

"We can help you," Flora said, but he shook his head.

"This is Lucy's mess," he admitted, "and now the responsibility passes to me. I'll work faster alone."

"Ariadne could be dangerous," Coral said, placing a cup of tea in the Druid's hands. "One of us should come with you."

"You'll need everyone to deal with the Coven," Gavin replied, "and Ariadne will be safe enough to approach in the daylight. I'll go alone."

He paused for a second before adding a final comment.

"Thanks for the tea, Coral; it's just the thing."

They all sat in silence for a few minutes before Gavin rose from the table, teacup emptied; there was still much to do before he set about his difficult and dangerous task, and he knew every moment mattered.

Leroy added one final piece of information as the Druid went to leave the room.

"If my memory is correct," he said, "I think the first sign of things being wrong here were around the time of the lunar eclipse, a couple of months ago."

"I'll bear it in mind," Gavin said, and went out into the foyer of the Montresor, but he soon realised Flora was hot on his heels.

"Gav, are you alright?" Her voice wavered nervously, and she reached out to him with a concerned hand.

"I'm okay, Flo," he lied, but she seemed unconvinced.

"Please, be honest with me."

"I think I just need to get some more sleep before I delve into the signs and records to work out who this is," Gavin said quietly, even though in his heart of hearts he already knew who their Hag was. He pulled Flora into a tight hug and kissed her on the cheek. "Please be careful out there, Flo; walking the Path of Mithras was said to be one of the most dangerous things a person could possibly do."

"I'll be fine, Gav," she said, beaming at him. "Besides, I can't let the boys down, can I?"

"It's coming home," Gavin replied with a chuckle. "I mean it, though, Flo; I don't want to lose you."

"Likewise, Gavin," she said, and then whispered her parting words into his ear. "I know you're angry and hurting, babes, but when you come face to face with Ariadne, please choose to be kind, for both your sakes."

I'll try, he thought as she returned to the others, *but I don't think I can let either of us walk away from all that's happened. I have to end this madness, for Lucy.*

Chapter Twenty Five – On the Trail

Flora

"You should get some sleep, Flora," Leroy said as she packed up her bag, ready to begin striking out in search of the Mithraeum and, by extension, the Hag Coven that dwelled within. "I mean it, Flo; you look dead on your feet."

"I'll grab some sleep on the way," she muttered, searching around her room for a torch. *Gavin said they would likely be underground.* "I'll find somewhere to take a nap on the trail. Besides, seeing as I'm no longer drinking Gavin's Sweet Breath, I can have these."

She held up two cans of Retribution, a new brand of energy drink that had reached out to her with a potential sponsorship deal some weeks ago. Leroy took one of the cans and looked through the ingredients.

"Flora, these can't be good for you," he murmured. "Hell, some of these chemicals sound made up; you have no idea what's in this! It could be Demon piss, for all you know."

"Yeah, it could be," she said with a tired chuckle, "but if it keeps me upright, I'll take it."

She packed the two cans in her bag and, after a few seconds of contemplation, seized a third and popped the tab, emptying the entire can into a glass beer stein. *Wow, that's a really vivid colour,* she thought as she stared, wide eyed at the sparkling pink liquid. *Raspberry Vapour is an appropriate name for something that looks like this.*

"Yeah, that's absolutely going to kill you the second you drink it," Leroy said.

"Oh, hush," Flora said playfully before taking a long, satisfying sip. The smooth and creamy raspberry flavour brought a smile to her face and she immediately felt perked up. *That's strong stuff,* she thought, *and it's definitely not just caffeine in there.* She decided to keep this from Leroy, however; she needed every edge she could get. "Let me have my indulgences."

"You're nothing *but* indulgences," he replied warmly. "Are you sure you don't want anyone to go with you?"

"I'll move faster on my own," she said firmly. "Besides, I need you, Rizz, and Coral feeding me whatever information on any missing Cep children you find; it'll be important to know what these Hags can do *before* I find them."

"And what about me?" asked a voice from the doorway. Flora turned to see Reggie standing there, coat of rags on and a strange machine strapped to his back, along with a pair of pistols at his hips. The long coat, ruffled shirt, and a dark purple homburg all combined to give him the look of a gruff adventurer, instead of a man who'd been half-dead mere hours ago.

"You need to rest," Flora said, but he shook his head.

"You took me in at great risk to your lives, and now is the chance for me to return the favour; trust me, Flora, I can help you." He pulled one of the pistols from its holster and twirled it in his functional hand. "Unfortunately, I can only shoot with my right nowadays, so how do you feel about being the left hand of the Devil?"

He grinned and offered her the weapon, which she took with a grim smile.

"Okay, you can come with me," Flora said as she buckled the holster beneath her light summer jacket. "Leroy, will you keep the others on task, please?"

"I will do." The Ghoul gave each of them a hug as they departed, and they made their way out of the Montresor. Once they reached the sunny street, Flora gestured for Reggie to turn left, towards the centre of Torquay, and they were underway.

"Reggie," Flora asked as she finally got a good look at the strange crank handled contraption that the Familiar carried, "is that what I think it is?"

"Which is?" he replied with a grin.

"A music grinder?" she said haltingly, fumbling for the right words. He laughed and gently corrected her.

"A Street or Barrel Organ," he said softly, "and the person playing it is the Organ Grinder."

"That's it! I always forget what they're called. I'm not exactly sure how that will help us," Flora said with a slight frown, "and aren't you supposed to have a monkey or something?"

"The monkeys will come when they're called," he said enigmatically, "and this isn't just an instrument; this is something very special, made just for me."

"If you say so," Flora said as they continued along the street towards the centre of town, "but I'm not going to carry it for you when your arms get tired."

"Shouldn't we work out where we're going before we-"

"I've already figured out where the trail starts," Flora said smugly, tapping the front of the book.

"You have?" Reggie asked excitedly. "Where is it?"

"Come along, Marianne Faithfull," she quipped,

"and I'll show you."

They made their way to the centre of Torquay without incident, although Reggie's appearance did garner some sideways glances; whether it was the hat that was so dark it was almost black, the strange instrument on his back, or Reggie's general attitude, Flora could not be sure. Still, they were not staring at her, which was a blessed relief.

"We're here," she said, gesturing to the building in front of them.

"A vape shop?" Reggie asked and Flora rolled her eyes. "What? This is just a fucking vape shop, Flora!"

"What are you, human?" she asked sharply, shoving him slightly. "Look with your mind, Kellogg, not your eyes!"

Reggie looked at her sheepishly for a moment, and then turned his gaze back to the space in front of the shop, his eyes slipping out of focus as he did so. Flora followed suit, tapping into the inherent gift that all non-humans possessed; the ability to see the Tangle.

The faintly shimmering threads seemed to coalesce out of thin air, draping over objects like strands of mermaid hair and cutting through solid matter as if it didn't even exist. A faint haze pulsed around them, deformed and shaped by the oblivious humans to its illuminating splendour.

They don't even know, Flora thought as her misty eyes beheld the endless aftershocks of creation as they played out before her. *How could they ever hope to understand?*

Suddenly the gulf between her and her friends seemed impossibly vast, and she began to tremble with isolation and fear. Before the terror at what she was witnessing could take the heart of her, however, Reggie slipped a hand into hers and the golden light began to fade; soon enough, the view in front of her was a vape shop once again.

"Thank you," she whispered, although whether it was the cosmic web or the man at her side she was grateful to, she did not know. She allowed her mind to recover for a minute or so before speaking directly to Reggie. "What did you see?"

"I..." he searched for the words, clearly awestruck.

"You've never seen it before, have you?" Flora said, suddenly aware of what a momentous occasion she had just been present for. "You didn't have anyone to show you, so you didn't even know it was there..."

"They never told me I could do that," Reggie said, although the sorrow in his voice quickly hardened into anger. "They kept me blind my entire life, all for one more iota of control. How dare they?"

"I'm sorry," Flora whispered. "I didn't realise that you'd not seen it before; I would've warned you."

"I had to open my eyes at some point," he said darkly. "Thank you for giving me the chance."

They were both silent for a moment.

"What were we looking for?" he asked, eventually.

"Hidden in the threads is a pattern," Flora said, "that forms the crude image of a sacrificial bull; one of the most widely known of the symbols of Mithras."

"This is the start of the path?" Reggie asked, and she nodded. "Why hide the start in the Tangle?"

"To keep out those who are not worthy," she replied softly, looking around at the people that bustled through their busy lives, totally unaware of the wonders and horrors that surrounded them. "Or to protect those without the power to protect themselves;

I suppose it depends on your view of the world."

"And which are you?"

Flora did not answer. Reggie's eyes slipped back into that strange blurry half-gaze as he glanced at the Tangle once more, but it was only for a few seconds this time.

"I see what you mean," he said, giving her a smile. "This is definitely the start, but where do we go now?"

"The next step on the pathway will be the Great Feast," she said, "of the slaughtered bull, partaken both by Mithras and Sol Invictus. However, I have no idea what the fuck that would look like.

"I only know about this place because I've seen it before." She frowned and looked around. "Something tells me that we're in the right place..."

"... but here at the wrong time?" Reggie suggested. "Sol Invictus; that's the victory of the sun, right?"

"Crudely translated, yes," Flora said, still searching the area for any signs or mystic symbols.

"Then we're supposed to be here at dawn," Reggie said.

"Fuck," Flora hissed, suddenly furious at their earlier dallying. "We've burned a whole fucking day, for naught!"

"This is too important to rush," Reggie said sagely. "If we go off half-cocked, we're liable to get ourselves killed, or worse. We should go back to the Montresor and get some sleep, so we're ready to deal with this when the sun rises."

"I just hope Gavin will have better luck than us," Flora said as she looked out through the fading afternoon sunlight. *Fuck it, we're already out.* "It looks to be a nice evening; how about we find a watering hole and have a few drinks before we head home?"

"Why?" Reggie asked. "Wouldn't it be more sensible to-"

"Yes," Flora said, exasperated, "it would make infinitely more sense to ration our time out here, but I don't want to go back to that fucking haunted hotel!"

There was a heartbeat of silence.

"Haunted?" Reggie asked softly.

"Buy me a drink," Flora said, leading him in the direction of a cocktail bar, "and I'll tell you all about it."

Flora sipped on her hurricane, enjoying the tropical sweetness that buried the burnt sugar bite of the rum. Passion fruit was a particular favourite of hers, and she adored any drink that managed to work in the delightful fruit.

Nothing else tastes quite so exquisitely pink, she mused, *except for that new energy drink.*

"So," Reggie said with a playful smile, "word on the street is that you had a tryst with Gavin the other night."

Does everyone know my fucking business!?

"And who told you that?" Flora asked haughtily.

"You don't just walk into a room and announce that you're gay without a catalysing moment," Reggie said, still grinning, "and the two of you have a certain energy about you."

"We're just best mates, Reg; that's all." She sighed heavily. "We almost did something, but thought better of it."

"I'm impressed," Reggie said softly. "I've never been able to pull myself back from that edge; I lost some incredibly close friends that way."

"You're biologically compelled," Flora said, placing a commiserating arm around his shoulder. "You're just made that way, even if it was cruel of them to do so."

"It was, but no longer," he said, taking a sip of his gin old fashioned before tapping the location of his wound through his shirt. "No heart, and no suicidal impulses; I'm free from them, Flora."

"What about the people you've already bonded to?" she asked quietly.

There was a moment of silence.

"I'm not sure about that," Reggie admitted, "but they're either dead, or they wish I was, so it's all the same really; I'm never going to see them again."

"I'm sorry if I upset you," Flora said after a few minutes. The sun had long since set, and the bar had switched to a more sedate choice of music.

I always liked Mazzy Star, she thought with a sad smile. *We should go home soon, though.*

"Tell me about the haunting." Reggie looked at her expectantly.

It was gonna come up eventually.

"Gavin is convinced that the mould and mildew that is currently rotting the Monty is a manifestation of the will of the hotel, or some bullshit like that." She shook her head angrily. "He has, somehow, managed to convince himself that the *soul of the building* has formed some kind of symbiotic connection with the psychic mould that runs rampant in the Montresor."

"That doesn't sound like anything I've ever encountered," Reggie said.

"Of course it doesn't," she said, glad that she could finally speak about it all, "because I'm certain it isn't. Yes, the Monty has always had a *presence,* but this is so much more than that ever was. Just look at the state of the place; the mould used to be unobtrusive but now it's black as night and everywhere! That kind of environmental degradation only comes from years of neglect or some kind of psychic corruption, and Gavin takes care of the Monty like it's his fucking child."

"You think it's the ghost of his wife?"

"Lucy, yeah," Flora said. "Coral has caught her on film a few times,but I didn't really believe what I was seeing. When the Ministry attacked, however, she absolutely came out to bat for us, but there's something really wrong with her spirit; she was a fucking saint who wouldn't say boo to a goose, but what's happening now, it's..."

"Evil?" Reggie said, and Flora nodded.

"Maybe death drove her mad," she said, "or this is some fucking hangover from Project Lamplight, but she didn't have a bad fucking bone in her body."

"Are you sure?" Reggie asked quietly.

"Of course I'm sure!" Flora said forcefully. "Gavin never said a fucking peep about anything like that, and he would've told me, for sure!"

Reggie was silent, so Flora gestured to his glass.

"Drink up, Reggie Brek; we better get a few winks of sleep before we hit the trail tomorrow. I still don't like the idea of facing the Hags, but I'm glad I won't be alone." She drained her hurricane and nodded to the bartender as the two Ceps headed out of the door. "A new day, a new challenge; let's see what fresh horror sunrise brings."

Chapter Twenty Six – Destined for the Scene

Gavin

"None at all?" Gavin said into the Bakelite handset as the darkness continued to deepen outside his window. Far beyond the sandy shore, the distant lights of ships burned like signal fires in the night, beckoning him towards the water.

"I'm sorry, Gavin," Arch-Druid Borage said, his rich voice flattened by the speaker of the antique telephone, "but I've pulled every string and called in every favour in an attempt to find your wife's daughter, all to no avail.

"It's likely that she either went through unofficial channels for the adoption, or the transfer was facilitated by the Ministry." Borage sighed heavily, his age apparent in the tiredness of his tone. "I'm not sure how you're going to be able to find her, especially without a concrete date of birth."

"Well, thank you for trying, Peter." Gavin tried not to stare at the shifting stars in the night sky, but the twisted constellations were impossible to ignore and they chilled his soul to the very core. "I have one final thing to ask of you, old friend."

"What is it?"

"Put the word out to all in the Dartmoor Circle to get the fuck away from the Torbay area for the next week or so." The receiver trembled against his ear as he spoke, his voice surprisingly even despite the dread that had taken the heart of him. "I think things are going to get much, much worse before this is over, and even if this shakes out the way I hope it does, there are still going to be deaths."

"Then we should be there to help you!" Peter said without hesitation.

"No!" Gavin ordered sharply before softening his voice once again. "No, Peter; you can help in the aftermath, but if you're all caught up in the storm that's coming, the Circle will perish. We're going to need one living Arch-Druid to shepherd the others when all the madness finally calms down."

"You don't mean to survive this, do you, Gavin?" Peter asked.

"I don't see any other way to make this stop," Gavin admitted, suddenly tired of the whole affair. "It's been an honour to serve the Circle alongside you, Arch-Druid Borage."

"Likewise, Arch-Druid Strangeways." Peter hesitated for a moment. "Gavin, may I offer you a piece of advice, not as a colleague or a Druid, but as a friend?"

"Sure." Gavin drained the contents of his glass as he waited for Peter's sage words. He looked at the empty bottle of Rock and Rye; it had been a present from Flora and he'd been saving the last of it for a special occasion.

The last night of my life seems fitting.

"When I was a young man," Peter said after a few seconds of silence, "with a faded photograph in one hand and a loaded gun in the other, I was told that the way out of the darkness is to seek out the sun, even in the deepest blackest night.

"In short, son, there's always hope of a better ending."

"Sometimes there isn't, Peter," Gavin said sadly, "but thank you for sharing that with me, all the same."

"Goodbye, Gavin," Peter said softly.

"Goodbye, old friend," Gavin replied, and placed the handset in the cradle of the telephone, ending the call. He sighed heavily and turned to face the turbulent celestial display of the night sky, contemplating another attempt at summoning the Illuminated Man.

No, he decided after a few minutes of silently mulling over his options. *Something has changed, and this roll of the dice is mine.*

"Well," he said, getting to his feet, "if the mountain won't go to Mohammed..."

He closed the curtains and slipped out of his comfortable tunic, opting for more typical 'civilian' clothes instead; maroon chinos and a faded Rainbow t-shirt, topped off with a black suit jacket. As a final touch, he selected one of the flowers he had picked from the Montresor's garden earlier that day and placed it into his lapel.

A pink carnation, he thought with a grim smile. *This one's for you, Lucy.*

"If I can't find Ariadne by more conventional means," Gavin muttered as he slipped the Berretta into the waistband of his trousers, "then I'll walk the streets until I catch a hint of her power or fate brings me to her door."

Yes, he thought, *we're destined to cross paths tonight.*

That much is certain.

"We had a good run," he whispered to the empty hotel room as he slipped his feet into his sandals. "It's a shame that it has to end so soon, but at least it will mean something. Take care of the others; I fear that they won't understand."

Courage, Gavin.

The Druid placed a hand gently on the frame of his bedroom door and bade a fond farewell to his home before heading out into the moody darkness of the summer night.

He passed a bar that was playing Mazzy Star and swayed gently for a few steps, enjoying the endless patchwork of sound and light that human civilisation spread across the land. *I know that, as a Druid, I'm supposed to view all this with disdain, but who am I to deny the beauty of humanity?*

A quiet smile crept on to his face as he strutted his stuff in the direction of more forceful music, drawn inexorably towards the horizon as if by the unseen hand of gravity itself. It was in moments like this that Gavin wished that he could witness the Tangle directly; he suspected that it would look a lot like a giant city seen from high in the air, or maybe a continent of light spied from space.

Something hopeful, he mused playfully, *and unmistakably human.*

He rounded a corner, and then another, still compelled into motion by forces nefarious or otherwise as he danced and sang his way towards Ariadne Havelock; the last living remnant of the woman he loved.

The woman who both raised me up and brought me low, he thought wistfully, a hint of winter melancholy adding a touch of cold colour to an otherwise oversaturated warm night.

"I think I might be a little drunk," he whispered to a moth as it fluttered past. It did not seem to hear him, instead continuing on its wayward journey from street light to street light, and Gavin let his eyes follow the insect's lazy flight until something caught his eye.

Deep down, I always knew I'd end up here, he thought as he approached the looming yellow blooms that Peter had spoken of; whether knowingly or not mattered little, as here Gavin stood all the same.

"Sunflowers in the dark." He sighed heavily. "I was really enjoying the walk, but I guess it's time."

He opened the well-oiled gate and reached the door of the little terraced house in a few steps, pausing only to gather his emotions before knocking smartly on the door. He quietly prayed that no-one would answer, but the yellow glow of electric light shone through the glass of the door and, with a simple turn of a handle, there she stood.

Lucy's eyes stared at him from the girl's face, much as they had done, day after day, for the last several years. She looked more tired than ever and the threadbare grey hoodie was stained with charcoal and blood as she trembled nervously in the doorway, clearly all alone in the otherwise empty house.

"Hello, Mr Strangeways," she said softly.

"Hello, Alice," Gavin replied, giving her a tearful smile.

The two stood in silence for a moment, just looking at each other, as if for the first time.

"I didn't hurt them," Alice said, as if she knew what he was about to ask. "My parents said that they had adopted me on the condition that I wasn't... wasn't one of *them* any more. When they found out what was happening, they left.

"They abandoned me," she said tearfully. "Just like my birth mother did."

I can't do it, Gavin realised. *There is no conceivable universe where I could harm this poor child.*

"Are you here to kill me?" Alice whispered.

"No, sweetheart," Gavin said. "I'm not here to hurt you."

"You have a gun." It was not a question.

"I..." He took a deep breath to hold back his own sorrow. "I made a mistake. I'm sorry, Alice."

More silence as all plans and preconceived notions were cast away.

"Do you want a cup of tea?" Alice asked and he nodded. She gestured for him to step inside and he did so, slipping his sandals off as she closed the door. The two quietly walked into the kitchen and Alice busied herself with making the tea as Gavin perched awkwardly on one of the rickety wooden chairs.

He glanced at the table, his eyes widening as he saw countless charcoal sketches of beached whales, mudslides, and false moons, along with scenes that he had yet to encounter; tornados, lightning, and a massive earthquake running through the heart of Torquay. *A hint of things to come, perhaps?*

"You're quite the artist," Gavin said, eyeing the blood on her sleeve and hand. "What happened to your arm?"

"This?" Alice said, idly holding up her left arm and pulling back the sleeve, revealing a bloody imitation of Lucy's Lamplight tattoo.

"Did you do that to yourself?" he asked quietly.

"I woke up with it," Alice replied. "Well, to be more accurate, I zoned back in at daybreak and it was on my arm. I haven't slept in weeks; not since-"

"The lunar eclipse?" Gavin asked and she nodded. He was unsure of how to phrase his next question delicately, so he just decided to be frank. "Alice, have you died recently?"

She nodded, as if she'd expected his question.

"A few friends and I were exploring one of the abandoned buildings up on the moor, and I got electrocuted." She sighed heavily. "My heart stopped, but one of them managed to give me CPR and brought me back. They all said that I should go to hospital, but I genuinely had never felt better; now I wish I'd just died there."

"Do you mean that?" Gavin asked quietly.

"No," Alice admitted after a tense few seconds, "but I don't understand who I am any more, Mr Strangeways!"

"You can call me Gavin," he said softly, and in that moment he knew that his life as a teacher was over. *My whole purpose now is to keep her safe,* he decided. "I can explain what you are and your place in the world, but I think this is the best place to start."

He reached up and unclasped the silver locket that he wore around his neck, the locket that he had held close every night since Lucy's death, and handed it to the girl without a heartbeat of hesitation.

"Here," he said, and she took the necklace.

"Is this my mother?" Alice asked, opening it to look at the tiny portrait within.

"Yeah, that's Lucy," he said tearfully. "That's a lock of her hair, and the whole thing is scented with her favourite perfume."

"She's beautiful," Alice said, almost reverentially, gently sniffing the lingering fragrance that clung to the hair. "What am I smelling?"

"Bluebells, by Penhaligon's. She always said it was the best bluebell scent in the world, aside from the real thing." He smiled sadly. "There's an inside-out bluebell hidden behind the picture; it's said that if you can manage to do that without harming the petals, you'll win the heart of the one you love."

"You're a romantic, I take it?" Alice said, risking a tiny grin of mirth.

"Hopelessly," Gavin admitted.

"Thank you for showing me this," she said, moving to hand the locket back to him, but he shook his head and closed her fingers around it.

"That's yours now, Alice; she would've wanted you to have it."

"Why?" Alice asked sharply, all the warmth leaving her voice. "She didn't even want *me*, so why would she leave this for me? If she really loved me, she wouldn't have just left me!"

Sometimes there is a place for a comforting lie, Gavin thought as he searched his heart for the answer to the girl's question, *but too many falsehoods have already been cast.*

This is time for a painful truth, which will hopefully stop the bleeding.

"She loved you," Gavin said quietly, "but was afraid of you. What you need to understand about Lucy is that she went through a living nightmare as a small child, and the spectre of that haunted her for the rest of her life.

"She saw what other Exceptions, people with special gifts, are capable of," he took a deep breath, "and it drove her mad. Lucy was a beautiful, kind, and special woman, but she could be fickle, cruel, and downright dangerous at times. Loving her was like loving the ocean, Alice; she could be warm, gentle, and inviting, or she could be a roaring monster that would shatter your bones against the rocks, all whilst telling you that she adored you more than anything."

Gavin wiped the tears from his eyes with a trembling fingertip; he had never told anyone about Lucy's darker moments, but he hoped that the truth would help them both.

"She would've been an awful mother," Gavin admitted, "and she knew it. Still, the way that she locked your abilities away and abandoned you in the world is inexcusable; I am deeply sorry that she did that to you."

"Did you know?" she asked, staring into the middle distance, clutching the locket in one white-knuckled fist.

"It was before I met her," Gavin said quietly, "but the first time I saw you-"

He finally succumbed to his tears and broke down sobbing for a few minutes, leaning on the little kitchen table for support. When he had recovered enough to talk, he realised that Alice had placed a comforting hand on his shoulder.

"I'm sorry, Alice," he whispered.

"You don't need to go on, if you don't want to."

"I do," he said, steeling himself. "It's important that you know what she was really like."

He took a deep, shuddering breath.

"When I first saw you, the resemblance was so uncanny that I thought I was dreaming." He looked her in the eye as he spoke. "That was her gift, you see; she could alter and control your dreams, like some kind of god. She wouldn't twist my mind often, but when she did...

"I lived for centuries in a single night, tormented the whole time, only to doubt reality when I finally woke up. Even now, I still wonder if this is just another of her tricks," he said, "and, if it is, then you would be the cruellest twist of the knife.

"I always wanted a child, Alice, and even when I asked her, she never mentioned you." He shook his head angrily. "She had every opportunity to trust me, but she left this for us to deal with in her absence."

"How do you not hate her?" Alice asked, and he simply shrugged.

"I don't know. Maybe I do, and I just don't know what that looks like any more." He sighed heavily. "There's still much, much more to tell you, but we can't stay here alone like this; it isn't safe.

"Don't worry, though," he said, trying to keep up appearances for Alice's sake. "My friends and I are going to help you get through this. I am sorry I wasn't around to guide and protect you sooner, kiddo, but I'm here now and I'm not leaving you to face the world alone."

"You're a good man, Gavin," Alice said, squeezing his shoulder.

"I don't think I am, Alice," he said with a forced smile, "but I'm trying to be."

"What do we do now?" she asked, looking around the house as the eastern sky began to lighten.

I set out to save a child, Gavin thought, *and even though Libby's gone forever, I can still finish what I started.*

I can save Alice.

"Are you certain your parents aren't coming back?" he said, wanting to be absolutely sure about his next suggestion.

"Even if they did," she replied softly, "there's no undoing what they said. We're done."

"Then pack your things," Gavin said. "You're going to come with me, and I'll make sure you're safe until we've got this whole thing under control."

"Where will we be going?"

"Home," Gavin said firmly. "We'll be going home."

Chapter Twenty Six – You Missed the Starting Gun

Lola

Lola cried out as she came once again; whether it was the tenth or hundredth time, she had long lost count. Her acidic tears continued to pour from her eyes, scarring the table that the Demon had cruelly pinned her against as he took his payment.

What am I even getting? Lola thought through the haze of abuse and physical pleasure. *How could I ever receive anything that would be worth this nightmare?*

Speedball raked his fingernails across her bare stomach, ripping her flesh with a touch so careful that it seemed almost tender. The juxtaposition of unspeakable violence and the gentle affection the Demon showered upon her was beginning to make her doubt her ability to discern the reality of her situation; nothing other than a literal nightmare could possibly go on so long, nor keep her in such an exquisite balance of agony and ecstasy.

"I'm beginning to lose my fucking mind," she murmured thickly, her addictive saliva overflowing from her intoxicating lips.

"Then we're done," Speedball said, and suddenly she found herself sitting at the feast laden table once again. She blinked in shock and quickly checked over her own body, but not a single hair seemed to be out of place. He was sat across the table from her, back in his original form, with a satisfied smile on his face. "Tell me how you feel, Ms Oriole."

"Violated," Lola said in a trembling whisper, "and used, although I'm not sure any of that was real."

"It was plenty real enough for both of us," Speedball replied with an almost dreamy tone to his voice, "and it sounds like I have extracted payment enough from you."

He sighed contentedly.

"Oh, my dear darling Lola, your lips are the sweetest that I have ever tasted. You truly are a goddess amongst mortals, and I am willing to offer you anything that you'd like in exchange for letting me experience such absolute ecstasy.

"Whatever you desire, simply name it." He smiled wryly at her. "I would suggest deciding quickly, however; time here runs a little slower than you might expect."

"You really aren't the one doing this?" Lola asked, and Speedball shook his head.

"I am not, nor is it any other non-human or half-breed mongrel; such destructive evil can only come from the most wounded of human hearts, and it can only be sustained by a powerful sense of denial.

"You're looking in the wrong place, my dear." He chuckled darkly. "Then again, blindly going through the motions is the key to this little mystery. Still, as I said beforehand, you did not come here just to peruse the menu and you have paid a considerable price, so I will ask you one last time.

"Lola Oriole, what is it that you want?"

There was a moment of silence as Lola considered the value of the offer, but in the end she decided to speak from the heart.

"I want to be free," she said firmly. "Free from destiny, free from the shackles of fate... and I want to escape what I am."

"And what are you?" Speedball asked, keenly leaning forward.

"I'm a monster," she said sadly. "I am the woman with the heroin lips and the black acid tears, when all I really want is to be normal."

"To be human?"

"Yes," she said, hanging her head in defeat. "I wish I wasn't an Exception, and I hate that I was born this way."

"Wouldn't you rather be *all that you can be*, as the Americans put it?" Speedball looked at her with a pensive smile on his face.

"I don't even know what that would be," she murmured.

"Then I'll show you, eventually," the Demon said quietly, "and then I'll let you make your choice. After all, Michelle, I said that I would give you fair terms."

"That's not my name," Lola said uncertainly.

"No, it isn't," Speedball said, gently taking her trembling hands in his own, "but it could be."

Lola paused for a moment and then looked at the shifting horn die that remained on the table.

"That drop of luck," she asked, "will I need it?"

"And then some," Speedball replied. "So, are you ready to answer my question?"

Lola took a deep breath and looked at the jar containing the heart; her seemingly endless sexual torment had given her just the jolt she'd needed to put the pieces of the puzzle together.

"The Beggar King is Reginald Kellogg," she answered. "He's a Familiar, yes, but I happen to know that he's more Demon than anything else. I know that he's somewhere out there, allied with Flora Cain and

Gavin Strangeways."

"Three out of four," Speedball replied. "Only the why of the thing to win the pot."

Time for a shot in the dark.

"Rakshasa have a certain amount of clairvoyance," she began, taking her time to choose her words carefully. "Desai must've seen that he would be important to you, so he bred him to be relentlessly loyal to the Ministry; a loyalty that you now have instead."

She pointed to the heart.

"How can you be sure it belongs to dear old Reggie?" Speedball asked.

"It's got that faint bronze tint that comes from the Djinn mixed into his biology," Lola said, "and it bears the scar Charity Walpole gave him when he tried to rape her."

Speedball was silent, so she went on.

"He came to you, cast out and mutilated, and you took him in as a brother," she said, growing more certain with each word. "He's prophesied to lead you to victory, so you freed him from the yoke of his conditioning. A penniless leader, come home at last; that is your Beggar King."

"Bravo, darling," Speedball said with a broad smile. "Now take your prize and get out of here; time runs differently in my little heroin den, and I already think you've tarried long enough."

"But my choice-"

"Will be presented to you when the time comes," he replied, getting to his feet, "and you won't have to make it alone; you'll be surrounded by those who love you."

"I..." Lola hesitated before pocketing the die, and the

weight of it vanished almost immediately; somehow she was certain that it would always be on her person when she needed it. "Thank you, for everything."

"Thank *you* for the horror you let me visit upon you," Speedball said warmly. "Now run along."

She nodded and, before she could even reply, she found herself in the chilly darkness of the Devil's Armchair, looking out at the inky sea once again. Miette was nowhere to be seen, but Thaddeus grabbed her as soon as he saw her, pulling her into a tight embrace.

"Lo!" Thad gasped as he held her close. "You're alive! I knew you'd still come back!"

"Thad," she said with a smile, "I'm sorry that took a couple of hours, but I did get some information-"

"Hours?" Thad said, his eyes wide with confusion. "Lola, you've been gone for two days!"

What!?

"I... we..." He tried to fight back his tears. "Lo, we thought you were dead! Miette went on to chase up other leads but I wanted to wait for you. I was beginning to lose hope, but you're back now.

"You're safe, and you're home."

"You've been waiting here for two days?" Lola asked the towering man, and he nodded. "Why?"

"You're my friend, Lo," he said softly, his words almost whipped away by the lively sea breeze. "I said that I would stick by you, and I meant it."

"Thank you, Thaddeus," she said, hugging him even closer than before. There were a few seconds of silence, broken only by the dull roar of the surf, and then Thad asked her a question.

"What happened in there, Lo?"

Instead of answering, however, all that escaped her

lips were the sounds she'd held back throughout Speedball's exquisitely applied torture. Thad held her tightly as she lost control, screaming madly into the darkness of the night.

"The Djinn was a bust," Miette said as soon as Thaddeus opened the door to the little Ministry safehouse. "It was just a regular man running a fucking scam, and with Oriole dead we are running out of leads..."

She trailed off as she saw the dishevelled Juliet shuffle across the threshold. The translucent woman stared at her for a moment before asking a single question.

"Did he hurt you?"

"I'm alive," Lola answered, her voice hoarse from all her screaming. The first glow of dawn was tingeing the sky through the living room window. "I got some information about the case-"

"Oh, fuck the case!" Miette said, crossing the room in a flurry of wind and placing a hand on Lola's cheek. "Did that monster hurt you, Lola?"

"It was necessary for the case," Lola replied, barely loud enough for the Sylph to hear.

"No," Miette said firmly, "it wasn't. I'm sorry that I put you in that position."

"It's not your fault," Lola began, but Miette shook her head.

"That's not true; you've been imprisoned and drugged and threatened ever since you were a fucking child, and I've only added to that. Everything I've said, everything I've done... it all led to you taking that fucker's hand and walking into that place.

"I've been treating you both as tools, rather than

people, and I'm so sorry." Miette wrapped her arms tightly around Lola, whispering her next words through her tears. "I thought I got you killed, and I felt so guilty..."

"I'm alive," Lola repeated, although a part of her felt like that was a lie. "I have some information about the case."

"It can wait," Miette said gently. "Let me make you a cup of tea first, okay?"

"That would be lovely, thank you." Lola staggered over to the sofa and collapsed into the worn cushions. She blinked in shock; Miette was not merely acting compassionately, but she was almost *human* in her emotions.

Something is happening here, she thought. *Something important.*

"Miette," Lola asked when the Sylph returned with a lukewarm cup of tea, "have you ever felt like this on a case before?"

Lola took a sip of the tea and had to choke it down; it was at least half soured milk by volume and contained somewhere in the region of eight teaspoons of sugar.

"I don't normally feel much," the Sylph admitted. "Sometimes there are shades of anger, or mirth, but this is so different to anything I've ever experienced that I'm not really sure how to cope with it."

"Describe how you feel," Thad said, "in one word."

"Like I'm running out of time," Miette said quietly, "and that I'd do anything to get away from this place."

"Desperate?" Lola asked, and the other woman nodded. The Juliet looked at Thad. "I feel the same way, but I'm assuming that you're unaffected."

"Whatever this thing is," Thad said, "it's twisting the

psychic subspace of this town to drive people out of their minds."

"Why?" Miette asked.

"Because it needs them to give themselves willingly to it," Thad said, "and desperate people do desperate things. Whatever-"

"Whoever," Lola interrupted. "The Demon confirmed that this is a gifted human, and a monstrously powerful one."

"Gift repression?" Miette asked and Lola shrugged.

"Could be, but either way I'm going to get Bright Eyes to trawl through the digital footprint of every single person matching the description of our suspect in a fifty mile radius of this town. Thankfully, at least half of that area will be the sea, but it's not going to be a trivial task."

"What will you need?" Thaddeus asked as Lola slipped on her special glasses and settled in front of the computer.

"Time, which we are pretty short on, the space to focus on this, and some music to get me in the zone."

"What do you like?" Miette asked, but Thaddeus answered.

"Arctics?" He asked and she nodded.

"Yes, or maybe Pendulum; I'm not sure yet. Another cup of tea wouldn't go amiss either."

"I'll get right on it," Miette said, already gliding towards the door, but Lola's next words stopped her in her tracks.

"Thank you, Miette, but if it's all the same to you, I'd rather you let Thad make it."

<u>Chapter Twenty Seven</u> – We Rise with the Dawn

Flora

Flora blinked in surprise when she walked into the lounge of the Hotel Montresor as dawn approached. Instead of Reggie, who'd arranged to meet her there, she found Gavin drinking hot chocolate with a tired looking teenage girl.

"You're the spitting image of your mother," Flora muttered. The girl's resemblance to Lucy was uncanny; no wonder Gavin had had little trouble in locating here.

"Morning, Flora," Gavin said with a tired smile. She frowned slightly; the delicate chain of the locket that he always wore was no longer visible. "This is Alice."

"Nice to meet you," the girl said, giving the Faun a sheepish little wave. "Where are you going? It's barely morning!"

"Reggie and I have a little bit of investigating to do," Flora said, carefully. "We think there's a group out there who might be able to help you learn to focus your talents in a less dangerous way."

"I think I know who you mean," Alice said, nodding. "I can feel one of them in my head, sometimes, like a whispering voice."

One of the Hags is a fucking telepath!? Flora thought nervously. *This is gonna be more dangerous than I thought.*

"Does, uh, does the voice tell you anything about the rest of them?" Flora asked, trying to hide her fear.

"There are five of them," Alice said. "Sister is the one who speaks to me, Brother is the one who found me, -"

A Tracer.

"-Babby can make fire, Mumsy can make you forget, -"

Inferno. Fugue.

"- and Aunty is big and scary. Mumsy is the one in charge, but Sister's more afraid of Aunty than anyone else. Does that help you?"

"More than you know," Gavin said; he'd clearly drawn the same inferences as Flora from the descriptions Alice had given. "Hopefully they'll be able to tell us how to help you."

"Then why not let me go to them?" Alice asked.

"Because," Reggie said, entering the room, "even though they might know how to help you, that doesn't mean they have your best interests at heart."

"And you do?" Alice asked, nervously eyeing the Familiar's devilish appearance.

"Yes, we do." Gavin's voice was firm and authoritative. "Reggie and Flora aren't human, Alice, but they're still people and, more importantly, they're our friends; they'll protect you. We all will."

"We need to go," Flora said, looking anxiously through the window at the rapidly lightening sky. "We still might not have enough time to get there, though."

"We will," Reggie said with a smile, and placed a hand on her shoulder. "This will feel a little bit weird,."

"What-" Flora began, but her words were swept away as she felt every atom of her being split apart, forming a nebulous cloud that raced along the threads of the Tangle like diffuse sheet lightning. Her mind was exposed to the sheer vastness of the web that connected everything and everyone in a way she had never though possible, but before she could even begin to fathom the experience she coalesced into being once again in an alleyway near the vape shop.

"You okay?" Reggie asked, as Flora stared dumbly into the middle distance.

"Yeah," she said softly. "I've seen the Tangle many times before, but I've never been *inside* it and..."

"It's a real trip, isn't it?" Reggie said, a broad grin on his face. The silver florin rolled gently over the back of his fingers as he spoke. "It's a shame you can't see the Tangle whilst you're racing through it; I'm sure that would be an almost spiritual experience.

"Still, it's the fastest way from here to there that I've ever found; none of the risks of folding and better range than the wormholes, but there's always the chance that you'll take the wrong thread. Even then, there's a certain allure to getting completely and utterly lost, isn't there?"

"Where would you, or indeed, *could* you end up?" Flora asked, keeping one eye on the eastern sky.

"Pretty much anywhere," Reggie said playfully. "Sometimes I think I'd like to go to the moon; the peace, quiet and solitude would do everyone some good."

Flora hesitated before asking the question that had been burning in her mind ever since she'd first heard Reggie's voice coming through the handset of her antique telephone. *I hope this isn't too fresh for him.*

"Reggie, why did you leave the Ministry?"

"Why wouldn't I?"

"They literally made you," she replied quietly. "I understand why you would resent them for that, but I never thought they would let you entertain the notion of leaving. What changed?"

"I hurt someone I cared about." He frowned slightly and looked at the floor. "Sure, my conditioning and what they did to me was part of that, but the Ministry's attitude of simply doing or taking whatever they want was so baked into me that I..."

He sighed heavily.

"She stabbed me in the heart, nearly killing me, and then I showed up at her father's funeral, where she did this." He held up his gnarled hand, full of shattered and misshapen bones. "She had every right to defend herself from me, but when I returned to Desai and Cherry, all they cared about was getting me functional enough to work again.

"I refused to let them heal my hand; I need a constant reminder of what I've done in order to keep the conditioning at bay." He smiled hopefully. "At least, that was the case up until now; maybe I've paid enough of a price to finally put my old ghosts to rest. Still, I came down here in the hope that I would be able to stay away from her for the rest of our lives."

Flora placed a hand gently on his shoulder, unsure of what, if anything, she should say in response.

"I'm nobody's monster," Reggie said defiantly. "Not any longer."

"The Ministry is the real monster, Reg," she said. "Never forget that. Still, it takes a strong person to admit what they've done. These gifts we've been given are a poisoned chalice and we all end up as the horror in somebody's nightmare. All we can do is try to save who we can, and hurt as few people as possible along the way."

Before he could reply, the sun crept over the eastern

horizon and the air before the vape shop began to shimmer faintly in the early dawn light.

Courage, Flora.

"Time to go," she said, grabbing his hand and striding into the distorted space.

Hopefully this goes somewhere safe, she thought, and then the ground fell out from beneath her feet.

"Nifty Ways?" Coral asked, scoffing slightly. "That's a fucking stupid name."

"It's what they've always been called," Gavin replied with a chuckle, "and we all know how well that esoteric muck sticks."

"It's not esoteric, Gavin!" Flora replied sharply.

"Is it explainable by modern physics?" Gavin asked, and Flora shook her head. "Then it's magic, ain't it?"

"It's not magic, Gav," Flora said testily. "It's just... beyond current science."

"And a bit off to the side, and you have to squint a bit whilst standing on one leg," the teacher quipped with a wry grin. Flora huffed and he let out a low chuckle. "Oh, I'm just fucking with you, Flo; no need to pout.

"Do go on, O Learned One," he said, doffing an imaginary cap.

"Would you two just fuck already?" Coral muttered, but only Flora heard.

"What was that?" Gav asked.

"I asked if they're like wormholes?" Coral said, keenly covering her tracks. "You know, bend space, shortest distance is zero, yadda yadda, where we're going we won't need eyes, et cetera."

"Not exactly," Flora said. "Firstly, only non-humans can use Nifty Ways-"

"Not true!" Gavin interjected. "Whilst non-humans can enter them whenever they like, humans can do so too, albeit when certain conditions are met; time of day, position of the stars, season, and so on."

"But what *are* they!?" Coral asked, teetering on the verge of exasperation.

"In short, they're routes through The Backrooms that don't match up with physical space or time." Flora held up a hand, anticipating Coral's next question. "The Backrooms are a single huge network of corridors, offices, and other spaces that exist just out of synch with the world that you know, housing all the *stuff* that makes the supernatural world work, which is collectively known as The Apparatus.

"The Apparatus includes infrastructure for the dead, psychic relays, billions upon billions of records, the Ghost Post, and a whole host of other gubbins that allows this weird world to function smoothly. It's full of people who live and work there, just like you would expect."

"Think of it like the servants' quarters for the whole of reality," Gavin said kindly, "in the same way that the Monty has back stairs and the hidden laundry corridor. Nifty Ways allow shortcuts through this place, or access to otherwise unreachable places."

"Is it run by the Ministry?" Coral asked, who had been staring unblinking into the middle distance ever since Flora had said *Ghost Post*.

"No," Gavin said. "The Ministry has absolutely no presence there, as much as it would like to."

"Then who's in charge there?" Coral said.

"Something else," Flora said enigmatically.

The starkly lit corridor was full of black clad people

bustling to and fro, so Flora and Reggie lingered in the shallow alcove as they got their bearings.

"I already fucking hate this place," Reggie muttered. A woman in a black uniform, carrying a satchel brimming with black envelopes, glared at him as she passed. "I don't think they care for us much, either."

"Etiquette is important here, Reg," Flora said, nodding at the next person who strode by them. They returned her nod with a wink, which calmed her racing heart a little. "The House won't mind us being here as long as we don't linger or get in the way, but if you start insulting people the Butlers will be on us in no time at all.

"So, Reggie darling," Flora said, putting on a performative grin, "big smiles for all the boys and girls watching at home, and off we go!"

She tugged on his hand and pulled him into the flow of people that moved through the white walled corridor. He kept pace with her, but she caught him staring through some of the open doors that they passed and she squeezed his hand in admonishment.

"Eyes front, Reggie Brek," she hissed through her false smile. "The House hates snoopers, especially when supernatural doings are afoot; you don't want them to take against us, do you?"

"Sorry, Flo," he whispered, falling into step beside her. "I've never actually been here before, so this is all new to me."

"You haven't?" Flora asked, almost coming to a stop with the force of her surprise.

"Ministry Agents are expressly forbidden from coming into The Backrooms," he replied, pulling her onwards. "Desai has an agreement with The House, but it's uneasy at best."

They walked on for a few more minutes before Reggie asked the question that Flora had been dreading.

"What are we actually looking for, Flora?" he said softly, and she pulled him into another alcove. This one was filled with various pigeonholes and mail chutes, so it was only a matter of time before they committed the cardinal sin of *Being In The Way*.

"I'm not actually sure," she admitted, pulling out the book of Mithraism. "There's something in here referencing a hidden path, but I was expecting a landmark or another Nifty Way or... something, I guess."

Another of the postal workers approached the alcove, their bag full to bursting, and Flora had a flash of inspiration.

"Good morning!" The Faun kept her voice bright and cheerful as she spoke, and the uniformed man smiled in return. "I was wondering if I could pop those letters in their pigeonholes for you?"

"Why?" the man asked suspiciously.

"To give you a little break from your hectic day, of course," Flora said sweetly. Money had no value in the chaotic maze of The Backrooms, but time was a priceless commodity. "Would that be alright?"

"Well, yes," the man said with a broad grin, handing her the heavy satchel. She handed the book to Reggie before she began to deftly sort the letters, placing them in their correct places with almost supernatural speed.

Being a Rusalka has its advantages, she thought with a grin. The need to compulsively sort items was a curse shared by many non-humans, but Flora had learned how to lever that particular quirk in her favour years ago.

"Whilst we've got you," she said, trying to speak in as casual a manner as possible, "does this mean anything to you?"

Reggie showed the postman the book, and the man nodded happily.

"Oh, yes," he said enthusiastically. "It's an older route, but I've seen people take it from time to time. Are you having trouble finding it?"

"We're turned around like you would not believe!" Flora said with a hollow chuckle.

"Oh, I know what that's like," commiserated the ghostly postie. "My first few months were an absolute nightmare, but now I know this place like the back of my hand. Now, if you follow this route as written, it'll take you somewhere in the region of a week to get to where you're going, in Overworld time, that is.

"However," he said with a smile as he scribbled a set of instructions in the margin of the book, "this route will cost you maybe a day, tops. One good turn deserves another, after all!"

"Thank you so much!" Flora said, handing the empty satchel back to the postman. "May I ask your name?"

"Jimmy Kitts," he said, tipping his cap. "Now, I best get on, as should you; this is no place to tarry! Thanks for the time!"

Before either Flora or Reggie could reply, the man marched swiftly away with a renewed spring in his step. Flora was about to look over the route that Jimmy had given them, but a shudder ran down her spine as she felt the eyes of The House look her over.

We've been here too long already, she realised. *We have to hurry.*

"Can you follow those directions?" Flora asked as a strange garbled voice echoed throughout the corridor, broadcast over some unseen loudspeaker.

"Yes, I think so," Reggie replied as a large shape loomed above the crowd, heading slowly towards them.

"Then let's go," Flora said, "before we end up tangling with one of the Butlers."

He took off without another word, and she stuck close behind him, hoping desperately that they could outrun the Butler and exit The Backrooms before they came into direct conflict with the masters of the strange liminal space they were racing through.

After all, Flora thought nervously, *everyone knows that The House always wins.*

Interlude Two – Behind the Mask

"Why did everyone believe that Gideon was the more powerful of the two of you?" Thad asked quietly as Lola continued to trawl through the data Bright Eyes had flagged as potentially useful. "I know that you said that you tried to construct that particular facade, but surely anyone that met you would've seen through that in a heartbeat."

There was a beat of silence before she responded.

"Did you believe it?" she asked, looking over her shoulder at him.

"I..." he began, preparing to justify himself but then he faltered. *Why on earth did I blindly believe everything I was told about her, even after she managed to capture me?* Miette seemed to sense his confusion and smiled kindly at him.

"There are Ceps, Thaddeus," the Sylph said, "and beneath them are the Ceps who are also women. Just because we move in a world of unimaginable horror and unbelievable wonder, men accepting the equality between genders isn't any more realistic to those in charge.

"If we were to encounter Agent Treen or any other senior operative, who do *you* think they would assume is in charge?"

"But Lola is-" Thad said, but Lola cut across him.

"I *was* a Ravenblade, Thad; I've been disavowed, after all." She chuckled darkly. "Let's not also ignore the fact that Miette isn't even human, which would most certainly be weighed against her.

"Let's face it, Thad; the Ministry is the instrument of a patriarchal society." Lola shook her head in bitter mirth. "Hell, even the highest ranking woman in the entire organisation secured her position before her transition! I'm not casting doubt on Harper's gender identity, but the fact that she waited for so long is a little telling."

The trio sat in contemplative silence for some time.

Something stirred in the back of Thad's mind as he watched Lola's monstrous computer sort through endless faces, and he sat forward in his seat, frowning slightly. On one small screen she was chatting to some of her internet friends, and his eyes were drawn to the avatar she used.

"Lo, do you still pretend to be a man online?" he asked, the wheels in his mind spinning at full speed now. She nodded and a look of slow realisation crept on to her face. "You mentioned before that you've been doing it since you were young; did you learn it in Lamplight?"

"I did," she said quietly.

"I wasn't aware that was part of the instruction you were given," Miette said.

"It wasn't," Thad said, more sure than ever. "Your dream-hopping friend taught you, didn't she?"

"Lucy often said that the superiors listened to her when she appeared as an adult man in their dreams; far more than when she was her true self, at least." Lola glanced at the descriptions of their culprit that they'd been able to obtain, shaking her head in disbelief. "There's barely any consistency to these, aside from the cloak of stars and the fact that our target is an adult man; no wonder Bright Eyes is having such fucking trouble!"

"You think our man is actually a woman?" Miette asked, and Thad nodded.

"Not just a woman, but one that was close with Lucy, or someone like her at least." Thad looked over at Lola, whose fingers were dancing over the computer keyboard at lightning speed. "Have you found something?"

"I'm just fact checking a rumour I heard some years ago," she replied, "although it's buried behind a bunch of security protocols that are above my clearance."

"We could request access to the relevant document or file, if it's pertinent to the mission," Miette said, but Lola merely grinned in response. "What?"

"Sure, we could do that, or you could just ignore what I'm about to do," Lola said gleefully.

Miette blinked in shock.

"You... you can't do that!" The Sylph was even more pale than usual. "You absolutely cannot!"

"Can do, will do, and..." There was a beat of silence, punctuated only by the rapid clatter of keystrokes. "...have done."

Lola pulled down her glasses for a moment to wink at Thad, who couldn't help but grin in response. *I'm really starting to like her,* he realised. *She reminds me a lot of Aunty Bella.*

"You have no idea what they will do to you if they find out what you have just done!" Miette said, her shrill tone bordering on hysterical.

"Then don't tell them," Lola quipped as she read through the highly classified file. Thad waited for her to summarise it for them, but the stunned look on Lola's face drew a question from his lips.

"What is it?" he asked, although he already suspected what the answer would be.

"Lucy Havelock has a daughter; she's a Cep, and her gift explains everything we've been seeing." Lola's voice was quiet, but Thad could hear the frustration in her tone. "How the fuck did we fucking miss this?"

"We were too busy looking at Gideon," Thad replied softly. "Does the file have an address?"

"Yes," Lola said, trembling as she continued to trawl through the file, "but this kid is a Shaper; she can alter reality when she's asleep. It's far too dangerous to approach her at night."

"I agree," Miette said, "but I would also counsel caution moving forwards; there's something else at work here, and if we go into another situation unprepared, we won't survive it."

"So what do we do?" Thad asked, and was a little surprised by the Sylph's reply.

"We rest," Miette said, "and then we review everything in the morning. We start from the very beginning and we make absolutely no assumptions. I have a terrible feeling that this is all coming to a very dangerous conclusion, and soon, so this is the time for patience.

"Time grows short, and we're only going to get one shot at this," Miette said, barely loud enough to be heard, "so we better get it right."

We're going to have to kill her, aren't we? Thad thought, and Lola's next words confirmed that she had reached the same conclusion.

"She's just a child," Lola said, staring at the young woman's school portrait.

"She's a killer nonetheless," Miette said sadly, placing a translucent hand on Lola's shoulder. "Sometimes there's no other choice."

"There's always a choice," Lola said, her voice shaking. Miette did not respond to this, however, and instead drifted upstairs to bed. Thad hesitated for a moment before planting a small kiss on Lola's cheek. He turned to look at her one last time before heading to get some rest, leaving her alone in the dark room.

  She was illuminated by the glow of the computer monitors and, try as he might, he could not drive the image of her silently weeping face from his mind.

Part Three: Night Terrors

Chapter Twenty Eight – A Bad Day to Die

Flora

How long have we been here? Flora wondered as Reggie led her through the starkly lit corridors of The Backrooms. It could've been mere minutes, but it just as likely could've been several years; as she'd said earlier, time flowed differently in the space between spaces.

I wonder if anyone has ever travelled back in time?

"They're getting closer," Reggie said softly as another Butler joined the pair that were already on their tail. "What will they do to us if they catch us?"

"If we're lucky, they'll just toss us out the nearest entrance," Flora replied, "although fuck knows where or, indeed, when, that will be."

"And if we're unlucky?" Reg asked nervously, glancing over his shoulder at the looming trio.

"Don't know," Flora admitted. "I've never met anyone who wasn't lucky."

"That does not fill me with confidence."

Flora was about to reply when the Familiar led her through several sharp turns in quick succession. Some part of her mind was certain that they should be back where they started, but the geography of The Backrooms was fluid and malleable at the best of times; especially so when a particularly esoteric route was being followed.

Suddenly the pair found themselves before a door emblazoned with seven symbols; a raven, lamp, drum, laurel wreath, sickle, torch, and a shepherd's staff. The faint golden threads of the Tangle overlaid the symbols, weaving together in the centre of the wood to create the image they'd seen outside the vape shop.

"Is this it?" Flora asked excitedly.

"I think so," Reggie replied, and eagerly reached for the latch, but the Faun grabbed his hand, pulling him sharply away from the door. "This is it, Flo; why are we waiting?"

"We need a plan," she replied, very aware that every second they lingered in the corridor made their situation more dangerous. She tried to gather her thoughts over the sound of her racing heart and took a deep breath before she continued. "From what Alice told me, they have a Tracer, a telepath of some kind, an Inferno, and a Fugue, along with some other Cep simply called Aunty.

"That's a formidable combination, even without the mystery fifth, and they are not going to be pleased to see us."

"Won't their gifts be underdeveloped?" Reggie asked, and Flora shrugged.

"No way to know. They'll be untrained and unpredictable, but that's no guarantee of how powerful they'll be." She glanced at the shadows on the corridor wall; they grew larger as the Butlers grew ever closer. "I'm tempted to try and hit them with a hypnotic song as soon as we go through the door, but if we're too far away it could tip our hand-"

"Just leave it to me, Flo," Reggie said calmly, patting his Barrel Organ. "I'll show them who's the boss around here."

"What is that thing?" she asked, but he merely

winked at her before opening the door. The two were dragged through into the howling darkness that lay beyond, sending them falling into the inky abyss.

Oh shit, Flora realised. *We're definitely gonna die.*

They hit the ground with a thud, accompanied by several sickening crunches. Flora screamed in pain as something punctured her abdomen, pushing all the way through her flesh and out the other side.

"FUCK!" She scrabbled in the darkness to pull out whatever had been driven through her, but Reggie stopped her.

"Flora, stop it!" he demanded. His demonic eyes glinted in the darkness and she realised that her own inhuman senses were adapting too; within a few seconds she could make out vague shapes and then details only moments later. He still held her trembling hand and, with a groan of fear, she looked down at her stomach.

"Is that a fucking bone!?" Flora said, disgusted. She looked around frantically and saw that the low room they were lying in was filled with skeletons and rats; in some places they were crammed in almost to the ceiling. "What the fuck? What the *actual* fuck?"

"It looks like the bone missed most of your organs," Reggie said, looking her over. "You might lose the kidney, depending on how quickly you can heal, but you'll live. We should leave it in, for now at least."

"No," Flora said, almost delirious with pain. "No fucking way."

"If we pull it out, you could die!"

"I won't die," Flora said, gritting her teeth. "This isn't how I die; not here, not today."

At least, I hope it isn't. The thought distracted her

enough for Reggie to pull the bone out of her flesh, and she let out another blood curdling scream as he did so. He tried to stem the bleeding with his hands, but she reached into her pocket and pulled out one of Gavin's special healing concoctions; enchanted moss covered with a herbal salve.

She plugged the wound with the sticky mossy mess and both the pain and bleeding began to subside almost immediately. *For all his faults,* she thought, *Gavin really is a talented Druid.*

Maybe the most skilled I've ever met, actually.

"Penny for them?" Reggie asked softly.

"Just thinking that Gavin is going to be unbearably smug that he saved my arse *again*, and from the comfort of the fucking Monty, to boot." Flora sighed heavily. "I kinda fucked our whole plan, didn't I?"

"We definitely don't have the element of surprise any longer," Reg replied diplomatically, "but we've still got a few tricks up our sleeves."

"That Inferno could just roast us alive," Flora muttered. "I can't drown, but I can burn as well as the next fucker."

"I'm fireproof," Reggie said with a small grin, "so I'd be fine."

"Bully for you, Devil Boy."

"Demon," he corrected.

"Different words for the same creature," she replied with a wave of her hand. "One just implies seniority."

"Who made you such an expert?" Reggie asked, raising an eyebrow as he helped Flora into an awkward crouch.

"I know people," she replied enigmatically, "and before you ask, our *association* is purely friendship; no deals, no bargains, and no sex."

"If you say so," Reggie said, clearly not believing a word she said.

"If you keep looking at me like that," Flora said playfully, "I'll kick you in the dick."

"Don't have one," he replied wryly.

"Want mine?" Flora quipped, and they both let out a small snicker. "Seriously, though, why the fuck did you bring that fucking hulk of a music box with you?"

"It was a gift from a friend," Reggie said. "He said that it would give me the power to turn the tide in our favour, especially if our only allies were dead. Speedy told me that-"

"Speedy?" Flora asked. "As in Speedball, of the Devil's Armchair?"

"Yeah, that's him." Reggie looked at her with a smile. "He's your Demon friend?"

"That he is, although he never lets me call him Speedy," Flora said almost jealously. "Small world, isn't it?"

"Sure is. Anyway, Speedy said that he managed to salvage some of the materials from something called Project Pandora, and apparently this will give the music the Barrel Organ makes supernatural properties.

"He didn't specify exactly what would happen, but he said that if I followed my instincts it would all work out just fine."

"He's a mad son of a bitch," Flora said as she began to clamber clumsily over the bones, "but he's rarely wrong about things like that. I actually feel a lot better knowing that he's on your side; Demons can be elusive and sly operators sometimes, but they're never dishonest.

"I'm glad you met him."

Project Pandora does ring a bell though, she

thought nervously, *and not a good one.*

The two struggled through the chamber of gnawed skeletons for a few minutes before Flora was finally able to see a sliver of sunlight up ahead. *Oh, please let that be some kind of exit.* She was so distracted by this that she barely noticed Reggie stop to examine the stone walls of the corridor they now stood in.

"What are you looking at, Reggie Brek?" she asked.

"Please stop calling me that," he replied, although his resigned tone revealed that he knew his request would be in vain. When Flora did not respond, he went on, running his clawed fingernails over the worn stone. "These walls are ancient; this must have been here since the Roman occupation!"

"How can you be sure?"

"The construction techniques are a dead giveaway, as is the mosaic work on the floor." He gestured at the filthy ground and Flora was able to make out a faint pattern of small tiles. "The architecture of this place looks like a cistern or sewer at first glance, but it has too many decorative flourishes to be just that."

"Do you think this is the Mithraeum?" Flora asked, and Reggie nodded. Something stirred in her memory, and her eyes grew wide with realisation. "Oh my god, Reggie, I know where we are! There used to be rumours of an old Roman drainage system under the town, and I found the entrance with Gav when we were just kids.

"This whole structure empties through a cave in the cliff side barely four hundred metres from the Monty! We've been staring right at it this whole fucking time!"

"If you knew about the entrance, why didn't you go in?" Reggie asked.

"Everyone said that the old Roman ruins were-" Her

words were cut off by a dark cackle from somewhere deeper in the ruins.

"Haunted?" Reggie whispered, and Flora nodded. He drew his revolver and handed it to her, taking care to place himself between the Faun and the source of the laughter.

Not a moment too soon, it seemed, as his motion was followed by a harsh cry.

"Abracadabra!" screamed a woman, casting a wave of bluebell flames down the tunnel. The fire illuminated her emaciated form; she was completely nude, covered only in filth and burn scars, and her sunken eyes were mad with murderous intent.

The fire parted around Reggie like water around a rock, shielding Flora from the searing flames. The heat still stung her skin and singed the tips of her hair, however, and she flipped the revolver's safety off, preparing to slay the Inferno where she stood.

"Tsk, tsk," Reggie said playfully. "That was not very nice of you."

"Go away!" shrieked the woman, readying another wave of fire in her hands.

"Somebody better teach you some manners," Reggie replied sharply.

"You and what army?" cried the Inferno.

I need to be quick, Flora thought, leaning around the Familiar to kill the pyrokinetic woman.

Before she could even take aim, though, Reggie had placed his clawed hand on the crank of the Barrel Organ, turning it at an even easy pace. The music that emerged from the instrument was unlike anything Flora had ever heard and it sickened her to the very depths of her soul; even her bones seemed to groan and scream in protest at the awful melody.

She caught a glimpse of jerky, unsteady motion in the tunnel behind them and brought the muzzle of the weapon around to fire on anyone who might be sneaking up on them. Flora was instead greeted to the sight of dozens, if not hundreds of quivering rats and twitching corpses surging along the tunnel towards her.

Is he controlling them!?

The Inferno seemed similarly horrified and took several fearful steps backwards, towards the light. It was only when Reggie and Flora were fully surrounded by the animated dead that he decided to address their assailant once again.

"We only came here to talk," he said with a grin, "so we can either do this the easy way, or the really easy way."

Moments later the Inferno was dragged aside by an older woman, equally ragged in appearance, with hands that ended in freakishly long trembling fingers. *The Fugue.*

"Set down your undead slaves," she said, her voice sharp and mean, "and then we will talk."

I still think this is going to end in bloodshed, Flora thought, but Reggie released his spell on the skeletons, sending them cascading and clattering to the floor. The Fugue grinned, steepling her terrifying fingers as she did so.

"A clever choice," she said. Her voice suggested that she was an older woman, but her intonation was almost childlike. "You can call me Mumsy. Welcome to my home."

Chapter Twenty Nine – Cargo Cults

Lola

"Oh, Bright Eyes, my wide eyes," Lola muttered in a singsong voice, "show me what you have seen."

Her fingers rattled over the keys and a sly smile crept on to her lips; her sneaking suspicion, the one that kept her up far later than Thad and Miette, had been correct. *Lola, darling,* she thought smugly, *you're a real marvel sometimes.*

"Tea?" Thad asked as he strolled into the living room, and Lola pointed at the freshly brewed pot on the table. "Not feeling chatty this morning?"

"I'm just pulling together some information for our briefing; I'll be more talkative shortly." She continued to bring up all the relevant information on to the various screens, including the crime scene photographs that tied the whole thing together.

Now all I need to do is find you, you slippery little fuckers.

"I wasn't aware that we were having a briefing today," Miette said as she drifted in, "but if you've found something important, please feel free to share with the class."

"So," Lola said excitedly, spinning around in her chair to face her colleagues, peering over her blue spectacles, "what do I know more about than anyone else in the Ministry?"

"Fucking hell," Miette groaned, pinching the bridge of her nose. "I hate games like these, Oriole, so please just get to the point."

"Fine." Lola tapped a few keys and the slaughtered

body of Elmyra Vane appeared on the screen, photographed from multiple different angles. "This is the murdered Arch-Druid. Please, tell me what you see."

"Lola is this really necessary?" Thad asked, rubbing his eyes sleepily. "We already know who our target is-"

"*One* of our targets, Thaddeus." Lola allowed herself a heartbeat of satisfaction as Miette looked on in shock, before continuing. "This is important for you to understand, so bear with me on this. I'll ask you once again; when you look at these photographs, what do you see?"

"Dismembered body parts," Thad said after a while. "Cannibalised, and arranged on the ground in a weird pattern."

"Same here," Miette said. "The arrangement of the body isn't of any Druidic significance, nor is the location particularly important."

They're so close, Lola thought, *and all they need is a change of perspective.*

"Thad, lovely, if you saw this," Lola said, tapping the screen, "in a horror movie, what would you think it was?"

"Given how deliberately the bones are arranged, I'd think it was some kind of ritual or magic spell..." His voice trailed off as he looked at Lola in shock. "Lo, you know more about magic than anyone else in the Ministry, don't you?"

"Bingo," she said, flashing Thad a wide smile. "After all, I was the head of a coven for a very long time and I managed to pull off some pretty spectacular witchcraft, if I say so myself."

"So this is a spell?" Miette asked.

"No," Lola said. "Not at all."

"Then why is this relevant?" Miette asked.

"It's not a spell," Thad said slowly, "but it *does* look like one."

"Go on, Thad," Lola said, enjoying the spectacle of the scales falling from his eyes.

"Whoever did this thought they were casting a spell, so either this person is deeply unwell or they have some kind of evidence that suggests their *magic*, for want of a better word, is working." He blinked for a few seconds as the pieces fell into their final places. "Whoever did this is a Cep, but I don't think they know what they actually are, so their gift seems just like magic."

"Bravo." Lola grinned proudly at him. "You've a real knack for this, Thane."

"But any adult would quickly realise what was happening, wouldn't they?" Thad asked.

"Normally, yes," Lola replied, "but you do get exceptions in certain insular religious communities. However, this is not that, which would mean what, Thad?"

A look of absolute horror crept on to Thad's face as he finally realised what had happened.

"This was done by a child, wasn't it?"

"I never realised that Hags were actually real," Thad whispered after Lola had finished explaining how such monstrous creatures were formed. He raised his voice to ask his next question. "So the Hag that did this is probably a physical adult, but it still has the mindset of a child?"

"Yes," Lola replied, "albeit a deeply disturbed one."

Miette had settled in the armchair in the corner of

the room, huddled up with her head in her hands and keening softly. *She's not taking this news well,* the Juliet thought, *but hopefully the rest of what I have to show them will make her feel a little bit better.*

"Do we even know where they are?" Thad asked.

"Not yet," Lola said, and Miette let out a wounded howl as she pulled at her thin translucent hair. The Juliet looked at the Sylph in horror. "What's wrong?"

"We're fucked," Miette moaned. "We had one fucking mission and we've fucked it. Desai will have us all fucking killed!"

"Miette," Lola began, but the Sylph stared at her with wild eyes, red rimmed from crying, cutting her off immediately.

"We can run," she said frantically. "You've both got a plan for this, haven't you?"

"A plan for what?" Thad asked.

"A plan to escape the Ministry," she shrieked. "You must have something; you were in that fucking prison for months!"

"I'm sorry, Miette," Lola said softly, "but all roads lead to home, and Betony Island is where we belong."

"You're like a kicked puppy," Miette spat at the Juliet. "No matter how badly we treat you, you keep coming back to do as you're told."

Silence.

"Maybe she believes that even though the Ministry has done some terrible things," Thad said eventually, "there's still something good at the heart of it. Maybe we believe in mercy, Miette."

"Besides," Lola said, entering a few commands into the computer to bring up a new image, "I think our friends from the Hotel Montresor might lead us right to them."

Miette leant forward to stare at the short clip of Flora Cain and Reginald Kellogg vanishing into a Nifty Way outside a vape shop in the centre of Torquay. A faint golden image lingered in the air behind them; a crude piece of line art of a man wrestling a bull, hidden in the very fabric of the Tangle.

"When did they go in?" Miette asked.

"Yesterday at dawn," Lola replied. "I've got a priority search on all the cameras in a hundred mile radius to find them when they emerge."

"Is the image of the man and bull important?" Thaddeus asked.

"It's a sign of Mithras," Miette said softly. "That means that there's a Mithraeum, an underground temple, somewhere around here. Do you think that's where the Hags are hiding?"

"Almost certainly," Lola said, "and when our friends find it, so will we."

"Have you considered pinging their phones?" Thad asked, almost off-handedly.

I am a fucking idiot, Lola thought, blinking in surprise. *Why did I not think of that?*

"Lo," Thad said, a quiet smile creeping on to his face, "you *were* tracking their phones already, weren't you?"

"I may have overlooked that," Lola said, rapidly updating Bright Eyes' protocols in an attempt to find mobile data for both Flora and Reggie. Thad snickered slightly. "Laugh it up, Skeleton Boy, but I'm still the one that cracked this case."

"Oh, I know," Thad replied, "but it's nice to know that I'm not lagging *that* far behind."

"What if they ditch their phones?" Miette asked. "I

don't even have a phone."

"Flora Cain is an influencer," Thad replied. "She'd sooner part with her heart than her phone. It might also be worth tracking everyone else at the Montresor, just in case Flora is out of service."

"How would that find the Mithraeum?" Miette said.

"If Flora is in trouble," Thad said with exaggerated patience, "her friends will go and help her."

"Got her," Lola said, tapping to a monitor with the map. "According to her location data, she's only been back on the grid for an hour or so, which is promising. The signal is weak, however, so we can assume she's underground.

"That does present a problem, however; Thad, you won't be able to take the route to the Mithraeum that they did, and even if you could it would cost us at least a day." Lola frowned. "We'll have to wait for them to come to the surface to find our way in."

"We'd still be walking into a fucking bloodbath," Miette said sadly. "We have no idea how many members this coven has, nor what gifts they possess."

"Don't we?" Lola asked playfully, tapping a few more keys.

"How?" Miette said as five different faces filled the computer screens.

"Missing persons cases, along with police reports that detail hints of supernatural gifts gone awry. Once I realised what we were looking at, it was actually quite simple to find them. So, lovelies, shall we meet our Hags?"

"Our first was the hardest to find," Lola said as she brought up a black and white photograph of a young woman. Both Thad and Miette flinched at the sight of her freakishly long crooked fingers. "Records state that her name was Dana Hall and she disappeared at the age of fourteen; this was almost forty years ago now. Strangely, her vanishing was never reported by any of the staff at the children's home she was living at; in fact, they had no memory of her whatsoever.

"This, combined with her physical appearance, suggests that she is a Fugue. I'd wager that she is the oldest and most senior member of the coven, able to manipulate their minds and memories to keep control of them."

"If we take her out, will they descend into chaos?" Thad asked.

"No way to be sure, but there's a chance that another of the Hags will assume her place fairly quickly." Miette frowned as she spoke. "Having a Fugue in the mix is not encouraging. We've never actually tested whether Tabs and Famines are immune to the gifts of a Fugue, so it's a real risk to put you into combat, Thane."

"He's a decent sniper," Lola said, giving Thad a smile. "He managed to score a hit on Gideon in very unfavourable circumstances. If there's a chance that we can put you on overwatch, Thad, we'll do that, just to be safe.

"Still, even though her powers are technically the weakest, Hall is the greatest threat; if you get the chance, nail her first."

"Will do."

"You'll need a suppressed rifle," Lola said, "and you'll need to get her with your first shot."

"Why?" Miette asked, and Lola switched pictures to another teenage girl.

"This is Emily Matthews. Her home was destroyed

the same day she disappeared; the type and level of damage to the building, along with eyewitness accounts of her behaviour as a child, suggests that she is telekinetic." Lola saw Thad's eyes widen. "She may even be a Fulcrum, so she'll be powerful enough to deflect your shots. Her lack of training will make her vulnerable, however, so I will deal with her in close quarters."

"Kill the Fugue, then let you two deal with the Fulcrum whilst I watch your backs?" Thad asked and Lola shook her head.

"The Fulcrum is one of the few types of human that could kill me outright," Miette said, "and you'll need a spotter with decent night eyes."

"Not to mention that you can calm the wind to give him an easier shot," Lola said. "Handling the close combat myself won't be easy, but I'll manage."

I got out of Lamplight, she thought, *and I'll get out of this just as handily.*

"What else are we looking at?" Miette asked, and Lola rattled through the rest of the Hags; the Tracer, the Inferno, and, finally, the telepath. "Will you be able to deal with her?"

"I've killed more than one telepath in my time," Lola said, shuddering with the memory. "I'll need a little time to get some toys together, but I think I can do it."

"And if you fail?" Thad asked.

"Then come in after me," Lola said with a grin, "and show them exactly what a Famine is capable of."

"That sounds like a plan to me," Thad said, and Miette nodded. "So what do we do now?"

"We search for the entrance, one way or another," Lola replied. "The phone ping is our most likely bet, so we just get our gear together and sit tight until our friends from the Montresor make contact."

"Hurry up and wait?" Thad said, clearly disgruntled.

"Welcome to the Ministry, kid," Lola said with a chuckle. "Now get to prepping your gear; we might have to go sooner than you think."

"What makes you say that?" Miette said, and Lola eyed the dark clouds that were gathering on the southern horizon.

"Just a feeling," she replied softly. "A very bad feeling."

Chapter Thirty – Better the Devil You Know

Flora

I don't feel good about this, Flora thought as she and Reggie followed the Fugue deeper into the maze-like Temple of Mysteries. She contemplated sending Gavin a quick message to tell him what they'd found, but her mobile signal was spotty at best.

A dark shape was shifting from shadow to shadow ahead of them, jabbering like some madman; she was certain that this was the Tracer that Alice had mentioned. Moving through darkness was not a common gift for that particular species of Cep, but it wasn't unheard of either.

Still, Flora thought, *if we were to suddenly illuminate the shadow he was moving through, there's a strong chance he would end up fused with the wall.*

That would certainly even our odds a little.

"You shouldn't think such nasty thoughts about us," hissed a voice from her right, and she turned to face a ragged woman in her early twenties, a mop of matted hair plastered to the sides of her face. Her pale eyes were constantly darting back and forth, occasionally squinting to focus on a particular person.

"Do you need to pin a person's thoughts down to hear them?" Flora asked, almost conversationally, in an attempt to gauge the skill of the telepath. "Or do they just drift in, like stray radio broadcasts or whispers in the dark?"

"I have to focus," the telepath hissed, "but when I

do, I can make you do or believe anything that I want. I can even make you hurt yourself."

There was a pause as the filthy woman leaned in closer, her fetid breath souring Flora's usually strong stomach.

"I like to make people hurt themselves, but I especially like to make them hurt each other."

I'm sure you do, you little freak, Flora thought, but there was no backlash from the telepath. Instead she stalked away into the shadows of the Mithraeum. She and Reggie turned a corner, and were suddenly confronted with the mouth of a wide cave that looked out over the sunlit waters of Torbay. The roar of the surf was almost deafening as it echoed around the rocky surface of the Mithraeum.

"Holy shit," Flora muttered as her eyes adjusted to the glare of the sun glittering on the surface of the sea. "You can see the Monty from here!"

"Is this close to the old entrance that you and Gavin found as kids?" Reggie whispered, and she nodded. "Well, at least if we need to get out of here in a hurry, I know I can make that trip."

"You shouldn't whisper," snapped the Fugue, glaring at them both. "Whispering children get punished. Now, tell me why you are here."

"We come on behalf of the young woman that you are trying to recruit into your coven," Flora said firmly. "You think that you can control her power, but she's already far too dangerous for you to survive her reaching the peak of her potential. Your coven will be destroyed, and you will unleash a tremendous horror upon this world."

"What is it you want?"

"We need your help to protect her," Flora said,

"whilst we help her get her power under control. She won't be one of you, but when we are done, we promise to leave you in peace."

"They're lying, Mumsy," hissed the telepath, a wicked grin on her face. Her eyes glinted with cruel malice as she spoke. "They want her for their own, and they won't leave us in peace. We should give them to Aunty.

"She'll punish them and make them pay for their lies and their whispers."

The Fugue, Mumsy, scowled at Flora and Reggie, before raising her twitching fingers. She took a step towards them and Flora raised the revolver, pointing it at the telepath, even though she could already feel the sinister woman's thoughts trying to worm their way into her head.

Reggie, on the other hand turned on his heel and scratched the crude outline of a door into the rock with his silver florin, before rapping on it smartly with the knuckles of his left hand. There was a sharp cracking sound and the rock door swung open.

"Morning, morning, one and all," said a cheerful man in a torn and crumpled suit as he swaggered through the newly created portal. His straw blond hair and gilded teeth were almost luminous in the golden morning light. "Deary me, what a pickle we seem to be in!"

"Abracadabra!" yelled the Inferno, but the fireball in her hand crackled and fizzled into nothing. The burned woman looked at her hand in horror, and then fearfully at Speedball as he grinned nastily at her.

"Fire is the Devil's gift, child," he said, his rich voice echoing around the cave far more than should've been possible, "and it's impolite to throw such a prize back in someone's face, either literally or metaphorically.

"As such, consider your pyromaniacal privileges temporarily revoked. As for you," he said to the telepath, "someone needs to teach you what happens to liars, especially little shit-stirrers like you."

Speedball raised his hand up into a sharply curled claw and gestured towards the telepath, who let out a shriek of terror just as he punctuated the gesture with a snide laugh. Flora lowered the gun as the woman scratched at her own face, almost as if she was terrified that it would vanish the very next second.

"Oh, do quit crying! I didn't *actually* do anything to you... not this time, anyway," Speedball said through his devilish chuckles. His eyes flashed with dark fire mere seconds later, however, and his voice grew considerably harsher. "Still, consider that your only warning, and the same goes for you, *Mumsy*; get your fucking house in order or there will be hell to pay."

"Abracadabra!" screamed the Inferno, throwing both of her hands out towards the Demon. Where she expected a fireball, though, there was only the barest crackle of sparks. Speedball sighed heavily, and held up a finger to Flora and Reggie.

"One moment, darlings," he said, before walking over to the burned woman, snatching her up by the throat, and slamming her head into the jagged stone wall, over and over again. "I. WILL. NOT. TOLERATE. THIS."

His words were punctuated by the sound of her shattering skull as it split under the force of his vicious blows; the noise grew wetter with each impact as flecks of blood, flesh, and brain spattered on his tattered suit. He let go of her ruined corpse with a disgusted grimace and turned back to face the Fugue, who had been watching on with horror.

"Now, you long fingered freak, as much as I would love to open up and unleash a spot of unspeakable violence on you and yours, I understand that my friends need your help, so I'll let you live for now." He let out a mirthful chuckle. "Besides, as much as I would enjoy myself, I'm always on the clock and this arse doesn't shake for free.

"Still, consider yourself formally on notice." He grinned at Mumsy and the other two Hags before turning to look at Flora and Reggie. "And people think the Angels are scary! Sure, those feathered freaks can fuck you up good, but they don't *enjoy* their work nearly as much as we do; I've been told that being flayed alive is horrifying, but nowhere near as much as being flayed by someone who so obviously gets off on it.

"Still, darlings, how are you doing," he wiped the gore from his suit, "violent outbursts notwithstanding?"

"As always, I'm glad to see you," Flora said, greeting the Demon with an exaggerated kiss to the side of each cheek.

"Yes, mwah mwah," Speedball said, "but get a little taste of this!"

He pulled Flora in close and kissed her deeply, sending her mind into a whirl of erotic bliss and agonising ecstasy. This kiss lasted only a few seconds, but it took almost a minute for her mind to clear completely.

"Fucking hell," she said softly, "what was that?"

"Lola Oriole," he replied proudly, "pure and unfettered. Oh, if you think those poison lips of hers are divine, you should taste her pussy."

"How?" The one word was all Flora could manage as thoughts of Lola filled her mind.

"Everyone needs something, babe," he said slyly, "and she asked so very nicely. Still, I think I got the lion's share of the bargain."

"Don't you always?" Reggie asked.

"Not always, Your Highness," Speedball answered, and then handed Reggie a faded piece of parchment. "You best go and tell your friends where we are; that map will show you the cliff path to get back down here."

"Will you look after Flora?" Reggie asked, and the Demon nodded. "Then we'll be back soon. One last thing, Speedy; stop calling me 'Your Highness'."

There was a crackle of static as the Familiar teleported to the Hotel Montresor.

"Yes, Daddy," Speedball said with mock innocence, before rounding on the Hags. "Time to hop to it, you mad wretches; we've work to do!"

"Are you jealous?" the Demon asked as they prepared a ritual altar at the back of the cave, near the entrance to the Mithraeum.

"About what?" Flora asked.

"You know damn well what!" he replied.

"Okay, yeah," she admitted, "a little, but why does he get to call you Speedy and I don't?"

"What?" Speedball blinked in surprise. "Oh, Flora, babe, you can call me whatever you want!"

"Oh," she said, surprised. "What were you talking about?"

"That I got to nail Oriole, obviously!"

"I'm not," she lied. "I'm not sure why you keep talking about it, though."

"A little post-coital cucking makes the fucking that much sweeter," he said playfully. "I'm serious, though, Flora; I can see why you like her so much. I could torture that little morsel from now until the end of time."

"I don't want to torture her!" she hissed, trying to keep their uneasy allies from hearing their conversation. "I don't see the appeal of that at all."

"You will, darling," Speedy assured her. "Seeing that impossibly beautiful face all bruised and plastered with cum, only for those black acidic tears to cut little channels through all that violence and spunk..."

He shuddered with pleasure.

"Darling, it's so repulsive that it goes all the way around to being arousing again." He sighed heavily. "She almost made me wish that I could feel love, just to make the betrayal that much sweeter. I'm serious, Flora, you have to fuck that violet-eyed confection of trauma and abuse; she will rock your fucking world."

"Are you this disgusting with everyone?" Flora asked, even as her cheeks flushed red with arousal. *What is wrong with me? I can't possibly find any of that appealing!*

"It's the company I keep," Speedy said with a wink, "and as for your little crisis of conscience, of course you're turned on by this. You're half Rusałka, babe; sexual predation is in your blood, so just enjoy the mental images. Deep down you know you wouldn't harm a hair on that little sugarplum's head...

"Would you?"

Flora couldn't bring herself to answer, so she busied herself in the preparations for that evening's ritual. The Hags had assured them that the rite would enable Alice to fully access her powers without limitation;

unfortunately, though, it would deepen her insomnia and she would need to consume the dreams of others in order to survive.

I don't think Alice would be comfortable doing that, she thought. *I hope Gavin and the others have some luck finding some other way for her to sustain herself.*

"Oh, before the others arrive," Speedy hissed in Flora's ear, "I should probably warn you that Lola and her posse are likely to crash the show this evening, and she might be feeling a little conflicted towards you."

"Why?" Flora asked, already dreading the answer.

"When we had our little... *interlude*, shall we say," Speedball said playfully, "I was glamoured up to look like you."

"Why the fuck would you do that?" Flora said, having to hold back the anger in her voice.

"The same reason I do anything, darling; because she wanted me to."

Flora stared at him in stunned silence as he winked at her before bustling over to help the Hags with the ritual preparations.

She wanted him to? Flora thought, both horrified and thrilled all at once. *She wanted him to look like me!?*

Does that mean that she wants me as much as I want her?

<u>Chapter Thirty One – All Hell Breaks Loose</u>

Gavin

"I'll need to eat dreams just to survive?" Alice asked, her face dropping. She idly played with the silver locket in much the same way Lucy had, and Gavin was too struck by the similarity between the two to answer her question.

"It definitely looks that way, but we'll figure something out, Alice," Leroy said kindly. "We're a resourceful bunch, aren't we, Gav?"

"That we are," Gavin managed to say. *You could've been my daughter,* he thought sadly, *but life never seems to work out the way it should.* He dug deep and gave Alice a reassuring smile. "You've certainly taken a shine to that locket."

"It's a lovely thing," Alice replied, but something in her expression troubled Gavin.

"What's wrong?" he asked.

"Did she give it to you just before she died?" Alice said, and he nodded. "I thought as much; there's a lot of her in it, but there's a lot of you in there too."

"I gave it to her instead of an engagement ring," he said quietly. "It was supposed to bind us together, forever."

"You're a hopeless romantic, brother," Leroy said with a smile, but Alice was still examining the locket keenly. "Careful, Alice; you might hypnotise yourself with that!"

"How long has all this been going on?" she asked

after a few minutes of silence, suddenly staring at Gavin. "All the supernatural shit; how long has it been around?"

"For as long as there have been people," Coral said, "and maybe even longer. Don't worry, Alice; you're not the first person to go through something like this."

"That's what's troubling me," she said, angrily fastening the locket around her neck before gesturing at the huge assortment of books and papers before them. "Humans tell stories, we keep records, and we write shit down!

"Why isn't there just one big fucking book of all this shit?"

Gavin and Leroy stared at her in stunned silence, whilst Coral let out a low whistle.

"I"m serious! Why isn't there some fucking encyclopedia of monsters and freaks? We've got Gray's Anatomy for medicine, but nothing for this!?" Alice slumped back in her chair. "I can't believe that nobody has put all the centuries and millennia of research into one place."

"From the mouths of babes," Coral said with a slight chuckle.

"What's so funny?" Alice snapped.

"There is a book like that," Leroy said, "and it is one of the most carefully guarded secrets in the supernatural world."

"Then why is she fucking laughing?" Alice said gesturing angrily at Coral.

"Because we got a copy of it about three days ago," Coral said through her giggles, "but given all that's happened between now and then, we fucking forgot about it."

"Good work, Alice," Gavin said, rising from his seat

to retrieve The White Book. "If you can sharpen that deductive instinct even further, maybe you could work for the Ministry one day."

Alice muttered a reply, but he didn't hear as he trotted upstairs to his room. He reached into his dresser after fumbling with the key for a few seconds and closed his fingers around the little tablet with an audible exhalation of relief.

He jogged down the stairs, taking them two at a time, and then strode across the lounge to hand the tablet to Alice. She hesitated for a moment before taking it, powering it on and flicking through the menu with all the skill and practised ease of one who has grown up with such technology.

"Don't you want to look it up?" she asked as she browsed through the entries.

"It's yours to know, not mine," Gavin said. "It would feel like an invasion of your privacy if I saw your entry before you did."

Alice looked up at him, blinking in surprise.

"Thank you," she said after a moment. "That's... yeah, thank you."

"Not a problem," Gavin said, smiling sheepishly. "You're a person; you deserve to be treated like one."

"Am I a gifted human, semi-human, or non-human person?" Alice asked.

"A gifted human," Leroy answered. "A Shaper, specifically. For what it's worth, I'm a semi-human, and Rizz is a non-human."

"What?" Paris said as he sat up suddenly at the mention of his name, dropping the book that he'd been reading for some hours already.

"Hey, Rizz," Coral said, "is there a copy of the Beano hidden in there?"

"He seems more like a Dandy man to me," Gavin said with a chuckle.

"Hey, you both know that I don't read comics," said the unnaturally beautiful man with a charming smile. "They have way too many long words in them for me."

"Then what have you been looking at?" Alice asked.

"One of Gavin's Druid books," he said, picking up the ageing tome to show them. The pages were covered in patterns of branching lines, and Gavin's eyes widened in surprise.

"That's Ogham, Rizz!" he said, barely able to contain his shock. "Can you actually read that?"

"Yeah," Paris replied. "One knock for yes, two for no; it's not complicated."

"That's not..." Gavin began, but he stopped when he saw the twinkle in Paris's eyes. *You're not anywhere as silly as you want us to think, are you?*

"Fucking hell," Alice said angrily, and everyone turned to look at her. "There are people that can turn invisible and mind readers, but vampires aren't real? That's such fucking bullshit!"

"You're supposed to be looking up your own entry," Gavin said, but he couldn't help but chuckle a little.

"I already have," Alice said. "It didn't have much in there, but it did say that I can subsist on something call Nyx's Nectar instead of eating people's dreams, but it doesn't say where you can get it, so I assumed it would be a dead end."

"That sounds familiar," Gavin said. "I'm sure I've heard of that before, but I can't quite remember where. Still, something is better than nothing. Maybe if I-"

"Moon Liquor," Rizz said, reading authoritatively from the book he'd been slowly working through, "also known as Dream Syrup, Orphean Slumber, or-"

"Nyx's Nectar!" Gavin said, getting to his feet. Paris handed him the book with a smile. Gavin marked the page with a finger as he checked the inside of the cover; the note was just as he remembered, and he read it aloud. "To my only son, who I'm sure will need this one day; dream big and live bigger.

"Much love, Dad."

"Malcolm's still taking you to school, even now," Coral said with a grin. "Do you think you'll be able to make the magic moonshine, Gav?"

"It's a very complicated process with an incredibly esoteric ingredient list," he said. "It would require either an extremely talented chemist or an extraordinarily gifted Druid; luckily, I happen to be both."

He closed the book with a sharp snap.

"So you can make it?" Alice said, looking hopeful for the first time since he'd brought her back to the Monty.

"Blindfolded with one arm tied behind my back," he said with a wide grin. "See, I told you we'd-"

He was cut off as Reggie materialised in the centre of the lounge, covered in stinking filth and tiny little fragments of what looked like bone. The Familiar took a moment to catch his breath and then grinned at the assembled group.

"We found it," he said gleefully. "We fucking found it!"

"Reg," Gavin said anxiously, "where's Flora?"

"She's safe; I left her with a friend. They're preparing things as we speak, and we'll need to head out soon, but we've got a real shot at getting this under control, Alice."

"Tell us everything!" Leroy said excitedly, but Reggie headed towards the Schooner, preceded by Coral, who clearly had anticipated his next words.

"I'll explain it all to you momentarily," he panted, "but first I need a stiff drink!"

The route along the cliff side was treacherous, especially for the sleep deprived Alice, but Speedball's map was highly detailed and did not steer them wrong in the slightest. Gavin kept hold of Alice's hand the entire way, which he would've done anyway with a smaller child, but what surprised him was the fact that she reached for him almost as soon as they left the safety of the hotel.

Colossal storm clouds gathered on the darkening horizon, plunging the otherwise bright summer day into an eerie twilight. His Druidic instincts told him that the turbulent skies were directly related to the power that resided in the conflicted heart of Alice Mann and, for the first time, he truly understood why Lucy had been so afraid of her own child.

Still, I will face this fear instead of running from it, he thought, steeling himself for the ordeal that was certain to take place that night. *I will succeed where Lucy failed.*

Gavin, Alice, and Paris continued to follow Reggie down the cliff path towards the mouth of a monstrous cave, taking care not to lose their footing on the slippery rocks, slick with spray from the churning sea below. Coral and Leroy had remained at the Montresor, but they had taken up sniper positions in the upstairs windows in order to provide covering fire for the others should the Ministry Agents try to interrupt the impending ritual.

Instead of being greeted at the mouth of the cave by Flora, they were instead ushered inside by a man with gold teeth who greeted Reggie like an old friend. *This must be the infamous Speedball*, Gavin thought; anyone who moved in the supernatural world of Torquay had heard of the Golden Grinned Demon of the Devil's Armchair. *I knew he palled around with Flora, but it's no surprise he knows Reg.*

"Good evening, darlings," Speedball said, and quickly introduced himself to Alice. "A pleasure to finally meet the Illuminated Man, herself. We'll have to skip the more formal introductions, I'm afraid, but you can simply call me Uncle Speedy.

"Unfortunately, the situation inside is somewhat tense and I fear that we'll have a few *agitating elements* bearing down on us sooner rather than later, so there's a good chance this is all going to go very wrong, but, dear Alice," he continued as he helped her into the mouth of the cave, "here's the plan, in the broadest of strokes.

"Flora's going to give you a little something to put you to sleep, and then one of the Hags is going to help you find the part of your mind that's divided. Whilst we do that, we'll be putting Gavin under, too, so that he can help you find and heal the wound that's making your power unstable."

"Are you sure I'm the right person?" Gavin asked. "Wouldn't you or-"

"It has to be you," Speedy said firmly. "Just trust me on this. It's normally one of the Hags, but you don't want them picking around in her head. Also, dream sharing is something that only humans have ever really been any good at."

There's something you're not telling me, Gavin

thought, but a deep rumble of thunder from the approaching storm sent Alice striding deeper into the cave, away from the churning sea. Gav went to follow her, but the Demon caught his arm sharply as he walked past. Paris and Reggie stood beside the two of them.

"Listen to me," Speedy whispered to the assembled men, "as soon as that girl is under, all that power is going to come out of her with the force of a nuclear fucking bomb. That storm is going to be unlike anything we've ever seen, along with who knows what else coming along for the ride.

"What ever is happening inside her head needs to be resolved quickly, Gavin," Speedy continued, "and *permanently*. If you don't manage that... well, I dare say there won't be much of a Torquay to wake up to."

"What about the Hags?" Reggie asked. "Will they attack when we put Alice under?"

"They might," Speedball said, "but if they do, Flora and I will fight them off to the best of our abilities."

A flash of lightning lit up the evening sky, and Gavin shuddered at the thought of such power coming from one frightened teenage girl.

"We can help-" Paris began, but Speedball shook his head.

"The two of you will need to hold back the storm as best you can," the Demon said.

"How?" Reggie asked.

"Music," Speedball said. "It's the stuff of dreams, and it can be used to keep the waking nightmares in check. Paris, Flora mentioned that you were a bit of a dab hand with a fiddle, so this is for you."

The Demon handed Rizz an instrument made of blackened wood, criss-crossed with bright white lines that resembled the burns a victim of a lightning strike would suffer. Instead of rosin, Speedy licked the hair of the bow, coating it in black fire. Paris looked at the fiddle suspiciously, but the Demon waved his concerns away with an idle hand.

"This is a gift, pure and simple," he said, "no strings attached, if you'll pardon the pun."

"What is that made from?" Gavin asked. "The True Cross?"

"Don't be so gauche, darling," Speedy said with a smile. "It's the fig tree that Christ cursed, struck down by Angelic fire. Don't ask me how I got my hands on it, though; it's too long a story for a single lifetime."

There was a huge boom of thunder, followed by a ripple through the Tangle that was so powerful that even Gavin could feel it. He looked deeper into the cave and saw Flora and one of the Hags standing over Alice's sleeping form.

"It's started," Speedball said, looking at Paris and Reggie. "Time to get you to bed, Mr Strangeways."

Before he could reply, Speedy turned and blew a handful of powder into Gavin's face. It quickly entered his eyes, nose, and mouth, causing his body to collapse to the ground with a painful thud. Try as he might, Gavin could not move as one of the Hags came closer; hopefully to guide his mind into Alice's dreams.

"Sorry, sweetie," Speedy said, "but time really is of the essence and you've some serious work to do. Now, you boys-"

The first of the gunshots were lost in the cacophony of thunder and waves that rolled in from the stormy sea, but Gavin saw the bullets rip through the Demon as he stood in the entrance to the cave. The Arch-

Druid tried to rise from where he lay, but the drugs were already working through his system, untethering him from reality.

The last thing he thought he heard before he succumbed to the dream state was Flora's voice, yelling musically through the roar of the oncoming storm.

"Play, Paris, play!"

Chapter Thirty Two – Ante Up

Lola

The first lightning strike knocked Lola's drone completely offline and she swore as she clambered out of the little beach hut, only to be almost swept off her feet by the force of the wind. It took her a few seconds to regain her footing, and then she took off running towards the cliff path that the party from the Hotel Montresor had taken.

If only I'd had thirty seconds more, she thought angrily, *the drone would've given me a complete map of the route down to the cave.*

As it stood now, she would just have to chance it, but given the way the tumultuous waves were slamming into the rocks at the waterline, any misstep would certainly be fatal. Lola tried to drive the image of her body being shattered against the cliff from her mind, but the fear of drowning in both seawater and her own blood almost stopped her dead in her tracks.

Get your shit together, Lola, she thought angrily, and continued on her way, hopping on to the first ledge that would eventually take her to the cave edge. *At least the Inferno is down.*

The drone had been hovering near the mouth of the Mithraeum when her demonic acquaintance had smashed the poor girl's skull to smithereens against the red rock of the cave walls. Whilst Thad and Miette had initially been sceptical about Speedball giving assistance to the Montresor crew, Lola had taken it as a good sign.

"He must've known that we'd be watching," she

muttered as she hauled herself up on to the next ledge. "I know he wanted us to see what was happening, to see his part in all of this; I'm sure of it."

Admittedly, she did not know why, and the possibility of coming up against an unleashed Reginald Kellogg scared the shit out of her, but she had a job to do. A part of her secretly hoped that Flora, Gavin, and the others would assist her in the fight against the Hags if it came down to that, but they most certainly would not let her harm the child.

That's fine by me, Lola thought. *I don't care what Thad and Miette said; she doesn't need to die.*

The Ministry has killed too many children already.

"Lola!" Thad called out, his voice almost deafening in her earpiece. "Lola, someone is shooting into the cave!"

"At the Hags?"

"No; the Demon is down. He took at least one bullet to the head!" Thad clarified. "Miette saw muzzle flashes from the Montresor; do you want me to take them out?"

"No!" Lola yelled as she picked up her pace, clambering down the slippery rock face as the storm exploded into life around her. "Do not reveal your position until you can kill the Fugue; that is a fucking order."

"And after that?" The man's usually calm voice broke as he spoke, revealing just how terrified he was.

"Just cover me when I'm inside the cave; the angle they'll have from the hotel means that they won't be able to shoot very far in." She paused for a moment. "Miette, throw some crosswind up around the hotel, though, just to be on the safe side.

"I'd rather not get nailed in the back as I'm climbing

down. Lola, out."

Her motions grew quicker and more reckless as she went, driven by both fear and desperation.

The faster you move, the less likely you are to fall, she thought, remembering one of Gideon's many lessons. *Until, of course, one day you plummet for the very last time.*

She reached for her next handhold, but a rumble of thunder startled her so badly that she lost her footing and her one handed grip on the cliff face was not enough to hold her weight.

Letting out a scream as she did so, Lola slipped off the cliff and fell towards the churning sea.

Lola was curled up in Gideon's lap as he gently ran his fingers through her hair, his nails trailing pleasurably against her scalp. Even though she'd had him under her spell for almost a decade at that point, there was still a surprising amount of his personality left; most people's minds were wiped away entirely after a few days, but the Vortex was, for better or worse, different somehow.

"How are you still here?" Lola asked, turning her head to look at him as the setting sun glittered on the waters of the Thames Estuary. As much as Lola would've liked to have lived on the mainland, until she was old enough for her partnership with Gideon to not draw any unwanted attention, they lived on a small island just down the coast from Allhallows.

"What do you mean, songbird?" Frost replied, using his favourite nickname for the teenager that was simultaneously his pet and captor.

"You're still you," Lola said, getting to her feet. "You can still think and act for yourself, even after all these years; how do you manage it?"

"I'm a good dancer," Gideon said wryly, before deftly hopping up from the armchair they so often shared. Lola was pleased to see that today was one of his better days, and he didn't seem to need his slender cane at all; her joy was brittle, however, as Gideon's good days were often followed by Lola's most horrific nights.

He held out a hand and she placed her fingers delicately in his. He tightened his grip suddenly and shoved her backwards, stopping her short of falling with a sharp tug on her wrist. She yelped in pain and he let go, sending her sprawling on the carpet. He bent down, his eyes blazing with the fire that had scared her as a small child and absolutely terrified her now.

"Try and hit me, songbird."

"Why?" Lola asked, her voice trembling as she rose from the carpet. "What's the point?"

"I'm teaching you a valuable lesson." His smile faded immediately. "Try and hit me, Lola, or this will only get worse for you."

She growled and lunged forwards, but he artfully redirected her momentum and sent her slamming into the wall. Lola roared with rage and snatched up an icepick from Gideon's small bar and tried to stab him with it.

Once again, he deftly used her own motion against her and brought the sharp implement mere millimetres from her eye as her breath came in ragged gasps. *Is he going to put that in my brain?* Lola thought fearfully; she'd seen what trans-orbital lobotomies had done to some of the children on Betony Island.

"What you need to understand," Gideon said, still holding the point dangerously close to her eye, "is that fighting someone or something is a dialogue; a deft debate, if you will."

He tossed the icepick aside and pulled her in close, leading her in a dance to a melody that only he could hear. The two moved as one, spinning and stepping with almost supernatural grace, and suddenly Lola began to understand.

"It's easy to move in synch with someone, my love, but much harder to suddenly break the rhythm and shout over them; your venom is constantly trying to speak over my own thoughts, but it will never be as loud as I am deft." He kissed her gently. "Fighting is a dialogue, a rolling rhythm of lethal motion, and if you give it just the right nudge, you can break someone's flow and end their life in an instant.

"You don't need to be a Vortex to master that, child."

"Sometimes you shout over me," she said softly, a single burning tear rolling down her cheek.

"That's only because you won't dance with me willingly," he said with a cruel smile. "Then again, that's the best part about it, songbird, which makes fucking you just as sweet as killing you, only I get to do it over and over again.

"You might've won the war, little one," he said softly, leaning in to whisper into her ear as his fingers began to creep underneath her dress, "but I'm going to make you pay for that victory for as long as you live."

Unless you die first, Lola thought defiantly. *In fact, I'm going to make sure of it.*

She locked eyes with Reginald Kellogg as she fell, and he flicked a hand out towards her. Lola's scream was cut short as she temporarily dissolved into the Tangle before reappearing in the mouth of the cave like a flash of lightning.

She blinked as her eyes adjusted to the gloom, and swept her gaze over the entrance to the Mithraeum, drinking in as many details as possible as she did so.

Look once, see everything.

The shadows immediately to her left seemed to quiver slightly and she pulled a blade from the bandolier on her black leather combat suit with her right hand, turning and thrusting with all her might. The Tracer stepped out of the shadow and directly into her strike, allowing Lola to use their combined momentum to drive the knife through his neck and into his brainstem, killing him instantly.

Tracer down, Inferno down, she thought. *Only three to go.*

She pulled her knife free just as a woman with long, twitching fingers lunged at her, raising her elongated digits to head height as she did so. Lola prepared to parry with her blade, but she felt a bullet whine past her ear and into the Fugue's skull, blowing the Cep's brains all over the cave wall.

"Nice shooting, Thane," Lola muttered, holding her left hand in a thumbs-up gesture that he was certain to see. *Now there's just the Fulcrum and the telepath; the hardest of the lot.*

Up against the wall of the cave, the bullet-shredded body of Speedball let out a wet chuckle as his flesh began to slowly knit back together. His one intact eye winked at her, as if to reassure her that their deal still held firm, and then he raised an eyebrow in warning.

Lola turned on her heel, dropping an eyepiece over her eye as she drew one of her two handguns; a bulky hi-tech contraption that Thaddeus had insisted would deal with the Fulcrum for her. The heads-up display immediately painted over a dozen targets on the looming figure that stood deeper in the Mithraeum, but the software quickly realised that the bulk of the creature moving towards her was simply detritus driven by telekinetic power.

Some of the targets did stick, however, revealing the small woman at the centre of the trash monstrosity. Lola squeezed the trigger and the handgun spat out half a dozen carbamate coated flechette rounds, all guided by the smart targeting system, at the Fulcrum.

The Cep held out her hands to stop the darts, but the distraction of her collapsing construct allowed at least one of the projectiles to strike true, and the neurotoxin soon brought the Fulcrum to her twitching, painful end.

"This is a fucking sweet piece of tech," Lola muttered, looking at the maker's mark on the gun before holstering it and flicking the eyepiece back up. "Reichardt; that figures."

Before she could do anything else, she felt the questing fingers of the telepath reaching for her mind. She took one final look to find her target and screwed her eyes shut as she tossed out a small device into the air between them.

The Party Ball was her own invention for dealing with telepaths, based on her own experience with photosensitive epilepsy; the rapid strobe lights and medley of piercing noises had yet failed to break a mind reader's focus, and this one was no exception.

The telepath's mind withdrew with a pained scream, and Lola pulled her other sidearm, a standard issue Taylor & Bullock Giantslayer, from its holster, firing three quick shots as she did so; a double tap to the chest, followed by a finishing round to the head. The

Mozambique Drill was a favourite amongst the Lamplight instructors and the only person that had ever carried it out better was Charity Walpole.

The Party Ball let out a low tone to let her know that the seizure trigger had passed, just before the sound of the telepath's body hitting the floor reached her ears.

She opened her eyes and allowed herself a small smile; all the Hags had been killed without harming any of the other occupants of the cave. *Oh, I am so fucking good.*

Standing between Lola and Alice Mann, the Shaper she had sought out, was Flora Cain. The Faun went to move towards her but Lola immediately held up her hands, making it clear that she only wanted to talk.

"What do you want?" Flora asked as the storm raged outside the cave.

"I want to help," Lola said. "I might not know this girl as well as you do, but I've dream shared before and I was particularly skilled at all the conflict resolution scenarios we ran when I was in training. Trust me, Flora; you want me in there helping him."

"If you hurt them-" the Faun began, but Lola shook her head.

"Look at what's happening out there!" Lola said, gesturing to the storm that now threatened to tear the town apart. "They need you to help hold back that madness, and Gavin needs me to help him free Alice from the evil that's taken root inside her.

"So, Flora Cain, are you going to trust me, or are you going to let everyone you care about die?"

Chapter Thirty Three – Chained to the Rocks

Flora

The dark spots on her eyes left by the strobe lights were only beginning to fade as Lola Oriole, a woman who stood for everything she disagreed with, made her ultimatum. She blinked rapidly to clear her eyes, and then stared at the Juliet's face, searching for a lie.

Much to her great surprise, she found only honesty.

"If I sing you to sleep," Flora said carefully, "you won't be able to wake up on your own."

"I know," Lola said softly. "Either Alice has to bring me out, or you have to release me; if I do anything to hurt them, you can keep me there forever."

"I won't," Flora said, holding out a hand, "because I know that you won't hurt them. Come, lay down."

She lowered the Juliet to the ground and helped her to get comfortable. Their hands lingered on each other's for a few seconds longer than necessary, so Flora decided to take a leap of faith and leant down to give the Ministry Agent a small kiss.

"For luck," she said, almost sheepishly.

"Thank you," Lola replied, her voice scarcely louder than a whisper, but the blush that crept on to her face screamed louder than the storm outside. Flora gently stroked the other woman's face and the two shared a smile that was more innocent and sincere than anything either of them had ever experienced before.

"Go to sleep," Flora said, before letting out a low whistle than set Lola's eyelids fluttering as she entered the depths of the shared dream that permeated not only the cave, but the whole of the bay area. "Travel safely, Lola Oriole, and come back to me when you're done dreaming."

Flora lingered over Lola's unconscious body for a few moments, watching the movement of her eyes behind their lids and the gentle rise and fall of her breathing. Unbidden, however, came the mental images of horrors her demonic friend had visited upon the poor woman, and she felt a violent longing stirring inside her.

I could do whatever I wanted to her, Flora thought, *and not a soul would ever know.*

I could hurt her just because I can.

"But you won't, will you?" The words were wet, malformed, and slightly garbled, but she recognised Speedball's voice immediately.

"No," she replied, giving him a smile as she rose to her feet. "I'm more than just an animal."

"This much is true," he said, dragging his healing body away from the cave entrance, just in case the snipers decided to shoot at him once again. "Animals kill what they need to survive, whereas humans have always killed for far more noble, yet infinitely selfish, reasons.

"You know what I mean, Flora."

I won't do it.

"Look," he said, gesturing limply towards the cave entrance. "Do you really think that Paris and Reggie can hold the line against such carnage?"

She remained silent.

"You need to help them, Flora, in the way that only you can."

"I never asked for this!" screamed the Faun. "I didn't

know this would happen!"

"You were warned," Speedy said. "You knew what happens when good little boys become bad little girls, especially when they have your blood in their veins and that stain on your name."

"I don't want to," Flora said. "I won't!"

"You will," the Demon said, almost sadly. "Everyone always does, and it will only get easier each time. Then one day, it won't ever fade away; it'll take you for good."

"Promise me something," Flora said, her lip trembling as tears beaded at the edge of her eyes.

"Anything, Flora, sweetheart."

"Don't let me kill my friends."

"I'll do what I can." He took her hand in his. "You always were my favourite, Flora Cain."

"I can do it without it," she said, wiping her eyes. "I know I can."

"No, you can't," Speedball replied quietly, but Flora had already stepped out into the howling gale of the storm.

The sight before her was a horrifying one.

The clouds were black as night, with lightning flashes peppering the surface of the sea and the buildings of the town almost every other second. The swell of the ocean was enormous and the waves were already tearing apart the beach and the sea wall; without assistance, the entire area would be obliterated by morning.

"I can do this without The Mark," Flora said as she began to inch her way along the cliff side towards where Paris and Reggie were valiantly trying to hold the line. "I know enough Druidic magic to supplement my own skills; I can do this without resorting to that."

Despite her words of encouragement, she did not feel particularly empowered.

Her feelings of helplessness were only exacerbated when the clouds began to swirl violently, sending two enormous waterspouts down to wreak further havoc on the few boats that still remained on the turbulent waters.

Atop the cliff, Reggie was grinding his Barrel Organ at a frantic pace, and Rizz's new fiddle was literally blazing with unholy fire, but it was all in vain; the Illuminated Man was too powerful and the storm was going to sweep them away at any moment.

The rock beneath Flora's feet was beginning to give way, so she wrapped her hands around a sharp chain that was anchored into the stone. Arms wide and bound to the cliff, she felt more like a sacrifice to Mithras than the saviour of her little home town.

She cleared her throat and began to sing, even though the harsh wind whipped away every word that left her lips. The spray lashed Flora's face, the salt stinging her eyes and choking her as she tried to hold a consistent tune.

Fuck the words, Flora decided, *I'll just sing something that I know and love.*

She launched into a series of her favourite songs, soon finding her rhythm. Moving easily between musicals, choral numbers, and Shirley Bassey classics, her power grew stronger with each passing moment.

As she launched into a short tune from her favourite film, a small smile crept on to her lips.

I might actually be able to do this.

"I am your nightmares coming true," Flora sang, pushing her voice to the absolute limit and straining against the chains that held her above the churning, foaming water. "I am your crime!"

The storm continued to rage in the bay, pushing the tides ever higher and the waves ever closer to the homes and hotels of the town; *her* home, where Coral and Leroy would be crouched in the bathroom, away from the flying glass of the shattered windows.

No, Flora realised, *song will not solve this. I am at the conjunction of land and sea; I am where my power is strongest and I will wield it like a fucking god.*

"This ends now," she said, barely raising her voice above a mutter, but the cliff trembled with the power of her words. "The time for illusion and subterfuge is done; shed the wind and the rain and your fucking cloak of stars and face me!"

The waterspouts seemed to tremble and the lightning dimmed for a moment, but they soon resumed their previous intensity. Flora heard a cruel, yet somehow familiar, laugh mixed in with the thunder and something inside the Faun stirred, filling her heart with hatred.

Images of taunting bullies, opened arteries, and dangling nooses flooded her mind and the small cut above her eyebrow was torn asunder, turning into the twisted shining scar that Speedy had always said she would bear; a source of shame for so many years had now become a wellspring of terrible power.

The Mark, she thought as her eyes blazed with the intensity of an exploding star, *it is on me, at last.*

The blood of the second born son is on my hands, and that curse makes me untouchable.

The sign of the forbidden one, the outcast, is scrawled in my flesh for all to see.

"Face me," she demanded, and the force of her

words shattered the waves and broke the clouds wide open, slicing the waterspouts to ribbons of spray and vapour. "Face me, you fucking coward."

The lightning strikes began to gather into a single spot, forming the faint image of a woman in the afterglow, hovering in the sky above the surface of the ocean. The Illuminated Man pointed a finger at Flora, striking her through the heart with a bolt of lightning. Her flesh seared and her skin blistered as a pained scream erupted from her lips, but she persevered.

The Illuminated Man faltered for just a moment, and then unleashed a dozen more bolts on the chained woman, but each did less damage than the last; already Flora's flesh was healing and a cruel snarl escaped the Faun's lips.

"The Mark is upon me, you fucking bitch!" Flora cackled madly as the torrent of hate grew stronger with every beat of her darkening heart. "You can no more harm me than you can stop the turning of the earth."

The Illuminated Man let out a howl and unleashed a flurry of wind, focussed to blade-like sharpness, at Paris and Reggie but these simply collapsed into the gentlest of summer breezes as soon as they reached the two men. Flora sneered as the glowing figure stared on in what could only be horror and disbelief.

"I hold them under my protection," she said, her words thrumming with power and darkness, "and for as long as The Mark is on me, they are kept safe until the very ending of the world!"

"Fuck you, Flora Cain!" screamed the Illuminated Man and, at long last, Flora recognised her.

"So this is who you really were, all along?" Flora shook her head in disappointment. "What a broken, shattered thing you are; so weak and cowardly that you would wield a child like a weapon against those that once loved you?

"It's little wonder you have no power over me." Flora released the chains from her bloodied hands before smearing the gore over The Mark, granting her more power than she'd ever felt in her life. "It is time for you to die."

"I will live forever!" screamed the glowing figure, but it was clear that her power was fading.

"Calm seas," Flora said, and the waves collapsed into the most tranquil waters Torquay had seen in weeks.

"No!"

"Still air," the Faun demanded, and the wind died down immediately.

"How are you doing this!?"

"Clear skies." The clouds dispersed, revealing the shimmering stars of the night sky.

"I HATE YOU!" screamed the woman as her light began to fade.

"I'm sorry," Flora said, and she began to sing once again, banishing the woman's physical form back into the starry vista, to be woven into the night sky for as long as the song was on her lips and The Mark burned on her face.

I have done all I can here, she thought as she resolutely held the line against the Illuminated Man. *The rest is up to you, Gavin.*

Good luck.

Chapter Thirty Four – You See Her When You Fall Asleep

Gavin

"Alice?" Gavin asked, getting up from the ground. He blinked in surprise for a moment; he could've sworn that he'd felt both sand and grass beneath his fingertips, but instead he stood in his classroom, with the morning sunlight streaming through the windows.

"I'm here," she replied in a small voice. He turned around to find her sitting in her usual seat, with her books arrayed before her and her mother's locket clutched in one hand.

"Why this place?" he asked. "Was it to make it easy for me to find?"

"No," Alice said, a sad smile on her face. "I used to dream about this room a lot, even before I was in your class; I guess if my dreams really can shape reality then perhaps I brought us together for this moment."

There was a moment of silence between the two of them.

"I used to dream that you were my dad," Alice said softly. "I know that's a strange thing to say, especially now, but it's true. Those were good dreams."

Gavin gave her a smile, but something told him that a simple change of expression wasn't enough, so he strode over and pulled her into a fierce hug. She held him tightly for a minute or two, and then they stepped back, both of them teary eyed.

"Do we have to go and find-"

"No." Alice sighed heavily. "She'll come to us soon

enough."

"With the rain?" he asked sadly, and she nodded.

"I was worried that you didn't know it would be her," Alice said, "and I didn't have the heart to tell you."

"I knew the moment I arrived on your doorstep," Gavin said, "and I think a part of me knew we'd end up back here. Things have a funny way of coming full circle, don't they?"

"It's been a weird fucking summer, hasn't it?" Alice said with a chuckle and Gavin nodded, smiling along. The first few fat drops of rain started to fall, pattering on the window panes. "I don't want to go outside in that, so I might just open the wall if that's okay with you?"

"You can do that?" Gavin asked, impressed, and she removed the wall with a wave of her hand, flattening a bunch of the desks as she did so. "That's amazing, Alice!"

"It's all so much easier when you know who and what you really are, isn't it?"

"That it is," Gavin said, "and most people go their entire lives without realising it."

The rain was pouring now, and the vague shape of a woman was approaching through it. Whilst there had been a point not too long ago when he would've run into her arms, Gavin stood at Alice's side instead, making it clear to the long-dead Walker that his loyalty to her memory was finally done.

"Look at you both," Lucy said, smiling as her features finally came into focus. "Together at last."

"Hello, Lucy." Gavin's voice trembled as he looked at his wife, and he realised for the first time that he'd spent their entire marriage living in fear of her.

"Did you miss me?" Her voice was warm and heavy, like a summer monsoon, but held terrible power behind it. When Gavin did not respond, her smile became a sharp frown. "I asked you a question, Gavin."

"No, Lucy," he said, speaking truthfully for the first time in years. "I missed who you could've been, who I wanted and needed you to be, but I did not miss you as you were.

"You always were better as an ideal," he said sadly. "As a dream."

Alice was silent, but she was fiddling with the locket in a way that seemed more deliberate than nervous, but Gavin was much too frightened to notice. Lucy stood almost ten feet tall, much larger than life, and she thrummed with seemingly limitless potential.

"Either way, you've brought my daughter to me," Lucy said grandly, "and now my family is gathered to witness my final ascension; the true zenith of my limitless power!"

How on earth are we going to get out of this alive? Gavin wondered, and then, just as he was about to panic, Alice finally spoke up.

"You might've been my mother," Alice said, breaking her silence as the delicate chain of the locket dangled from her white-knuckled fist, "but you were never my family."

"I am more than your mother!" Lucy roared. "In this world, I am your god! I gave you this power and I can take it away just as easily!"

"Yes, you did give me this gift," Alice admitted softly, but there was a hint of threat to her tone. "The Illuminated Man taught me so much about this world, just as Gavin taught me all the chemistry that I know.

"I was the weird kid, however, with interests that my parents deemed freakish; occultism, witchcraft, and Druidic magic. Turns out I've got a real knack for spotting things of that ilk, especially binding spells," she said, looking meaningfully at the locket, "which I learned to dispel by the time I was thirteen."

"You," Lucy said, a flicker of fear flashing in her eyes, "you wouldn't dare!"

"Are you sure?" Alice asked. "After everything you've done to me, are you so *fucking certain*?"

"I-I made you!" Lucy hissed as the rainy sky around her darkened.

"Fucking *oops*," Alice replied, and the ghost of a smile touched Gavin's lips.

Go get her, kiddo.

"You ungrateful child!" Lucy screamed.

"Hey, *mum*," Alice said with a snide grin, "get the fuck out of my room."

The necklace began to glow in the teenager's hand, but little else happened. Lucy laughed darkly and the tumultuous sky began erupting with flashes of purple lightning, striking the rocky ground closer and closer to the Gavin and Alice with each bolt.

"You foolish child!" Lucy said viciously. "You think that a few weeks of power and a beginner's grasp of witchcraft would give you the authority to cast me out?"

Alice stared at Lucy with horror as the lightning struck mere inches from the girl's feet.

"As for you," the monstrous woman said, rounding on Gavin now, "all you ever were was a human; little more than a toy for me to play with. Even allied together, you are helpless!"

"This is a place of power," said a voice from behind Gavin, and he turned to see Lola Oriole walking towards him, a smoking censer in one hand and a dripping honeycomb in the other. She was clad entirely in a black robe, embroidered with golden bees that seemed to buzz and vibrate as she moved. "This is a place of power, child, and the power comes from within you.

"Do not believe her lies," Lola said as she swung the censer above her head, shrouding them all in the scented smoke. "You have the strength to cast her out, and I will show you the way."

"Who are you?" Alice asked.

"She is merely a frightened girl in a mask," Lucy sneered. "Nothing more."

"I am the last living heir of the Honeysweet bloodline," Lola replied.

"And this makes you a witch?" Lucy scoffed.

"No," Lola said softly. "Once, yes, but no longer."

"Then what are you?" Alice asked.

"An exorcist," Gavin answered, and Lola nodded. He placed a firm hand on Alice's shoulder as he realised what needed to be done. "I stand beside this child not as a friend or father, but as an Arch-Druid. I speak for the time in the stones, the tide in the seas, and the tithe man takes from the land. I speak for the fur, the feather, the blood, and the bone of all who grow in nature's grace.

"You, Lucy Havelock, are in defiance of the natural order," he said sharply, "and it is my duty to restore the balance. I cast you out!"

The necklace in Alice's hand trembled and grew brighter.

"I am the sun and the moon, the man and the

woman, the good and the evil," Lola said, "and all that lies between. I move in the magic as grass moves in the morning breeze; I stand for life and vitality and the power that binds us all together.

"You are as an autumn leaf in that same wind and, like that life, you too will fall." She dropped the comb and placed her honey-slick hand on Alice's other shoulder. "I cast you out."

The necklace was thrumming with power, yet one final push was needed. Gavin's heartbeat thundered in his ears as he wondered if the young woman's nerve would hold against the titanic threat they faced, but his fears were allayed when she spoke.

"I stand here, in my own mind," Alice said, almost in a trance, "and I speak only for myself; for my power, for my life, for my *authority* over this place. I dreamed of you so often as a child and in doing so, I summoned you.

"Your being is my doing and you turned out to be a nightmare; this I must undo. Mother, I cast you out." Alice held up the necklace between her hands as it glowed brighter than ever before, and a mirror image appeared wrapped tightly around Lucy's neck. The teenage Shaper tugged the silver links and they sliced through her mother's ghostly flesh, dispelling the Walker's form and leaving little more than vapour behind.

"Lucy Havelock," Alice said softly as the necklace crumbled to black dust in her hands, "die in peace, and be reborn no more."

There was a beat of silence as the two adults looked proudly at the feisty teenager stood between them, and then Alice spoke once again.

"Now, dreamers, awake."

Just as suddenly as the dream had begun, it ended, and Gavin opened his eyes.

"Are you both alright?" Alice asked as she helped Gavin and Lola to their feet.

"I'm a little groggy," Gavin said, "but I'm sure it'll pass."

"You did well," Lola said warmly. "You are an impressive and talented young woman."

There was a pause as the Ministry Agent listened to an earpiece before going on.

"Yes, Miette; the situation is over." Her reply was short, and Lola gave the other two a smile as she pulled out the earpiece and switched off her radio. "Technically, I'm supposed to bring you back to the Ministry with me, Alice, but I'm not going to do that."

"You're not?" Gavin said, raising a shocked eyebrow.

"You and I both know what they'll do with someone with skills like hers," Lola said, meaningfully glancing at her left wrist. "I know that she'll have a chance to truly grow into her skills working for the Ministry, but I think she'll be safer with you."

"Will they send other people after me?" Alice said, suddenly afraid.

"I won't let them," Lola replied, "and if they try, I'll be right back here to protect you."

"You know that you're always welcome to stay here with Flora, Leroy, and the rest of the gang," Gavin said, "but if you still want to be a midwife, I'll make sure that happens. I can afford to get you a little flat somewhere in the town, and I'll pay for your education; I just want you to be happy and to have the life you want.

"If that life does involve heading off to London to become some super skilled Ministry top operative, though, will you do one thing for me?" Gavin asked.

"What?" Alice said softly.

"Write to me every now and then; I'd like to know that you're getting on okay." He was surprised to find that he was on the verge of tears, and Alice nodded.

"You'd go far in the Ministry, Alice," Lola said, "but it's not easy work, and sometimes you'll end up in situations that have no good outcomes. It's important work, but it's not for the faint hearted. Still, I think you'd rise to the occasion admirably.

"Either way, the choice is entirely up to you."

"What do *you* think I should do?" Alice asked Gavin, and he couldn't help but smile at the familiar tentative tone of the girl he'd taught for so many years.

"You have the power to shape your own dreams, Alice," Gavin said, "so follow your heart and do whatever feels right to you."

"But what if I pick wrong?"

"Then you pick wrong," Gavin said. "You're always allowed to change your mind, and there's plenty of time to change the road you're on if you realise it isn't for you."

"You promise?" Alice asked, and both adults nodded.

"So," Gavin said, taking her hand in his, "what does your heart tell you to do?"

"Something I heard in a dream once, when I was a small child," Alice said softly, placing her free hand on her chest. "It's telling me that my father would always look after me."

It took Gavin a few moments to realise that she was looking directly at him.

"But I'm not-" he began, although his words faltered as she spoke.

"Not yet, no," Alice said gently, "but do you want to be?"

Epilogue – Someone or Something to Show You the Way

The Deputy Director's exquisitely manicured fingernails tapped the pen in her hand as she stared at Lola with harsh grey eyes and a stony frown on her face. The two women sat in the Project Operator's office on Betony Island; one of the few places untouched by the fire that had occurred so many years earlier.

"And you let her go?" Harper Cherry asked sharply after Lola had finished giving her mission debrief.

"Yes, Deputy Director." Lola's gaze was fixed on the wall behind Harper's head, her expression one of grim professionalism.

"Despite your express orders to either capture or kill the individual behind these deadly occurrences?" Harper tutted disapprovingly. Lola's eyes briefly drifted to stare at the comparatively fresh scars on the Deputy Director's face before returning to the wall.

I wonder who did that to her? Lola thought. *And how on earth did they actually manage to wound her?*

Lola's mind filled with memories from the final day of Project Lamplight; Harper Cherry walking unscathed through a hail of bullets and shrugging off the roaring inferno as if it wasn't even there. It had long been whispered that the Deputy Director was invincible, but Lola had not believed the rumours until she had seen them with her own eyes.

"Agent Oriole?" Harper snapped, impatient for a response.

"I did what I thought was in the best interest of both

the child and the Ministry," she said, only half lying. "She was too volatile for us to use in her current state, and she's too old for a Ministry *education*, ma'am."

"You could've killed her."

"I'm not sure I could've," Lola admitted, "and I don't think Thane would've got close enough; Miette can back me up on that one."

"On that matter, she has," Harper confirmed. "She also said that you have concluded that Kellogg was not a threat, once again in defiance of orders."

"I thought-" Lola began, but Harper brought a fist down sharply on the table.

"You are supposed to act, not think," the Deputy Director growled. "Would you give the same excuses to Director Desai?"

"Yes," Lola answered without hesitation, "and they are *reasons*, not excuses."

She saw something flash in the older woman's eyes and a small smile crept on to Harper's lips. *She's going to have me executed,* Lola thought, but the realisation was unaccompanied by fear. *Perhaps that's for the best; better to die here than in Prague.*

"Do you accept personal responsibility for the eventual outcomes of your decisions?" Harper asked softly, and Lola nodded after a few seconds of consideration. "Would you agree that it would fall to you, and you alone, to destroy Alice Mann and Reginald Kellogg if they proved a danger to the public?"

"I agree that it would be my task alone," Lola said shakily, "but I don't think it will come to that."

"But you would do what was necessary, if the time came?"

"*If* the time came," Lola replied, stressing the fact

that she did not believe the worst would come to pass, "I would do whatever was needed of me."

Harper considered the Juliet for a moment, before nodding curtly.

"Thank you for submitting your report, Agent Oriole." She gestured towards the door. "Please return to your quarters; I've no doubt we'll be calling on you again soon."

"I... Thank you, Deputy Director." Lola turned on her heel smartly and walked towards the door, only stopping when Harper spoke once more.

"Lola?" Harper said, and the Juliet looked over her shoulder at the Deputy Director. "Bloody good show; you've done Lamplight proud."

"Thank you, ma'am."

"That's all," Harper said dismissively. "Now, run along."

As Lola headed back to the shared dwelling on the edge of Betony Island, she felt a strange feeling creep over her.

All roads lead to home, she thought, *but now I'm not entirely sure where that home will be.*

"So you used to be a Chemistry Teacher?" asked Barney Parker, Gavin's new therapist.

"Yeah," Gavin said as he sat in armchair in Barney's office. "Is that important?"

"What made you stop teaching?" Barney said, giving Gavin a warm smile. The man was getting on in years, but Peter Borage had recommended him highly; that, as well as the fact that Barney was a werewolf, was why Gavin had agreed to see him. "Aside from the lure of the supernatural, of course?"

"I had a bit of a shake up in my personal life," Gavin

said sheepishly. "One of my A-Level students, Alice, turned out to be my late wife's daughter, and she needs someone to guide her through her blossoming gifts."

"One nurturing path for another," Barney said with a nod. "Does seeing Alice regularly make you feel closer to Lucy?"

There was a minute or two of silence between the two men

"No," Gavin said after much consideration. "Every day that I spend with Alice seems to make my life with Lucy seem a little further away."

"Is that a good thing?"

"Yes," Gavin said with a small smile, "even though the change is painful. It doesn't do anyone any good to live in a haunted house forever, otherwise you'll wake up one day and realise that you're now one of the ghosts."

"Are you a ghost, Gavin?" Barney asked, and the Arch-Druid shook his head. "Then what would you say you are?"

"Now, I'm..." he trailed off for a few seconds, and then smiled as he thought of Alice. "I think I'm starting to be a father."

"Now, the top floor belongs to me and Reggie," Flora said as she led Alice around the Montresor, making sure that she was properly settled in. "Gavin and Leroy live on the floor below that, and Rizz on the first floor; Coral finds the stairs troublesome, so she lives downstairs.

"That gives you a decent amount of space on the first floor, if you don't mind Rizz's music, or we can reconfigure the ground floor and convert either the dining room, lounge, or the Schooner into a room for you."

The Mark throbbed slightly on her brow as she spoke, but this did not trouble her; the curse was sated, for now.

"Thank you, Flora," Alice said somewhat sheepishly, "but Gavin has already told me that he'll get me a little flat somewhere in town, so this is all a bit unnecessary. Thank you, though, all the same."

Flora blinked at her in surprise, although not at the news regarding the flat; Gavin had already told her about that.

"Darling, don't you want a space here?" the Faun asked, clutching her hands to the hollow of her neck, suddenly afraid that she'd overstepped.

"I don't want to get in the way," Alice said quietly. "You've already done so much for me... I don't want to impinge on you any further-"

"Alice," Flora said firmly, taking the girl's hands in her own, "the Hotel Montresor belonged to your mother, which makes it as much yours as ours. You will *always* have a home here, darling, and we will *always* help you, no matter how deep in the shit you might end up.

"We're a family here, and we fucking act like it." She looked Alice in the eye. "As far as we're concerned, *you* are family, now, darling. Is that okay?"

Alice nodded, and after a moment Flora gestured to the wallpaper in the Silver Schooner, which was cleaner and clearer than it had been since the onset of Lucy's slow decline. The air was fresher, and the lingering black mould and mildew was fading away, almost as if it had realised that the time for change had come at last.

"This place has been in decay for what feels like

forever, but now things are finally coming back to life; in no small part thanks to you."

"You really mean it? You actually want me here, even after all I've done?" Alice asked, as if she could scarcely believe what Flora was saying. The Faun nodded, and Alice allowed the faintest hint of a smile to creep on to her lips. "You promise?"

"Absolutely," Flora said, "and it seems like the Monty does too; even the building has decided to smarten itself up for your arrival! Come on, let's go pick you out a bedroom."

Besides, Flora thought as they continued to stroll throughout the ageing hotel, *a touch of youth always makes a home more liveable and does wonders to keep old ghosts at bay.*

"Hello?" asked the voice on the other end of the phone. "Who is this?"

"Mallory?" Thad asked, his voice cracking a little.

"Thaddeus?" Mallory's words were hushed, as if he'd just received a message from the great beyond. "Thaddeus, you're still alive?"

"Yeah, Mal," he replied, already tearing up a little. "I'm sorry I didn't call you or Jess sooner; everything was in such chaos from the moment after we last spoke, when we first arrived in Torquay, that I just didn't get a chance."

He sighed tearfully and leant his head on the cool glass of his bedroom window.

"I honestly wasn't sure if we were going to get out of that one alive, Mal." He heard his partner's quiet sob on the other end of the line. "Hell, if it wasn't for Lola, I think I'd be in a shallow grave somewhere up on Dartmoor."

"Lola rescued you!?" Mallory replied, shocked. "After everything that happened with the Coven?"

"Yeah, she actually saved my neck more than once." Thaddeus paused for a second, wondering who else was listening in on their conversation. "I don't think I'm going to be coming home for a while, Mallory; there's so much more to do here."

"I see," Mallory replied, his tone indicating that he very much didn't.

"Something feels off about Lola," Thad said, lowering his voice. "I'm starting to think that what happened with the Hivemother wasn't entirely her fault; I think there's someone behind the curtain of all this, Mal, pulling her strings.

"I can't offer you any concrete proof, though, but my gut says to stick around here a while longer and to help her through whatever happens." He shook his head sadly. "She seems to think that she's doomed, Mal, but I... I think I can save her."

There was a moment of silence before the Artist replied.

"You're a good investigator, Thaddeus," Mallory said with quiet pride, "so trust your instincts and do whatever you think is necessary. I trust you to do the right thing, but I only have one request."

"Name it," Thad said, "and I will do whatever you ask."

"When all this is done, come back to me, please," Mallory asked. "I want to see you again, alive."

"I will if you will, Mal."

"Promise?"

"I swear it," Thaddeus said, before adding a final message. "I love you, Mallory Marsh."

"And I you, Thaddeus Thane. Stay safe and I'll

hopefully see you soon."

The line clicked and Thad held the phone for a moment in a trembling hand before wiping the tears from his eyes. Lola knocked on the door, calling him for dinner, and he replied that he'd be with her soon; he still had one final message to send. He rummaged in his field rucksack for the cheap burner mobile he'd surreptitiously purchased in Torquay.

His fingers danced over the keys as he rattled out a cryptic message, and then hit send.

Here you go, he thought. *Let's see what you can do with them on your side.*

Gavin answered the door as the bell jangled for a fourth time, sighing heavily as he looked at the small woman who stood on the doorstep; an easy smile was on her face and broad sun hat perched atop her head.

"Good morning," she said warmly, clearly enjoying the last of the summer's fine weather.

"I'm sorry, but we don't have any vacancies, I'm afraid," Gavin began, pointing at the sign in the window. He stopped, however, when he realised he held a business card in his hand. "What on earth...

"How did you do that?" he asked the woman, who was now grinning mischievously.

"I've got quick hands," she said enigmatically, "and I'm not here for a room."

She gestured to the card, and Gavin looked it over.

"Cherry & Understudies, Private Investigative Detectives," Gavin read aloud. He frowned suspiciously. "Are you looking for someone?"

"After a fashion," the woman replied. "We heard about the good that you and yours did for this town, and we'd like to offer you the opportunity for further work. I'm not saying that we'll be your bosses, but rather you and your friends will be equal partners in our organisation, with the right to refuse any job we send your way.

"You'll have access to our considerable pool of resources and talents, to boot." The woman grinned at him. "So, Mr Strangeways, what do you say?"

"I'm not one for violence, I'm afraid," he said, and went to hand the card back, but her reply stopped him short.

"We know, and that's why we're asking you to join us," she said. "We believe that violence is an absolute last resort."

Gavin considered her offer for a moment before speaking.

"I don't even know your name."

"I'm Tabitha Godfrey, but all the people that matter simply call me Mouse. Pleased to meet you, Gavin." She reached out to shake his hand and, after a heartbeat of hesitation, he greeted her warmly. "I hope you'll all agree to be a part of CUPID; from what we've heard you'll fit right in."

"Heard from who?" Gavin asked.

"We have eyes and ears inside the Ministry," Mouse said in a conspiratorial whisper, "but this particular information comes from Thaddeus Thane; he was very impressed with your combined skill set. He did mention that your methods were a touch unorthodox, but that's only yet another plus in my eyes."

Thane recommended us!?

"So, Mr Strangeways, what do you say?" Mouse asked as she leant against the door. "Care to play in the shadows a little longer and get filthy rich whilst doing so?"

"Keep the money," Gavin said firmly. "I'll do it just to help those that the Ministry leaves behind in the darkness."

"An agent of the light," Mouse said, revealing her Lamplight tattoo with a wry chuckle, "just like me. I think we're going to get along just wonderfully, Gavin. I'll swing by tomorrow morning, when you've had a chance to talk things over with your friends."

"You're so certain that they'll join?" he asked, impressed with her confidence.

"Of course they will; the only one I had any doubts about was you." She tipped her hat and began to back away into the bright sunshine. "I'll see you in the morning, Gavin, and let me be the first to welcome you to CUPID."

So much for the quiet life, Gavin thought as he closed the door, but try as he might, he couldn't keep the enthusiastic smile from his lips.

The air was still warm in the centre of Oxford as the middle of September approached, but the threat of autumn was carried on the wind; never more so than at sunset, when the creeping chill of winter made its first threatening overtures towards the Dreaming Spires.

The man kept his head down as he hurried along the High Street, eager to be away from the snuffling masses and their disgusting infectious breath. He pressed a lavender scented handkerchief to his face as he passed a gaggle of school children as they laughed and caroused down the pavement; it would not do to get sick now, not when he was so very close to salvation.

Thankfully he was able to enter the sandstone venue before he encountered any more foul and filthy pedestrians, causing him to let out a deep sigh of relief. He doffed his coat and hat before pulling on the ceremonial gown and polished copper mask that were required for the evening's festivities.

"I say, North," said another of the participants as he shuffled into the shadowy room, "I thought you weren't coming tonight!"

"No," North rasped as he choked back a cough, "I would not miss this for the world."

"A pleasure to have you, then," another said raucously, raising a glass of wine. His eyes glinted menacingly through his gleaming hyena mask. "To your health, North!"

The chorus of cruel laughter that emanated from the nearby masked participants made North scowl, but he nodded along all the same, raising his own glass to the powerful man that had mocked him.

Better a part of the pack than their harried prey.

"Hey, chaps," one of the anonymous celebrants called out as a medical trolley creaked into the space, "I think we're about to begin."

"See you on the other side," North muttered, holding his handkerchief to his nose once again as he let out a small cough, wincing in pain as he did so. He shuffled to one side, craning his neck to get a clearer view of the proceedings.

The vaulted ceiling was high enough to accommodate a gallery but, aside from a few eager souls stood atop chairs, there was no vantage point from which the masked horde could watch the impending carnage.

Their leader soon entered the room to much hooting, hollering, and whooping. He raised his gloved hands high over his head as his assistants laced up his surgical gown and walked him to the table.

The energy in the room grew more palpable with each step towards the sedated sacrifice the surgeon took. Soon there were wild cheers and snarls of desire as several of the celebrants were driven over the edge of bloodlust and headlong into the waters of sexual ecstasy.

I worship at the altar of violence, North thought reverentially as he bounced lightly on the balls of his feet, *and tonight this is my church.*

He scarcely noticed the first cut; so lost was he in the heady hedonism of the crowd. When their leader spoke, however, North's mind was suddenly clear as polished glass and he looked at the makeshift operating table with hungry eyes.

"Only from the glory of death can the miracle of life be renewed!" cried the masked surgeon as the first of the kidneys was carefully placed in a gleaming steel dish. "Only through the knife can flesh be made whole once again!"

The masked celebrants continued to scream, laugh, and cheer as the pain and horror of the procedure finally reached a crescendo in the sacrificial patient, breaking through the haze of drugs and sorcery that had held them silent the entire time.

As the surgeon reached down and began to cut out the victim's liver, their eyes snapped open wide and they began to cry out in agonising terror. Their screams were immediately drowned out by the mad rhythmic laughter of the hyena-faced crowd and their eyes darkened as their lifeblood began to pool in their abdominal cavity; no more sounds would ever be uttered by this one, no matter what horrors were visited upon their harvested corpse.

Go in peace, wretch, North thought feverishly, *and may your unworthy viscera snatch me from the grave, one last time.*

More screams and bloodshed are to come in...

PRESS THE FLESH

Acknowledgments

This one got away from me a little, and I was unsure of just how it was going to end until I got there, and I did not realise just how twisted a tale this was going to be until I was well underway. Speedball, The Place, and even the coven of Hags were conceived of in the moment, which might be why this book feels like such a visceral journey to me. Combined with my own personal knowledge of Torquay and its environs (my paternal grandparents lived there for many years), this story became weirdly real for me. Even though this might be one of my less planned stories, I found great joy in fleshing out Lola, as well as introducing the Montresor gang; worry not, you'll see more of them soon enough.

There are people I must thank, of course, because such a book cannot be written alone..

Firstly and most importantly, I would like to thank my partner, Syd, for the love, support, and the tremendous help with this story. She has listened to me talk about this for months, and has given me both inspiration and encouragement in spades, as well as suggesting that I take breaks from writing when I did not realise just how much I needed them. I love you, darling, and I am so lucky to have you in my life.

Likewise, I would like to thank my metamor, Ben Wright. Thank you for all the support and discussion that has helped this book become the nightmare that it finally grew into. I especially valued your input regarding Mithras (which I knew nothing about going into this) and for explaining various aspects of computing to me in order to make Lola's expertise something vaguely believable.

I would like to thank you both for inviting me into your life and our home; I feel loved, wanted, and cared for, which I am grateful for beyond measure.

I would also like to thank our guinea pigs, both for their reassuring presence and constant source of amusement. There will continue to be references to you scattered throughout my writing.

A big thank you goes out to my best friend, Dr Georgia Lynott. You are a source of light in my life and always a joy to spend time with. I hope you will enjoy this book, and the series as a whole.

I cannot write a horror novel without thanking my parents, Steve and Samantha Farrell, my grandparents, Frank and Lorraine Keeley, and other members of my family; you have all played a crucial part developing my absolute love of horror. From late night films to tatty paperbacks read in the car on long journeys; it all has culminated in this book, and all those that follow it. Thank you.

I would like to extend my thanks to my childhood friends, James Bullock and Colum Taylor, for all their support and all the horror films we watched together over the years.

Once again, I would like to thank my therapist, Zayna Brookhouse, for her help in turning my fear and grief into something constructive that I could share with you all.

I'd like to thank all the musicians, artists, writers, and cinematographers that have contributed to the horror genre. I write to music, so your help was invaluable in the creation of this work. I know I've name dropped a few artists in this one, but if you really want to get a feel for my mood writing this, I spent a large portion of the first drafting listening to *Knees Socks* by The Arctic Monkeys and *Angel of Small Death & The Codeine Scene* by Hozier on repeat.

Of course, I'm sure that I have missed people off of this list; it is not exhaustive, after all! So, to all the other Parrots out there who helped to make this work a reality, I thank you.

And, last but not least, you, dear reader, for choosing to read this book.

Thank you.

About the Author

Eleanor Fitzgerald is a polyamorous non-binary trans woman living in and around Oxford. Eleanor uses any and all pronouns, and is neurodivergent and disabled. Eleanor is hard of hearing, and completely deaf on one side.

They have a fascination for all things weird and wonderful, and have thoroughly enjoyed writing this work for you. Rest assured, it will not be the last!

Eleanor also paints (physically and digitally), and created the artwork for this book's cover illustration. This was one of their first all-digital covers, and there are many more to come! Their particular style is impressionism, which they love immensely.

If you have any questions or comments, they can be reached at the following email address:

eleanorfitzgeraldwriting@gmail.com

Printed in Great Britain
by Amazon